Russell Celyn Jones is the author of five other highly acclaimed novels. He is a regular book reviewer for *The Times* and is Professor of Creative Writing at Birkbeck College, London University.

'Celyn Jones excels at giving his creations an unheralded extra dimension . . . and in his evocations of a family life thrown mysteriously out of kilter . . . an arresting amalgam of anger and unease set in motion by the past's intrusive hand' *Independent on Sunday*

'More than just a clever psychological thriller, this novel is a terrifying exploration of how we define guilt and innocence, truth, fiction and memory' *Observer*

'Breathtakingly visceral and utterly compelling. The combination of the narrator's intimate, confessional approach, unsentimental yet profoundly moving, with the author's gift for narrative and swell of riverine detail, is a winning one' *Independent*

'Fascinating . . . *Ten Seconds From the Sun* is a tightly written story that delves into one of the few real taboos left in our plundered stock' *Sunday Telegraph*

'Celyn Jones, rather like Ian McEwan, has a knack for inducing paranoia, getting unsettlingly close to his audience and cutting moral certainties adrift. Noirishly gripping, *Ten Seconds From the Sun* is a must' *Daily Mail*

'A grim and gripping read, which, quite unexpectedly, at its conclusions, allows a flicker of light and hope' *The Times*

Also by this author

Soldiers and Innocents
Small Times
An Interference of Light
The Eros Hunter
Surface Tension

TEN SECONDS FROM THE SUN

Russell Celyn Jones

ABACUS

First published in Great Britain in July 2005 by Little, Brown
This paperback edition published in May 2006 by Abacus

A CIP catalogue record for this book is available from the British Library.

ISBN 10: 0-316-73081-5
ISBN 13: 978-0-316-73081-5

Typeset in Sabon by
Palimpsest Book Production Limited,
Polmont, Stirlingshire

Printed and bound in Great Britain by Clays Ltd, St Ives plc

Abacus
An imprint of
Time Warner Book Group UK
Brettenham House
Lancaster Place
London WC2E 7EN

www.twbg.co.uk

For Kate

Men have what the time is.

Shakespeare, *King Lear*

Sweet Thames! Run softly
Till I end my Song.

Edmund Spenser, *Prothalamion*

1

Two men sitting at the next table along are way out of their habitat. Off the ships, maybe. They are sunk in shadow and I can see no more than a black leather jacket zipped to the throat and a tight-fitting t-shirt. But something about them hair-triggers my instinct for preservation. We've been regulars at this Italian family restaurant for many years and I know when I'm in the presence of itinerants, people passing through.

The remains of our starters of salami and potatoes, anchovies with butter, ravioli dressed in olive oil, lie spread on the table. Lily prods her main-course salmon on a bed of linguine. An investigation with the fork reveals the fish is undercooked. She makes a comment I'm too self-absorbed to catch first time around, and I ask her to repeat it.

'I said it looks like Franco's fallen out with the chef again.'

The proprietor is a hot-blooded Venetian who treats his chefs so badly they keep walking out on him, sometimes in the middle of a shift, leaving the boss to cook for the rest of the night. But he hasn't the right temperament for the kitchen.

'You want to send it back?'

'No. How's the lamb?'

'Undercooked too.' I pour wine and watch Franco, pad and plate of bread in hand, approach the two men beside us.

The one in the leather jacket commands him to bring the shrimp. His voice is cracked and dusty. Not a sailor's voice.

'No shrimp,' Franco explains.

'What you mean, no shrimp?'

'Is off.'

'*Ease* off,' the man mimics Franco's Italian-English. 'Then why is it on the menu?'

Franco can keep his cool because the hostility goes over his head. He cannot hear the intonation of these men leaning on the table with their elbows. Smoke from their cigarettes agitates Lily. I fear she is going to say something to them about it.

Instead she raises the subject of her brother, who is trying to quit smoking. 'Colin likens his smoking life to an old friend constantly in and out of prison that he can't afford to see any more. He calls smoking a weasel behind plate glass. I quite like that, don't you?'

I don't like it as much as she does. I can feel the chill behind that plate glass.

The man in the t-shirt grunts, 'The spaghetti carbonara, is that still on?' The voice conjures the same arid geography as his companion's.

'Yes,' says Franco.

'Well, that's something. I'll take a carbonara.'

'Make that two.'

'Two spaghetti carbonara.' Franco writes down their order. 'You want something to drink?'

'Do we want something to drink! Do we want something to drink!'

'What do you think about chartering a Thames launch for their anniversary?' Lily asks me, apropos something we were talking about earlier.

'Your mother won't like that. She'll complain.'

'My mother would complain about the dust in heaven.'

My eyes are veiled but I can tell the one in the leather jacket is looming hard in my direction. I can feel his breath upon my neck, like the strong hot breath of a horse. Because he can't draw me in by sight, he asks: 'What you drinking, chief?'

The silence lasts a few seconds until Lily answers for me. 'The Cipress della Court.'

'I was asking your boyfriend.'

I stare down at my plate. The lamb sits in a pool of blood.

'We'll have what they're drinking. And cancel one of those carbonaras. I'll have what he's eating as well.'

'The lamb?'

'Yeah, lamb. Jesus Christ.'

'Would you like the lamb penetrated?'

Even I stir, curious to know what he means.

'*Penetrated?* Just cook it, chief. No need to shag it for me as well.'

Their laughter paints the walls. I hear a jacket unzipped. Franco minces away. The room cools off as they lose interest in me and my shoulders fall in my shirt. I steal a glance at a hand making a fist around a hunk of bread. The way he makes a barrier with his arm around the side-plate and bullies that bread, suggests etiquette taught by men. And the way they don't talk and eat.

I struggle to find my way back into Lily's company. Her head is in profile, staring down her long curved nose into the restaurant. She feels none of this tension that rakes and bruises me. Her flesh is loose on the bone, her eyes like swallows. I want to go back to where we were, discussing her parents' forthcoming wedding anniversary. But I can't find the page.

The mobile phone with its winking red eye sits on the damask tablecloth. Our electronic link to the babysitter back home reminds us that our most precious cargo lies in bed a mile away. Every few minutes one or the other of us evokes them by name. Simply saying, 'Flora and Eliot' purges them out of our systems for a while and allows us to live this moment tonight.

But this moment tonight keeps drifting into trouble and when Lily next mentions the children, it sounds like a prayer to me. 'What did you make them for tea, Ray?' Whatever one of our children orders for tea the other is guaranteed to contradict. So it came to pass, I say, that I sailed fish fingers *and* chicken nuggets on to the oven shelf. 'You spoil them. You should make them eat the same thing.' I don't protest, and never do. I can't remember the last argument we had because it wouldn't have been important. I've never once raised my voice to Lily. 'And lighting candles for them every night, is that really necessary?'

Two hours ago, I was much happier, standing with my back to the cooling oven as the children ate like primitives in the kitchen, listening to them telling jokes, recalling school folklore. They kept blowing out the candles so they could light them again, so they could play with matches, play with fire.

I tell my wife, 'Flora said her Miss Mansfield is getting married in the summer and when she returns to school in September, will be Mrs Scott.'

Lily twirls linguine on her fork. 'Did you know she wants to go to the wedding?'

'Yes, I did. But she can't.'

'She could go to the service I suppose.'

Eliot our son couldn't care less about Flora's teacher's

wedding, and talked over his sister in the kitchen about losing a trainer from his sports kit. Flora shouted at him, 'You always do that, ruin what I say,' and called him 'fat-boy'. Eliot, conscious of a few excess pounds, took it to heart. As he fled the kitchen he threw a punch at his sister. She tried to make the most of it, clutching the injury in both hands.

'Okay,' I said. 'You've secured the penalty. Now stop it.'

'No, but how would you feel if your only brother hated you?'

'Eliot doesn't hate you.'

'Yes he does. He'd be happier if I was dead.'

'That's a terrible thing to say.' And it really is – a terrible thing that kids can say. Her words aged me.

After tea, the eighteen-year-old babysitter arrived from her house across the road and the children tried being conciliatory. From the landing upstairs I overheard Flora announce to her brother: 'Eliot, I think we should agree to stop fighting and save ruining our childhood.' Within ten minutes all was calm again, all was well in the household. Eliot decamped to his bedroom, erecting SimCity on the computer screen. Flora began practising for her Grade-1 flute exam. I stood in the bathroom, naked from the shower, unravelling from a twenty-four-hour shift on the river, the ground still moving beneath my feet. Green, blue and purple bottles lined the glass shelf. Pink conch shells, polished moonstone, topaz and peridot in a Sicilian bowl – all my wife's touches – coloured the bathroom like an ocean. A sea breeze blew in through the open window and rattled the sash frame. Outside, the garden lawn was cracked and parched from drought and littered with bikes, climbing frame, paddling pool, water pistols, footballs, badminton rackets. Seeing these children's things lying out there, lovely in the evening light, so intoxicated me it took minutes before I could respond to Lily calling me out for dinner at Franco's.

From our table Lily is looking around the restaurant, trying to guess who among the crowd is out on a blind date. As the director of an introduction agency (for 'professionals too busy to find love') she may have even fixed them up. Academics, television producers, lawyers, bankers, architects pay a grand for a year's membership and then she gives them access to the files, in which hordes of lonely hearts are profiled according to their interests . . . and their baggage. Clients are offered a minimum of thirteen dates for their money: a baker's dozen chances to find true love. For an extra five hundred quid she makes telephone calls on their behalf. Another five hundred and you get a personal matchmaking service to do all the prep work. Some cynics would say that's paying top dollar just to get laid. But I'm not one of those cynics. It's Lily who sometimes worries, prone as she is to self-criticism. 'I tell these men on the phone, "Come in and have a look at all the lovely ladies on our files." Like they're hookers.' She matches her clients according to lifestyles, aesthetics . . . and then they terminate the arrangement when one or the other lights up a cigarette.

It's her nature to scope a room to see who's in, if there's someone she might know, and it's mine too. Except I look through my ears and nose. And I don't scope a room to see if I recognise anyone. I scope it to see if anyone recognises me. Right now, I'm trying to be as inconspicuous as possible, unmemorable, and watch her watching others. It's a view I like the most. Three prominent scars on her face – split eyebrow, one-inch cicatrix below her bottom lip and a diamond on her chin – catch the candlelight flickering in a blue glass vial on the table and give her otherwise unremarkable features a lift, some piquancy. They dramatise the conventional picture. My wife is pretty in obvious ways. There is nothing predatory or sexual. Her eyes show the strain of someone who's spent a lot of time around unhappy people, the lonely and unloved.

She has two expressions: one of dispassionate interest she uses at the office so her clients don't get the wrong idea, don't confuse her for a woman who can be taken away from the premises for £1000. The other expression she reserves for me. It implies there is only clear water between us. To see myself numbered in her eyes is the only security I have in the world. We've been together twelve years and married for ten, and all the trust I've earned, I've earned in that time.

The life she led before me is all around us in this town, where she was born and raised. The life I led before her, she takes on faith is what I say it is. Which is true for most people, other than childhood sweethearts, before their slow tango down the aisle.

I pour Lily more of this lively red wine from Piedmont with a nose of blackberry, liquorice and wet fox. 'Any of these your clients, then?'

'I have eight hundred clients. There's got to be a good chance one or two might be here. I'm sure I know . . . Or is it need I recognise, you know, written on the faces?'

A birthday party seated at the middle table put their hands together in applause. I twist round in my chair and see a dour-faced and perspiring Franco arriving with a candlelit cake. I wince as a camera flash fires off in my direction. I'm on celluloid, irrevocably. The man in the leather jacket sees something too, something like my after-image in the dying glare. He comes after me again. 'Hey, chief. Haven't we met before?'

It's a gauntlet, thrown in from a dark corner. This time I do say something. 'I don't think so.'

'Yeah, we have. Same school maybe.'

'I didn't go to school round here.'

'Who said anything about round here?'

Short bursts of laughter, the clinking of glasses, a plate crashing to the floor, pyrotechnics. 'Okay,' I say, 'then where *did* you go to school?'

'In a convent.' His laughter runs down my back like cold water.

I stare into my wife's eyes – 'Then we didn't go to the same school' – right through to the back of her skull, until something on the next table short-circuits and I feel a cool breeze of withdrawal.

He rises to his feet and stands behind my back, then moves away seeking the toilets.

Lily determines the birthday boy over there is fifty tonight and tells me the over-fifties don't get filed in the agency. Such a person would have to place a classified ad, or go on a Saga holiday to find a partner. 'Some tribe in Africa used to throw their fifty-year-olds off a cliff,' she tells me. 'Did you know that?'

A few minutes later he is back from the toilets, all frisky and sniffing, and reconnects the circuit. 'Globe Town!' he says from behind my chair. 'You went to school in Globe Town, near the Mile End Road.'

Again it's Lily who answers him, directing her remarks into the space I cannot see. His broken symmetry reflects in the retina of her eyes. 'That's in London. He went to school two hundred miles away from London.'

For the first time I stare across at his friend, who is smoking hard and watching hard. The smile on his face is twenty years in the past.

'Now could you please leave us to finish our dinner,' she says, and this time I hear the shake in her voice. Her confidence dealing with men, this man, is waning and I don't know how to help. My heart's pumping so hard it makes my ribs ache.

The man slides back into his seat.

It is finished. But it will be months before I venture into Franco's again.

'Yes, there are lots of lonely people out there,' Lily sighs with a quick glance across to the next table. 'It makes me think I'll always be in business, don't you agree?' The smile is still live as she turns her attention on to me. Whatever she sees in my face wipes the smile off her own. 'Are you tired?' she asks.

'Yeah, I'm tired.'

'You want to go home?'

'Do you mind?'

'My *darling*. You've been working for twenty-four hours. Let's go home.'

I make a gesture to Franco as he passes along the floor. He reappears from the kitchen a few minutes later with the two men's bottle of wine and our bill. He looks hammered and unable to share platitudes with us as he normally does. But I'm not looking to delay our departure. I pay cash just to get out faster.

A last broadside is made as I am steering Lily towards the door, one voice only crawling up my neck. 'See you again, chief.' There is no possible reply to this but the taunt goes all around the room.

The sky is hot and flammable as we step outside the restaurant. The wind has swung round in the past hour and carries upon it a smell of oil and molasses. It rattles the foliage of the trees and muffles our footfalls as we walk through town. But the streets fail to resurrect me. I have not recovered from those two men and start looking for shadowy places to hide. But we live more in history here than in shadow. Much of the architecture has had more than one life. For instance, the Heritage Centre we pass to starboard has been a leper hospital, a chapel, a tavern and a barracks. Our only hotel was built as a residence for the Duke of York before he became King James II and later used as an ordnance storekeeper's quarter. The Mission Church, now an arts centre, was first a public house where services for new immigrants were held in the bar.

Even Franco's restaurant used to be a fort. Beneath its parquet floor the dead lie stacked up like coral.

I hear arid voices borne on the dirty wind. We may be leading danger to where our children lie sleeping. I would rather not go home just yet and suggest to Lily a wander down by the river. She takes this to be an amorous suggestion.

Five minutes later I hear the river breathing in the dark like a caged animal. Its pulse quickens as it runs to the sea, cleansing itself. A spirit tanker glides up-river from the deep, past a church ship anchored up on the north shore. I embrace Lily, since this was her expectation, and put my hand up inside her shirt to feel the skin on her back. I kiss her with my eyes open and stare out into a reach so wide and deep, sailors could throw a corpse overboard and still call it a burial at sea. People once came here from the far corners of the earth and created a restless asylum before moving on. Others came seeking refuge from East End industry, and shrivelled from the loneliness and quiet before tailing it back to their old jackspaces. Prison ships, asylum hulks, were anchored off our shores. This is where the trauma was sent, where nightmares refuelled on exhalations from the Channel. The river brings them in and moves them on again. When I came, I came by river too, in the middle of the night. Now I've settled here, settled at last in this town on the River Thames, twenty miles downstream from the City of London and twenty miles upstream from the sea.

On our return to the town centre I anticipate two men

springing out at us. But then, as our street comes nearer, mercy is extended: a blackout. The lights are out in all the houses and the street lamps are dark.

Lily says, 'What's done this?'

On winter mornings you can lose your children from under your nose in the mists drifting off the flood plains.

I say, 'Our children are in the darkness,' then navigate our way home by my love of them.

Lily lets us in with her key and I ram home the bolts. Through the dark a smell of smoke is sharp in my nose. Lily shouts out the babysitter's name. Flora screams and we hear feet running. Within seconds Flora, Eliot and the babysitter are in the hall with us. I feel Eliot's fingers clutching my leg.

'What's happened?' Lily's voice is on the edge of hysteria.

'I think it's a power cut.'

'Why didn't you call us on the mobile? What's that smell of burning?'

'We tried to light the candles in the kitchen' – this is Flora 'and Eliot set the tablecloth alight. *Stupid boy!*'

'Flora, no . . .' the babysitter says, still on our payroll.

'Why aren't they in bed?'

'They were,' she defends herself. 'I was reading them a story when it happened.'

'You should get home. Can I pay you tomorrow, when I can see my purse?'

'Yes of course, Mrs Greenland.'

After Lily cuts the babysitter loose and I've re-bolted the door, Eliot says through the pitch-black, 'I was frightened that burglars would come in and steal everything.'

'Was it Al Qaeda who did it?' Flora asks.

'No, darling. Just a common-or-garden power cut.'

'Tony Blair said a terrorist attack was . . . was . . . imminent. That means right away, doesn't it?'

'Tony Blair doesn't always know what he's talking about, Flora. I'll take you up to bed. You too Eliot, wherever you are. It's past ten already.'

I get the candles from the kitchen while Lily is settling the children and place one in their bedroom, the bathroom and on the stairs. The last of the candles I take to our room. Lily comes in after a few moments and sits on the bed, loosening her clothes in the light of the flame. 'I left the candle burning in their room. Will you go in there and blow it out?'

'Of course.'

'Then I can go to sleep. I'm bushed.' She covers her naked body with the duvet. She seems to have forgotten I've been up for twenty-four hours.

In a little while I pad softly out of our bedroom, into the children's room and find them asleep. Then I do what I often do when I've had a scare: perch on the edge of the lower bunk-bed and listen to them sleep; Eliot above and Flora below. His arm hangs down the side of the bed. The duvet is twisted around her waist. Her blonde hair spun on the pillow is as ephemeral as cloud.

I blow out their candle and inhale the smell of hot wax. The outline of toys and furniture hardens as my eyes grow accustomed to the darkness. My agitation drips away slowly. Then the house lights come back on – forceful and sudden. The children stir in their sleep before I can hit the light in their room. I draw the curtain tightly over the window and hear my heart pounding.

In our bedroom Lily sleeps in the candle's lambent glow. I snuff out the flame between my fingers and move to the window. Outside, the street has a totemic menace. An echo from that world finds its way into the bedroom in a motion of air particles.

By rights I belong out there in the dark streets
Instead of on this island normal
I gatecrashed twelve years ago,
On false pretences.

2

Five years before *my* slow tango down the aisle with Lily, I was being assessed for risk. I went before a committee comprising the prison governor, a local GP, headmaster and solicitor. They examined the progress reports from my counsellor and my wing probation officer, and looked at me closely to see if I resembled the written word.

For nine years their aim had been to return me to the community.

But after killing once you can never return to innocence.

You cross a line and the landscape on the other side is lost to you for ever.

The committee acknowledged this when it said, 'Even if you are released from custody, you will belong to the Lifer Unit until your death is notified. You remain subject to recall to the end of your days.'

The governor made it clearer still: 'Your life will never be your own.'

At twenty-one they asked me what I was going to do when released, *if* I got released. I'd been in custody since the age of twelve. I completed all my schooling inside, and from seventeen, studied for an inshore navigation certificate by distant learning.

I told the committee that my aim was to become a river pilot. One day.

They knew this already. But inside, repetition of future aims is a sign of recovery from past sins.

It was prohibited for a Category-A prisoner released on licence to work with people along the lines of education or psychotherapy. But a blue-collar job would suit fine, working with marine machines. Out on the river I'd be no risk to the community. But the fishes better watch out.

Nearer still to the time of my tariff date, the governor told me I needed a new name. The world outside was baying for my blood and my old name, Mark Swain, was a noose. He said, 'You're interested in charts and maps, what about a country?' I chose 'Greenland' as a surname, because fire can't rage in the ice and snow. Raymond . . . 'Ray' was the name of his favourite uncle. Then Social Services paid me a visit with a National Insurance number made out in my new name. I was issued with a passport too, but if I ever wanted to travel abroad, say for a holiday, the home probation officer would first have to do a risk assessment. Would I come back? Would there be hostile media interest?

As my day to be released approached and I could smell the roses, the press – who could also smell something – opened up the case again. The shout lines referred back to a boy who 'killed without remorse'. They reported on the preparedness of vigilantes awaiting my release, and how patient they'd been. Some of the papers tried to tip them off on what I looked like now. Newspapers have their own men inside.

So who were these vigilantes? Certainly not relatives of the victim. We all want to kill somebody sometime.

But only people who actually have known what it's like on the other side: dark, barren and windswept and very, very lonely. If I could convince anyone tempted to kill me that it only results in eternal shame and ruined families for generations to come, I would. But you can't talk people out of doing something if they are set on finding these things out for themselves.

With so much hostile pre-release curiosity, the official solicitor issued a seven-year injunction against the media disclosing my new identity or whereabouts. While the news editors fumed about the injustice of this, I went out of prison a couple of times on day release. In the last phase of my custody, the people upstairs were arranging my acclimatisation. They found a volunteer to chaperone me. An Anglo-Indian final-year sociology student at Essex University helped me learn what it was like on the outside, about fashions and trends. I suspect I became the subject of her thesis but never mind. On my first day release she took me to a party where I met some of her friends. I don't know what she knew about me, but in any case I found it very easy to put people off the scent. I fitted in with her friends by smiling, laughing and having something to say. People trust a party animal. They suspect someone too grave and sincere. Then a month later, in November, she took me out again to a Guy Fawkes bonfire party. *Interesting*. We held sparklers and discussed how fire has many symbolic definitions: to purify and give light as well as to heat. She told me the story of Phaethon, who got permission from his father to drive the horses of the sun for a day. But he couldn't control them and would have set the world on fire if Zeus had not killed him with a thunderbolt. He fell from his chariot into the river and his sisters mourned for him until they turned into trees.

Then early one morning I slipped out through the main gates and never came back. I began my supervision with a home probation officer. He would own me now, until he saw fit to cut me loose.

Tom Reeves was the home probation officer. He was plunging a chocolate biscuit into a mug of tea as I walked into his office. I sat on the opposite side of his desk and the first thing I heard him say was, 'Do you believe in the intrinsic goodness of a child?' But not before he'd finished that biscuit.

'What do you mean?' I asked.

'I know very little about you,' he continued, 'apart from what's in the CPS Bundle.' He patted the pile of papers on his desk that had been maintained and updated and followed me wherever I moved. 'But this is mainly offence analysis – statements you made before and during your trial, CATS team interviews, prison reports. What they don't really tell me is: are you still a risk?'

'I'm not. I don't think I am.'

'You're going to have to talk to me.'

'I am talking to you.'

'About your childhood, things that happened *before* you committed this . . .'

He couldn't finish his sentence. So I finished it for him. 'Murder.'

'I'd prefer to call it a killing, wouldn't you?'

'You can call it a killing, but I did time for murder.'

'Adults commit murder. You were twelve at the time.' His eyes locked on to mine. 'At some point I'm going to ask you to revisit the moment of the offence.'

'Okay,' I said, even though I'd forgotten that moment, all ten seconds of it. I'd spent a year in custody for every one of those ten seconds, and I still couldn't remember one of them.

Tom repeated his earlier question: Did I believe in the intrinsic goodness of a child?

I looked for an answer in the calming reproduction Monets hanging next to anti-racist, anti-sexist posters behind his head.

'Thing is, Ray, when you're serving a long custodial sentence for doing a bad thing, after a few years you often forget what it was you did that put you in there. Maybe you have to forget it, because what you did makes you feel ashamed. In any case, you begin to think you're in detention for being *who* you are. Not for what you once did. You think you're a bad person.'

'Okay,' I said. 'Now I'm with you. I do believe in the intrinsic goodness of a child. Yes. Definitely.'

'Do you know what intrinsic means?'

'No.'

'You're going to have to start talking to me . . . *truthfully*.'

I'd got into the habit of telling officials what I thought they wanted to hear. But Tom always seemed to know the difference, and in time so did I. What happens then, when you begin to tell the truth, is a lot more interesting than when you tell lies.

I said, 'I don't want to live. But I've left it too late to kill myself. That would be too good for me.'

Tom called this my depression talking. My one act of homicide was analogous to suicide and I didn't need to kill myself twice. This was my second life, second chance, and instead of feeling guilty to the end of my days, he suggested I should find a nice wife to love. But that would involve me making a disclosure about the past, wouldn't it? And I wasn't ready for that. I had yet to convince myself I wasn't intrinsically *bad*. All I could hope for was that my guilt and shame might help me become a good citizen, maybe a better citizen than most.

I was only happy when talking to Tom; chronically depressed the moment I left his office. Then I would go to a café across the road from his building and from where I could see his window. I'd sit there for an hour or more, or until someone in the café scrambled a memory. *You look like someone I know* – I've been told a dozen times. Then, back in my digs I'd look at myself in the bathroom mirror. I wanted to see if anything of the child still survived in my adult face, but my eyes frightened me. They were shifty and dark. I practised a look that wasn't my own and thereafter, whenever I felt someone's eyes on me, would work up the same tension in the muscles across my forehead and under the base of my nose. Why do some people think they know you anyway? How do people, who hardly know themselves, think they know who you are? Is it they can only recognise themselves in others?

Meanwhile I was going out of my mind for want of someone to share myself with. The loneliness was sending me crazy. I'd come home from work and wash up, then watch hours of TV until my jaw sagged from ennui. I'd take myself off to bed and sleep with silence. Every night I'd lie awake listening to it in the dark.

I saw Tom once a week for twelve weeks, then once a fortnight for the next twelve weeks and monthly thereafter. One hour per session. This went on for four years, in the same late-Victorian building, with its cold, disused fireplaces, bottle windows and dark green walls – the colour of suspended punishment.

Nearing the end of four years' supervision, we still hadn't cracked open the 'moment of my offence'. I asked him why.

He asked me why. 'I've been waiting for you to start, Ray.'

'I can't remember it.'

'You won't leave here until you do. You've got to go there sometime.'

'I don't know *how* to go there.'

'Is it because you don't want your supervision to come to an end?'

'Why wouldn't I want it to end?'

'Because it's the only place you can be true to yourself.'

He was right of course. Truth was the lingua franca in my supervision periods, while lies kept me alive outside. And it was Tom who taught me how to lie as well as tell the truth. From the age of twelve I'd lived inside institutions. I needed a back story, to be deployed whenever someone – struggling with their memory to locate me, where they'd seen me before – asked about my life. So Tom 'lent' me his. Month by month he guided me through the geography of his hometown of Oystermouth with the aid of Ordnance Survey maps. He enrolled me into his grammar school, introduced his school friends and teachers. He told me how to tell stories. 'If you can tell stories well, people tend to believe you.' We worked on the detail about friends and what they did, where they did it. Gradually that town of Oystermouth became my town. It was a happy place and a happy time. I borrowed everything but his family – mum, dad and siblings. His family was not for trading and I understood why.

Then finally under his guidance, I did revisit the 'moment of the offence'. It took a long time to get there. And I never want to go back.

That is one story I never want to tell again.

Ten seconds that shook the world.

After that watershed was passed, Tom said I was clean. Recalling the moment of my offence was the final piece in the jigsaw needed to convince him I was risk-free, and to prove it, he called a case conference with members of the Multi-Agency Public Protection team. His colleagues in health, police, Social Services and their solicitors all agreed that nothing about this meeting should go on to the computer. They weighed up my progress against the original offence. Then he proposed the suspension of my supervision.

He told me the result in his office a week later. After four years' 'trouble-free existence in the community' my supervision was to be cancelled. The licence would remain in force and I could be recalled to prison at any time. But I was free to go. Tom no longer needed to see me again.

In our time together I'd learnt few facts about Tom, while he learnt everything there was to know about me. But he never complained our relationship was one-sided, said he was just doing the job, of which listening was the primary component. No one says anything until someone listens.

And so after four years' listening, what did he do?

He stopped listening to me for the first time.

I didn't want to let him go. I was dependent on him. Tom Reeves was the only person I didn't have to lie to. He alone knew how it was for me in the world. This was the worst possible news.

I wept in his office and banged my fists on his desk.

Tom sat there passively. After all his years of support, he refused to acknowledge my cry for help.

He said, 'You've complied with the terms of probation and are free to go.'

'Free to do what? No, Tom, no, listen to me . . .' Tom saw the big picture. He knew the thing about me no one else knew. 'I'm lost without you.'

'You have your own life now, a job on the river. You've been promoted twice. You don't need me.'

'No, you're wrong. I can't have any of those things

without you. I'm like a munitions ship people believe is a Cunard liner.'

'You've earned your place in the world again, Ray.'

'I'm on licence in the world. I belong to *you*.'

'You don't belong to me. No. That is wrong.'

Tom was married with three grown-up sons. He was a trained psychiatric nurse. He spent his childhood by the seaside. Now the other thing I learnt, so late in the day, was that I did not belong to him.

'Am I wrong?' I asked. 'Whose personal history is it I'm lugging around and calling my own? I'll forget what I am if I lose you. How many times do I have to say this? I do belong to you.' Then I added provocatively: 'In the same sense you belong to your wife and kids.'

He didn't like this, my bringing his family into the room. But he never said anything.

'My birth certificate is a lie. My National Insurance number is a lie. I don't drive because I can't bear holding yet another fake document.'

'But you've worked so hard to establish yourself, Ray.'

'Oh, I know . . . I'm so full of love for life, euphoric about the order of things. But only when I'm on the river, Tom. Only when I'm away from straying eyes. No one can come after me when I'm on the river.'

'That's more than most men feel, that joy of being at work.'

'It's not joy. And I have to go home sometime. Then I'm not safe. I leave work and I'm not safe. Don't you see? The river and your office are the only places where I can be myself.'

For four years Tom's office had remained more or less the same. It never had a paint job. The same green walls surrounded us. Except now they were closing in on me. Beyond the window rain-clouds moved sluggishly across the sky. I felt the barometer pressure dropping in my blood, felt the river outside at low ebb.

'All these people asking probing questions year in, year out . . . it's only a matter of time before someone fingers me. Someone who knew me back then. The stress is bringing up bad things in my head.'

'Like what?'

'A deep soulful sensation. Like the sensation of warmth that killing brings.'

Tom's eyes magnified through his spectacles. He watched me closely, my whole person – what my feet and hands were doing, as well as my mouth and eyes. He once claimed he could tell I was withholding something by the way I crossed my arms.

'Are you just telling me this, Ray, so I'll not cancel your supervision?'

Like I said, I couldn't lie to Tom. 'I no longer live with those impulses. I will always be at risk, but not *a* risk.'

'I am going to cancel your supervision. I want you to try it for a trial period at least. After a year you can come back in if you wish. If I don't see you in a year, I'll take that as a positive sign. How does that sound?'

'Like death.'

'Oh come on.'

'Can I keep seeing you as a friend?'

'I can't be useful to you as a friend.'

'I could listen to you for a change, Tom.'

'Not on, Ray. I think you know that.'

I started to panic, clutch at straws. 'Do you know, you've far too much hair at your age. How many of your friends have told you *that*? It's immodest.'

'That's what my wife says.'

He smiled at me. A result . . . a chink of light. But too little, too late.

* * *

I went about my life in a permanent state of self-absorption, only free of it when working. Navigation is a defence against self-absorption. The river persuades you into its way of thinking. Motion is a state of optimism and everything about the river lives in the present. Off the river the past catches up with you again.

I was struggling with this crippling depression that prevents a person from seeing a thing for what it is when I met Lily at a Christmas party in Waterman's Hall, a few months after I'd been released from supervision. While she flirted with me, I was measuring up the risk involved to me in taking this further. After the first year of our courtship I began measuring up the risk to her as well. I didn't imagine she'd forgive me if she discovered I was once that boy called Mark Swain. I was convinced she'd decide the past still lived within me, as a primordial force, and run a mile.

Without knowing what lay behind my reserve, she wore it down and helped me rise above this self-absorption. I still had no ego, no self-love. She was the only thing around worth a damn. I didn't go back to see Tom because Lily was now my holding ground. And I had done what he suggested I do. Rather than shroud myself in guilt and shame, I loved someone to the very best of my abilities. And I didn't go back to see Tom because I was in breach of the terms of my Life Licence. I should have made a disclosure to him about Lily and one to her about myself. Failing to do so was what they referred to as a Recallable Offence. I'd be put back under supervision again at the very least, or returned to jail. I was the property of the Lifer Unit 'until my death is notified'. So that's how it stood – I was in breach of certain codes and practices when I went off with Lily. I wasn't breaking the law, wasn't a risk to society. But I was a risk to Lily. She'd been tainted by my past without knowing it, like someone catching a sexually transmitted disease.

We dated for two years and got married when she was pregnant with Flora. Now how could I tell her? It would crush her, crush this new family. My daughter's life would be cursed if the truth were revealed. Two years later Eliot was born and I suspended the decision to make a disclosure indefinitely.

All Lily's ever said is there's something about me she can't work out, a dark streak on my psyche, but admitted it excited her. Women like men to be a little dangerous, and that has never been difficult for me.

There are a thousand lifers like me out there on licence, their supervision cancelled. Who do *you* think you are married to?

I am guilty of an unspeakable crime, but it was committed in another age. I tell myself all the time, we can have more than one life. We all deserve a second chance. So that thing is over, there is nothing of that past bleeding into this present. What was true then is false now. My wife is Mrs Ray Greenland and she sleeps with the angels. Mark Swain, if ever she remembers him, is that infamous boy who disappeared long ago.

But one slip, one mistake, and it will all be dust. The tension continues to mount. If I'm vigilant it's not because I prefer to live than die, but because the preservation instinct is embedded in the genes.

So here's the thing: if that day comes and I'm cornered in some dark street and know I'm in the final seconds of my life, I'm not going to panic. If you're not scared of death you'll never die.

But until that moment arrives, I'll be fighting to stay alive with everything I've got.

3

Noon on Saturday, and the heat presses down like stone as we arrive at Flora and Eliot's school for the occasion of the summer fête. In the playing fields under every dark tree there is a darker shadow. At the south end of the field a game of boy football teeters, without a referee, on the verge of anarchy. We give our children five pounds each to spend and they fly off towards the stalls that are set out like a wagon train. I wander lethargically after Lily as she makes some early purchases, a five-thousand-piece jigsaw and a homemade chocolate cake, which is going to melt before this day is through. I make for the bar and return with two glasses of Pimms clutched in one hand. Mine does not last long. I catch a glimpse of the sun as I am draining the cup. The kids return spent out. I replenish their pockets, then get another one of those Pimms. I watch where Eliot runs off to and see him hook up with his school chum, Jamie Fox, admiring the McLaren F1 and the 1949 Frazer Nash on display. I see his sister with her own posse gathered by the coconut shy. I look for any men unaccompanied by children walking in the shadows under the sycamore boughs.

Parents congregate around the white plastic garden

tables seeking the shade of umbrellas. The sun makes everyone subdued and swollen in the neck. Only Jamie Fox's mother has any energy and greets Lily like a Latino with brown smoky edges to her voice. Lily doesn't like her because she married a stockbroker for his gold. He reminds Lily of her own bad time with a man in the same line of work. Both the Foxes are overdue for a coronary: she spends all day in the gym while he is pounding the trading floors. Because Lily doesn't like her, I pass her over to greet Larissa Osborne, who is Eliot's best friend's mother. Like my wife, Larissa was born and bred in this town. She even went to this school herself as a child. I bend down to stroke her golden retriever puppy and he nibbles my fingers. Larissa pushes the dog off and smacks his nose. 'He's got to stick to the rules,' she says. As I unfurl to full height along comes a cheeky cockney whose name I can't remember, bursting out of her blouse. She kisses me on the cheek, which is a first.

The ceremony of motherhood emits a powerful force. All that unconditional love they give to and receive from their children makes them arrogant. Even this early in the day, women are chanting accounts of their children with priest-like piety, while their husbands jostle at the bar stall, their business mobile phones firing off in their holsters. But in the real business of children, these men are just messenger boys.

Neither Lily nor I have brought our mobile phones. This is not a place of work. Only by leaving phones behind can you distinguish a day off from a day on.

I like all the women, even Jamie Fox's mother, who I overhear tell someone that she never wears knickers. Now I'm going to spend the rest of the day thinking about her taking a leak. I like these women and these women like me. I don't threaten them as some men do – househusbands who can turn in decent fairy cakes – who stand in the female preserve of the school playground at closing time.

As I'm beginning to relax, Lily reminds me I'm on barbecue duty. I'd forgotten she'd volunteered me for this. I'm comforted to see Larissa's old man, Peter, on the same shift, and join him at the grill, where he hands me an apron. Native families like the Osbornes are reliable in my view, because they prefer the hermitage to a life at sea, and can flip hamburgers and chicken drumsticks all day without hankering for views of the horizon.

But what goes up comes down. A new volunteer joins us at the fire, wearing Paul Smith cufflinks in his shirt. The thick hair on the backs of his hands could hide a muskrat. His small and remote eyes settle upon me, prickling the sweat behind my ears. He asks Peter what he should do in a pungent South African accent, and is put to work. We take so many orders in the next ten minutes that soon I am wading through the crowds to fetch more supplies from the back of a refrigerated van parked in the field. Returning to the barbecue with stacks of chilled hamburgers and chicken drumsticks I hear the word *explosives* on the South African's lips. This is what happens when you walk away from an otherwise manageable situation: it moves on and becomes something you don't understand and can't control.

It seems they are in the middle of a story Peter is telling, about making pipe bombs as a boy, using sulphur, potassium nitrate and charcoal for gunpowder. The South African, whose name is Deke, asks him: 'How old were you when you began your life of crime?'

'Ten or eleven.'

'Christ, man, you started late.' Deke laughs with an easy, Southern Hemisphere informality.

'My parents called a cop to our house. He asked if I

was an IRA sympathiser.' Peter holds on to a nostalgic smile. 'I said I was. Then he goes, "Do you know what sympathiser means?" *No*.' Peter turns to me. 'What about you, Ray? What's your confession?'

The whole lying opera of memory: 'I stole a bus when I was sixteen.'

They both laugh at this, but Peter's laugh dies in his throat. He knows a little more about me than Deke. A hamburger falls between the grill to be consumed by flames. 'But you can't drive, Ray.'

I look Peter in the eye. 'I can drive. I just don't have a licence.'

Peter waves a spatula in the air and says in his good-natured way, 'Slightly hypothetical anyway, as you wouldn't have had one at sixteen.'

'So tell us how you stole this bus,' Deke pursues me.

They want a story, a tale to take their minds off the hot coals and the heat of the day.

'I was with some friends trying to get home one night so we stole a bus . . . a works coach. All you needed in those days was silver foil from a cigarette packet between the contact points. Janway Davis was the thief. I was the driver.'

'Is that his real name, Janway Davis?'

'We were driving along the Oystermouth Road, singing, "We're All Going on a Summer Holiday", when a police car pulled us over. And these friends of mine jumped out the door, ran across the golf links on to the beach and started swimming out to sea. The cop came to my window and said, "You're driving without any lights." He looked at me closely and said, "How old are you, son?"'

'Oystermouth Road . . .' the South African trickles the words out on his tongue; a man trying to remember something.

'What did your parents do?'

'The magistrate said he could see I was from a good home and went to a good school, and didn't want me back in his courtroom again.' I strain for a laugh. 'But I never snitched. My friends still owe me for that.'

'What was the school called?' Deke asks.

'Emanuel.'

'In Oystermouth?'

Deke has this way of asking the difficult questions innocently, and now I am uneasy and look for Lily in the crowds.

'Yeah, in Oystermouth. The town was called Oystermouth.'

'Oh, man oh man! I was a boarder there.'

'Were your parents missionaries?' I ask swiftly.

'Yes, they were.' Deke is overjoyed to have his past recognised. Then he looks at me, his eyes like fishing hooks reeling in the years, trying to locate my face in a different time and place. But I am the one schoolboy Deke has never met. I'm standing in for Tom Reeves here. This is an awkward moment but not a life-threatening one.

He explains to Peter that Emanuel was a Christian school that took pupils as boarders if their parents were missionaries.

'That's unusual . . . your parents being missionaries,' says Peter.

Deke turns to me again, excitement rising in his nasal voice. 'Do you remember the science teacher, Gobbers? I ran into him about a year ago. Hadn't changed a bit.'

'I think you're a bit younger than me.'

'How old are you?' he asks.

'I'm thirty-eight.'

'Then I am younger. But Gobbers was there since the Flood.'

'My science teacher's name was Goldberg,' I say. 'Close.'

'Are you sure?'

'Sure I'm sure.'

'Gobbers . . .' Peter says. 'Was that his real name?'

'We called him Gobbers because he had protruding bottom teeth. Every time he talked he'd spit up his nostrils.'

The queue for hamburgers and chicken is getting longer. We are not keeping up with demand. I want this conversation to end but I don't know how. Scorched by both fire and sun my blood runs thin through my veins. I slip an undercooked burger into a roll and sell it.

Deke chants as a way of remembering: 'Goldberg . . . Goldberg . . .'

'It's possible he left or got sacked. He was shagging one of the sixth-form girls.'

This little anecdote animates Deke. 'Shagging his pupil? Man, that's heavy for that old place. For a Christian school.'

'How come this missionary school turned out misfit atheists like you two?' Peter jests.

'I'm not an atheist,' Deke says.

'And it wasn't a missionary school,' I add. 'We saw them necking in his car. Goldberg and this sixth-former. After that we skipped science whenever we liked – down to the beach and there was nothing he could do. Lounging about, diving off Donkey Rock.'

'These the same friends who stole the bus?' Deke asks.

Noises rising off the baking field become congealed and distant as a crowd at the seaside.

'Or if it was raining or winter we played snooker in Overland Road.'

Why do I push this? Why can't I stop?

Deke points a finger in my face. 'The Churchmen's Club, yeah?'

'Opposite St Mary's Church.'

He pauses for a split second. 'St Peter's.'

'St Peter's . . . you're right. My friend's dad was a member of the club. He used to keep the key in a cigar box.'

Flora appears, pulling at my shirt tail, and makes me feel uncomfortable. I don't want her hearing this story. But she soon goes when I give her a hamburger.

'You see your old *poes* still, Ray? Janway Davis and those other guys?'

I look at the spatula in my hand, trying to remember how to use it. Lily appears at my elbow and announces my shift is over. She has overheard part of my story, about keys in a cigar box, and looks a little hurt that after ten years of marriage there are still accounts coming from my mouth that are new to her. With Deke's last question still hanging in the air she looks at me, and detects trouble in my eyes.

'I've never heard of Janway Davis,' Deke reprises the issue. 'But what about Brush, who was as thick as one? You must remember him? Or Bottom Turn Ern . . . a surfer who could pull a big turn on a wave but fell off each time. Remember Shirt and Buster who spat into their own fish and chips? Or Plank, a.k.a. Bill Sandries, the only ex-Emanuel schoolboy to be sent to prison for GBH. Or Pixie Hardy who went to Australia because everyone called him queer, and Glanmor Thomas who followed him out there. Jonah, Digger, Jubilee . . . these guys were larger than life and all ages. And Smudge! The cockney hiring out deckchairs. Surely you remember him? Smudge was well into his thirties and dating sixteen-year-old girls. What about Coochie Bear, the ugliest kid in Oystermouth and his best friend, Noel Morgan, the most beautiful boy in Oystermouth?'

I say simply, 'I don't see anyone any more. I've lost touch.' I bow my head and feel the heat of the barbecue on my already burning face.

He makes one last passing shot. 'What about the girls? You must have old girlfriends.'

Lily hears a hint of malice in this. 'Talking to me about his old girlfriends won't win him any beauty contest.' She peels off my apron like I'm one of the children, takes the spatula out of my hand and pulls me away.

I am sometimes amazed at Lily's capacity for knowing when I need her, without knowing *why* I do.

'I don't like him,' she says when we are out of earshot. 'I mean, where was he when Nelson Mandela was in jail?'

Still dazed by the interrogation he was giving me, I say, 'His parents were missionaries in South Africa.'

'Then I rest my case.'

It's not much longer before the children – having eaten what is on offer, seen their friends, completed the circuit of stalls several times over, and now burnt out by the sun – want to exit. Moments later, we stand outside Lily's car with the doors open to expel the trapped heat. What strangeness presses down on my mind in that minute I will never be able to understand; a mood that forewarns of something failing in the psychic universe. A sort of epitaph for the future, in which I sense the trees exfoliating around us.

The car is still as hot as an oven as we drive off and puts the kids into a warlike state. They needle and pinch, kick and scratch in a series of attacks and counter-attacks. Lily's over the rack from the tension and claims other drivers are steering straight for her. Eliot elbows Flora in the chest and I twist round in my seat to face them screaming in the back. 'Hey! Hey! Let your mum drive safely.'

At a set of traffic lights, a young man materialises and begins to wash the windscreen with a sodden towel. Lily tells the bloke to push off through her open window. When I hear him call her a cunt I open the passenger door. '*No!*' Lily grabs my arm. The lights turn to green and she guns it. 'That would be a stupid thing to do.' She is, of course, correct.

I try to distract the kids again, attempt to calm them down with a story about the Norwegian barque *Sophie*, found dismasted off the Scilly Isles in 1896. 'It's early in the morning, right? The islanders board the ship and find the dinner table laid, a lamb stew simmering on the stove, the log up to date, a hold full of coal. But no crew on board, just a dog wagging his tail. If a ship is abandoned, it's within the law for anyone who wants it to take the cargo, so they take all the coal off the ship.'

'What kind of dog?' Flora asks.

'Border collie.'

'Why did the crew leave the dog behind?'

'That's *the* interesting question. When the owners of the vessel laid claim to its cargo, those islanders wound up in court and had to pay for the coal they took. And you know why? Because the court ruled the ship had not been abandoned because the dog was left on board.'

'Lots of Lassie for him,' Lily says.

'Why are they called the Scilly Isles?' asks Eliot.

'Because it's a stupid place to put them,' Flora laughs.

Eliot hits her and she hits him back. Then we all hit something.

We hit something. A loud bang outside is synchronous with one inside as the airbags inflate. The car has stopped but the forward momentum has yet to cease. I'm pushing deeper and deeper into the soft plastic shell of the airbag. It is deathly quiet. Only the engine purrs like a kitten and then that cuts out. My head and torso are jammed between the seat and the airbag. I'm still facing the back so can see the kids are fine, albeit with desperate countenances. They think they caused this by fighting. My next thought is about the airbags. I never quite trusted there was anything behind the dashboard until now.

Then: '*Is everyone all right!*' Lily shouts.

'What did you hit?' I ask, but she doesn't know.

I open the door and ease my way out to discover we have driven into the back of a gold-coloured Sports Utility Vehicle. The nose of our car is peeled back and the radiator exposed like snarling teeth. An old blue Toyota is beached in the middle of the road with its front bumper on the tarmac. A bicycle lies on its side with the wheel spinning. A woman on her back kicks her legs in the air. Five feet away, a young girl of no more than three is face down on the road. She wears a helmet and a turquoise dress and one of her shoes has come off her foot. Cars begin to build up in both directions, horns blaring. Whoever is inside the SUV hides behind smoked glass. The driver of the Toyota materialises and holds his hands over his ears. Lily is still prising herself out of the car while ordering the kids to stay put. She sees the woman and the girl. I hear her intake of breath. She reaches the child where she lies faster than I can think. The mother screams for the first time, breaking a very long silence of maybe fifteen seconds, and crawls over to where her little girl is being comforted by Lily. The Toyota driver – West African at a guess – has startled eyes. He keeps repeating in heavily accented English: 'This is not close to the pretty. This is not close to the pretty.' The SUV engine idles, but still no show from the driver. I don't know what's happened but when the child's voice changes tone from rasping inhalation to a loud cry I think it's going to be all right. She's going to be all right. The mother is now cradling the girl in her arms. 'Jesus Christ, oh . . . oh . . . my sweet . . . there, there . . . oh Jesus . . .' The little girl's face is cut and grazed. Blood and road dirt on her face is a very upsetting sight for the mother, whose arm looks deformed, broken at the wrist. For the moment she is anaesthetised by worry.

I ask her, 'Did he hit you . . . the Toyota?'

It's another voice from behind that I hear. 'No one hit her.' I turn to see the SUV driver, now out on the road and leaning against his vehicle. 'She fell off the bike and Uncle Tom here swerved to miss her, then went into me.' His words run round my head like dogs on a track, the *sound* of his words. I've heard this voice before. 'Cycling with a kid on the back . . . How stupid is that.'

'Maybe this is not the right moment for criticism?' Lily remonstrates with him.

I don't look at him closely because I don't want him looking too closely at me. His voice, which conjures desert spaces, reminds me powerfully of one of the two men who sat beside us in Franco's last night. If he wore a leather jacket then, now he wears a dark blue suit with a faint red pinstripe, and shoes that boast a high military polish. His canary-yellow tie is screwed round the neck in a Windsor knot.

Lily does what she can but the woman is beside herself with worry and guilt. The kid's going to be all right, but will need some first aid. The mother's going to need emergency first aid. My kids are trapped in the heat of our car. The West African still looks frightened. I explain to him they're okay, the mother and child, and he backs away from me. I look through the window of his car and notice from the radio equipment that he's a minicab driver.

The other party wants to swap insurance details, even though I can't see any damage to his SUV – his tank. The African shakes his head vigorously and won't give his name. 'Look, chief, this is not my vehicle, all right.' The man asks once again for his name and address. When he tries to read the minicab's registration, the African steps in front of his number plate. He's wearing new trainers and old brown trousers that are greasy on the thighs.

I'm pretty sure I know what's going on: he's an illegal, working under an alias. Can't speak English very well but understands the danger he's in.

The SUV driver produces a mobile phone from his breast pocket. 'Give me your name and address, chief, the company you work for. Do you understand? This is a minicab, right?'

'I send you money.'

'No, no. Name and address. Or I'm calling the Bill. You with me? The filth. The men in blue.'

Lily looks up from the ground. 'Have you called for an ambulance?'

I turn to the SUV driver and risk all: 'I don't think he's insured.' His eyes dilate in the glare. They look burnt by the sun, with brown freckles in the corners. He bows his head to study his phone and key in numbers. His head has been shaved close enough to bring the blood to the surface of the skin. 'You'll get him into a lot of trouble if you make that call.'

'That's not my problem, is it?'

As he is waiting for the phone to fire up I stroll over to the minicab driver. 'Go now, if I were you. Do you understand?'

'Sorry. Yes. Sorry, sorry.'

'You've got nothing to be sorry about. Just fuck off.'

The engine of his car has been running the whole time. He gets in and abandons the scene and his fender on the road.

'Hey!' the other driver shouts. 'Where's he going?'

Lily stands up to him and says with suppressed anger, 'Are you calling an ambulance?'

Our car is as good as beached, with the airbags sitting perkily in the front seats and the bonnet rolled back. I make a suggestion. 'Might be faster if you give them a lift to the hospital.'

'I've got a prior engagement,' he says.

Lily stamps her foot. '*Cancel* it . . . on that mobile phone of yours.'

I look for our kids to see how they're doing, and their faces are pressed against the side window. The fight is all knocked out of them, their drama subsumed in the epic one outside the car. Then, too late to stop her, Lily writes down our address for this man. It makes the hair stand up on the back of my neck. She is insisting that we go to the hospital with the injured cyclists. But someone has to take our children home and I have no choice but to volunteer for the hospital run because I don't want her travelling alone with him. She gets the kids out of the car, remembers to take the chocolate cake she bought at the fête out of the boot and starts to walk the mile to our house.

The cyclist's arm is so swollen and painful she can't do much for her little girl, so I carry her and put her into the back seat. I ride up front in this Mercedes with tan leather seats and Global Positioning System. It's showroom-clean and spotless. We are silent driving, while outside the streets brim with life, like a movie watched through the windscreen. The air-conditioning is cold. I use my advantage as a passenger to look him over.

Shaved head, long nose and serrated jaw.

'Haven't we met before?' I tempt him out. Want to see if I am right.

He takes his eyes off the road and briefly they fall on me. 'I don't think so, chief.'

'Same school maybe?'

He twists round to face me, his new leather seat screeching like old ravens. His eyes scroll down and settle on my mouth, like a woman flirting. 'I said, I don't think so.'

I press my back hard against the door. The injured passengers in the back are still in shock, curled up together, subdued and silent.

'You a family man?' I ask the driver.

'Like we both are, chief.'

'So who's looking after the kids?'

He slows down a tad. 'My ex-wife. For my sins.'

'But you know where they are? A man should know where his kids are at all times.'

He exhales long and hard and loses direction crossing a double white line. He begins to sojourn into the past, his voice freighted with depression as he confesses to the last dark hours of his marriage. Words fall like dust from his mouth. He offers up a self-portrait of a dead man walking into the foyer of the Principal Registry. 'They even X-rayed my bag, chief. Like an airport, but without the Duty Free.' He remembers sordid details – like the security guard's short-wave radio squelch in the court foyer; his married life with children reduced to a number printed on a schedule on the wall; solicitors drifting in and out like undertakers.

He drives straight up a ramp to the A&E. I fall out of the vehicle and offer assistance to the still silent woman by taking her child in my arms. Her hair is warm and soft. I smell blood on her face. The driver shoots off without saying goodbye. He fails to wish them good luck, or even good riddance.

An air of calm efficiency prevails in the A&E; a lull before the storm of a Saturday night. I wait while a nurse makes an assessment. Not long after that a doctor calls them through and I leave. A minute later I'm walking through the streets in the heat of the day. Then I'm running along the thoroughfares with a pounding thought: where has that driver gone with my address on a piece of paper in his pocket?

I get home and find Lily and the children eating melted chocolate cake in the kitchen. In the lounge I pour myself a Macallan straight up. It's only four in the afternoon but it's been a heck of a day already. Lily joins me with a cup of tea. I tell her that the mother and child are going to be okay and she says, 'She was telling me she fell off going over a drain. Stupid woman, riding a bike on the road with a three-year-old on the back.'

'That's what he said . . . the bloke in the SUV. Do you think he was one of the men in Franco's last night? One of the two sitting next to us.'

'Oh, I don't remember, Ray. All I remember is we had a power cut.'

Her lack of interest in him comforts me. It brings me back to earth.

I spend the next half-hour arranging for the car to be towed to a garage, then work off some anxiety playing outside with the kids, who are being unnaturally polite to one another, the car crash still fresh in their memory. They sit on the swings comforting themselves with chocolate cake. When the neighbour's cat jumps over the fence into our garden, Flora breaks off a piece of cake for him. The ginger tom's a regular visitor, but never before has Flora fed him. She has acquired a dutiful concern for vulnerable things, and while she offers the cat some of her cake she asks about the girl who was knocked off her mother's bike. She trembles asking the question and her eyes look hollow. Whereas she can ask questions that go directly to the heart of the matter, Eliot deals with it by obsessing about the damage to our car, perhaps the only way he can understand the violence of the event. Forces that bend metal are supernaturally powerful, and he shivers as he repeats over and over how the bonnet peeled back and exposed the engine. He wants to know if the car will be all right. Flora wants to know if the little girl will be all right – which is really one and the same concern, expressed differently, for their own safety in the world. When I assure them both that the girl will get well and the car will be repaired, I wish it could guarantee their safe passage through life as well.

From what Flora says next, I know she's beginning to recover. 'I saw something just now I've never seen in my life before . . . a squirrel taking a pee.'

Night falls, it remains hot and close, and the children sleep without their duvets. Lily is naked upon our bed as I enter the bedroom. The candle on the bedside table has not been removed since last evening's blackout and I light it again. She smiles at me expectantly. But I'm trying to dampen steel-stark visibility in here, not create an ambience. A single yellow flame is kinder on frail emotion than one hundred white watts.

I play my fingers along the inside of her thighs and kiss her pointed knees. And then, out of the blue, she asks me to trim her pubic hair. Not a request she's ever made before.

I have never denied my wife anything and after finding a pair of hairdressing scissors from the bathroom I start to trim carefully. There are two scars on her belly illuminated by the flame, legacies of her deliveries by Caesarean section. Pregnant with Eliot, she told the surgeon not to open up the original scar but to give her a new one. She felt it wouldn't be respectful to our first-born. So now she has two parallel scars to remember both children by.

I make a neat triangle about the size of a bikini and cut the wispy hair around her labia. She yelps when I snag a hair in the scissors.

'That put tears in my eyes!'

'Sorry. I can't see too much in this light.'

'You're no hairdresser, Ray.'

'I hope you don't let your hairdresser do this.'

She settles again, sinking her head back on the pillow, and yawns deeply as I brush the hair off the sheet into my hand.

I lose the hair down the bathroom toilet and stow away the scissors. When I return to the bedroom she is asleep. People asleep are very different people from when they are awake. In sleep you glimpse the pure form. And it makes me want to sing, knowing she'll still be here in the morning, all funky and warm by my side. I settle myself on the edge of the bed and examine the scars in her eyebrow, lip and chin. I am not the only one with a past, and the soft flame provides a reading light by which to study the history in her face.

Before we met, Lily was in a tryst with some financial securities specialist fourteen years her senior. He looked into her dark brown eyes as I do, played with her chestnut hair that I have seen grow highlights of grey. But what he saw so enraged him it made him want to deface her. Her scars are what he left behind as my dowry. And I tell you this: if ever we meet one dark night, I'll want to return the favour, dramatise that merchant banker's face.

It's all talk, all hot air from me. I just wish him dead.

He sold futures on the stock market and neglected his children from a previous marriage. His former wife was out of the picture and he was raising them alone when he met Lily. He tried palming them off on her, while he made his mint, and she got to love them as if her own.

But blood is thicker than water and from the moment she split with their father, all contact with his kids was lost.

She wouldn't be fooled again into watering someone else's garden. Other people's children became abstractions, proto-citizens not worth a second glance. One of my attractions, she said, was my virginity: no ex-wives or children.

Virginity is one of those words people think they understand.

The truth is, she liked me because I didn't have what the other guy had.

She liked me for what I was not.

Maybe it pleased her too, that her blue-collar man didn't resemble a single professional on file in her pink offices.

A few years after we were married she got to like someone else – for what he was. A widower she met in a bar. The affair lasted four months and I was only told when it was over, although I knew something was going on from the drop in temperature as she moved through the house. The children were very young at the time. I held them close and waited.

When Lily finally confessed she was remorseful about the hurt inflicted upon me. But she was most sorry for herself. Her affair was not a small thing, was not immaterial, and she withdrew from me. This was an affair of the heart and so much more dangerous already than if it had been sexually motivated. She was filling a void and I feared the void was me.

I watched her getting lost. Then thirty-one years old, she was not yet in her life. Her job with a cosmetics company did not satisfy, while I went to work on a river vessel and entrusted my life into the hands of other men; a relationship she said looked more profound than our marriage. A marriage based on entertainment: restaurants, cinema, walks in the park.

She said she could feel time rushing by. She spoke about wanting to do something to make a difference, make a mark. Her ambitions were abstract until one day at home she began talking about the widower. She was drawn to his loneliness. A good man with a thirst for love after such a long drought. At first she'd had nothing on her mind but to counsel him. Then, feeling moved by his sadness, offered sexual solicitude. But sex was no substitute for the love he was seeking.

Hand in hand on the sofa, I asked: 'Would you do it again?'

She shook her head slowly. 'I gave something to him that rightly belongs to us. I plundered our joint account. But was it so terrible, what I did? Like giving someone a pint of your blood.'

Our blood, I thought.

She confessed after it was over, but it was not over for me. Forgiveness was not the point. I had no right to deny anyone forgiveness and Lily had mine in the bank. She hurt me, but no more than I deserved. Every punishment I get takes into consideration crimes committed in the past.

As the weeks passed, a new idea began to take shape in Lily's head. She was fermenting something, based on her experience with the widower. She made connections. In less than a month she evolved the first plan of action. Lily was going into business. She paid for advertising space in magazines and newspapers and began organising discreet liaisons on commission from our house. She called her operation Bliss, a name that remains today.

I didn't like my wife organising sex among strangers. I wanted her to organise love between us. And when she did shift the onus on to love in this new enterprise, it became a respectable and profitable company. When you 'find' love for others they will be eternally grateful, at least as long as the love lasts. Lily's clients were grateful and she came home fulfilled. She settled down at last when marriage – other people's – became her entire focus.

In time, what she learnt from her lonely hearts she brought home to share with me. Conversely, when she said things to me like 'The difference between men and women is, men are selfish and women love selfishly,' I assumed she was rehearsing what she would tell her clients another day. 'The two natures can balance out in a relationship until children come along,' she continued. 'Young children are a threat to a couple, like guests who never leave. That's when marriage goes pear-shaped – when the wife transfers her love on to the children and the husband assumes a foetal position for the next five years. Or gets a mistress.'

If our children tested us once, in those mind-numbing routines of babies, they now sealed the marriage. Doing right by your children is complex and important work, a profound job we were sharing down the middle. 'Do men have affairs,' I asked, 'only because they're jealous of their children?'

'Why do men have affairs . . . Men have affairs so they can confess. So they may bleed.'

Lily regards herself to be a good judge of character not so much from personal experience (there had been too many mistakes) but from her professional experience, from other people's mistakes. But no human judgement is foolproof. Lily is a good judge of character, except for my own.

'How do you know,' I asked, 'that I don't have a mistress?'

She just looked at me in that way I knew so well, a look of the faithful.

Lily believes she has grounds for this trust because I do not look at other women. She never worries that I might drift off to find a mistress. About that she is not wrong. If I'd had different life experiences I might be less faithful. What I do know, though, is monogamy requires stiffer penalties than divorce if it's going to succeed. Prison would be an effective sanction. Love is safer when propelled by guilt, and guilt that predates the marriage – all the better.

Without guilt there is no hope.

4

One privilege of being a lifer is going straight to the top of the waiting list for training courses. I was moved to a prison from the young offenders' institution when I was seventeen and the governor asked me to think about what apprenticeship I'd like to pursue inside, to help me on the outside. But I didn't have to think about it very long.

I said I wanted to work on the river. I wanted to be a pilot.

That might have raised a laugh anywhere else, but not with the governor or my wing probation officer who worked so hard to remove the stain from my soul. We can't bring the river in to you, they said, but we can arrange for you to study all the shore-based navigation courses.

Taking the shore-based course first was in reverse order to the way things are usually done. Normally I would have had to do six to twelve months' watch-keeping time at sea or on the river, and then the theory. But someone in the DTI had a sense of humour and I was allowed to study by distant learning for my STCW 95 certificate in association time, while other inmates watched TV, phoned home or used the gym. I explored the deck of a ship without being seasick; studied the movements of the tides without feeling their hydraulic pull against the keel; read meteorology and stability charts without a drop of rain falling upon my head. Deep into the night I read in my cell about cargo handling and stowing, the ARPA Simulator (radar), Global Maritime Distress and Safety systems, personal survival techniques. I even read the 1836 Select Committee Inquiry into the causes of shipwreck – as though it was an ongoing investigation. I felt my bile rising when I learnt about nineteenth-century ship owners putting profit before crews, employing masters without navigation skills, some as young as fourteen. Wrecks were always cargo issues, crews expendable. I found that deplorable.

During the time I was inside there were several train and plane crashes and the outrage that followed on the radio and on TV astounded me. Why do people refuse to acknowledge that if you are going to travel across land at a hundred miles per hour or above the earth at thirty thousand feet, an element of risk is involved? Yet when the *Doña Paz* collided with a coastal tanker in the Philippines with the loss of 2,749 lives, the public reaction was muted, as though the seamen had it coming.

What I liked most though about this shore-based course was the chart work. I navigated the world in my cell. I worked out passages far beyond the home waters of the British Isles, escaping into the Baltic Sea to the Sweden/Norway border, to the Mediterranean, the Atlantic as far as the Equator, the Chinese coast, the Falklands coast, the Caribbean and South China Seas, the North and South Pacific.

A chart is different from a land map. Unlike cartographers, hydrographers calculate that which cannot be seen, the invisible forces of nature below the surface of the seas and rivers. And if land maps can sometimes be dishonestly drawn, when inaccuracies are shrewd political decisions, charts are always honest. They are personal assurances from the hydrographer to the mariner, more reliable than love letters. Their corrections to new charts and caveats in the weekly *Notices to Mariners* could mean the difference between some sailor coming home safely and dying out at sea. Changes at sea and on tidal rivers like the Thames appear like autumn leaves falling from a tree. I learnt that no chart can ever be safe unless corrected on a daily basis, and scored on my practice ones alterations to buoyage systems, changes in light and fog signals, jetty construction, shipwrecks and information about the shifting seabed supplied by survey ships.

Each night as I drifted into sleep surrounded by navigational aids, I'd sail into the past and change the order of events there.

I came out of prison at twenty-two with eight GCEs, two A-levels and an STCW 95 certificate from the Department of Trade and Industry. Tom Reeves helped me get the practical experience by arranging my first and only job interview. A difficult hour with the boss because a disclosure had to be made to him by the Lifer Unit. I don't know how much he was told about me or even if he knew my true identity. But if he did, he never let on. All he said was, 'Eighteen year I were in the merchant navy, son, flying under all kinds of flags. Worked with a lot of ex-cons too. All that mattered was, were they conscientious seamen? You do the job properly, that's all I care about. If you don't, you'll be getting your cards.'

I began as a deckhand in seven twenty-four-hour shifts every three weeks. From the beginning I never missed a day's work, was never late. I did everything I was told, and more. Occasionally I heard my name, my old name mentioned, or thought I did, in conversations amongst the crews and I'd wait for the blow to the back of the head. But it never came. The boss could have ruined me by spilling a few words but he never told the crews I had previous and nor did he bring up the disclosure again.

If my face barely resembles the one I had at twelve, other things in nature stay the same. Such as the Thames, a seminally unchanging mass with subliminal internal movements and minor disturbances. It was the same as the river I'd studied inside prison. Except now when I read about it on my days off, I could hear it. I could taste it.

I lived in a probation hostel for the first six months and they had to issue me with an overnight pass to get to and from work. Penal conditions still applied to my life – night curfew, and a ban on drugs and alcohol. I had a room the size of my old prison cell, with yellow walls, maroon carpet, sink, wardrobe, my own pots, pans, crockery and a fridge. A PVC bin-liner over the door window reduced the glare of the twenty-four-hour hall light. The light throughout the hostel was strangely grey, like a winter cathedral.

Even though no one said so, all the other residents were ex-Rule 43. I could tell by their eyes (averted), behaviour (compliant), and medication (antidepressants stowed away in the main office). They rolled up an entire half-ounce of Golden Virginia tobacco into cocktail-stick-thin smokes, still rationing the weekly issue of snout that they could now buy at will. In prison they would have been segregated from other inmates for their own protection, and their freedom to roam this hostel (and my freedom to attack them if I wished) made me uncomfortable.

At first I avoided them by holing up in my room with my library books on the Thames and cooked for myself while they were asleep. That was another thing I owed the library. I used its cookery books to make dishes that didn't in the slightest resemble prison food, and with no ground glass either. I used herbs for the first time in my life, and it was the smell of cardamom, paprika and cumin that drew the creatures I lived with out of their lairs and into the kitchen. At first I resented them, then I fed them. Cooking *pour un* is never fun, and the truth was, these fat nonces with childlike voices were the only family I had.

5

Sunday is family day, cordoned off from the rest of the world. The bells of the Dreadnought Mission are ringing out my relief.

It begins with me going by taxi to collect my mother and father-in-law and bring them home for lunch – a detail I volunteer for to reduce the stress on my wife, whose relationship with her mother has always been so-so.

Lily's father, Aubrey, has been in a wheelchair for as long as I've known him. A stroke left him one arm and one leg to work with. Everything else is in the waxworks. Lily's mother, Rose, cares for him at home with some help from the local authority. She can just about lever old Aubrey from his bed to the commode, but the two nurses who call in each day do the grunt work, such as giving him a bath and providing some cleaning and cooking, which Rose maintains is substandard. She follows them around the house as they work, making veiled threats behind their backs. The two Jamaicans, who trapped Aubrey's thumb in the hoist last year as they were lifting him out of the bath, said they were being dogged by her. But this didn't stop Rose firing them on the spot. Over the ten years of his illness she's sent packing seventeen nurses from the local authority, and continues to accuse the help of steaming open her mail in the kitchen and stealing her jewellery from the bedroom.

'It's all junk,' Lily says of this jewellery. 'Five-bob trinkets and plastic pearls. You couldn't pay a thief to take that stuff. It might even be funny if she wasn't chasing off the girls. Soon there'll be no one left who's willing to come.'

But Rose will not hear of it when Lily suggests, as she does from time to time, that Aubrey should go to a nursing home.

'Over my dead body!'

'It may well be, Mum. He's ageing you fast.'

'He makes me feel older than my years. I don't deny that.'

Lily tells me her mother has always been a difficult woman who goes out of her way to find faults in others, a habit that has become pathological with age. No one is immune from her misanthropic opinions and conspiracies. On the day Lily and I got married she took me to one side at the reception and declared: 'I'll be watching you in the future, my boy.'

It's not my future that needs the watching.

Ten years on she is still waiting for me to trip up. So far, though, she has seen nothing much with meat on to really complain about.

I arrive at their postwar, semidetached, pebbledashed house and ask the cab driver to wait. I ring the front doorbell and listen to Rose spring the multiple locks on the other side. She is a sharp-featured woman with a healthy polish to her face; a person who knows she's going to live for ever with a little extra effort. But today there is less polish than usual and I can just tell I'm in for some histrionics.

'*What* a day! What a day I'm having already.'

'What's wrong, Rose?'

'What's *wrong*? Where do I *start*!'

She turns her back on me and retreats into the lanolin-smelling house. I follow her into the lounge, which has been converted into Aubrey's bedroom, and find him sitting up in his wheelchair, smiling at me. Father-in-law to go. On the wall behind his head is a reproduction painting of nineteenth-century ocean-going schooners moored up outside The Prospect of Whitby, and a daguerreotype of Brunel's steamship *Great Eastern* in construction on the Thames. The flock wallpaper makes me go cross-eyed.

Before I can properly greet him, she says, 'This morning I found a mouse living in the bottom drawer of his chest, eating his supply of chocolate. It's even made a nest out of his tissues. None of those useless nurses found it.'

What redeems Rose is her devotion to Aubrey. He is the only person beyond criticism. And it becomes evident to me after a while that he's known of this mouse for days. While Rose is out of the room, he whispers to me, 'I called him Mickey.' He was keeping the mouse for company, even feeding the critter chocolate.

All that is contained in those three drawers is all that he has control over.

Rose returns with his medication – antidepressant, blood pressure, cortisone and heart tablets in a jar – and a cashmere coat that she begins to pull over him.

'It's thirty-two degrees outside, Rose. Do you really think he needs that?'

'It might be hot for you but not for him. He can't move around like you can.'

'You're the boss.'

'At least you got something right.'

I push Aubrey outside as Rose locks up the fort. The driver helps me lift the wheelchair into the cab. As we get going, Rose finds the register that she will sustain all day. 'Lily was looking terrible last Sunday, I thought. What's wrong with her, Ray?'

'Nothing. Lily's fine, don't worry.' Lily and I have a prior agreement not to mention our car accident yesterday. Whether the kids can keep mum is another thing.

'I *have* to worry.' She catches my eye with a severe look. 'If I don't, who will?' She brushes Aubrey's shoulder with her liver-spotted hand, removing the dandruff invisible to the naked eye.

The route we take gives us a few glimpses of the Thames shining like a silver dish under the sun. Rose sighs, looking through the window, and says glumly: 'The river is something you can never quite describe.' Then, as we near the house, she rallies again. 'Who's cooking lunch today? Not you, I hope.'

Cooking Sunday lunch is one of my regular routines I share with Lily's younger brothers. Of the two, I find Colin easier company than Jerry, who is very competitive. For instance, when we play snooker once a week he wants to win so badly we usually throw the match just to keep the mood sweet for when we have a pint afterwards. Colin is also funnier. He has a big spirit that he often has to suppress to prevent laughter leaking out of him all the time.

Colin sells computer software and Jerry works in public relations. I have no idea what their jobs entail in detail, but whatever it is they do, something's turned them both prematurely bald.

Jerry is better at keeping in touch than Colin, which extends to him calling me every week, even when I'm on the river, via my mobile phone. He starts by asking the same question. 'How's the water today, Ray?'

And I give the same reply. 'Flowing nicely, Jerry.'

As we prepare the meal in the kitchen, the wives keep out the way in the living room, enjoying the role reversal and the white Rioja. I often wonder what they talk about on Sundays. Lily assures me they only talk about us, which I find hard to believe. When Jerry, Colin and I are cooking we talk about them twenty per cent of the time and sport eighty per cent.

We like cooking for the women because they really appreciate the effort. Lily in particular is still quite shattered by her parents' culinary habits. 'I worked it out once that in forty years of marriage Rose has cooked for Aubrey fifteen thousand meals. And not once have I heard him say thank you.'

Today we are making tea-smoked chicken with chorizo and artichoke pilaff, from a recipe Jerry took off the BBC web page. The print-out sits on the counter, and we keep consulting it every few minutes. Colin blends with olive oil a herb mix of parsley and chives, while Jerry mixes sugar and tea leaves in a bowl. As I line the base and sides of our large frying pan with tinfoil, Colin regales us with an account of some programme he watched last night on television, about men and women in sexual relationships with animals.

'What time was this?' Jerry asks.

'About two in the morning.'

'What were you doing up at two?'

'Do you want to hear this or not?'

'Do we have a choice?'

'This woman was talking about sex with her golden retriever and her husband saying how he likes to watch. That was bad enough, but when she started on the subject of intercourse with her stallion, I had to hide behind the sofa.'

'Colin, we gotta eat later.'

Colin ignores Jerry. 'The men all looked like werewolves. One of them was describing how his horse likes to come when he's fucking her, and another how he has to stand on a bucket to reach. Then his wife said, "In our eight years of marriage I've had to share my husband with three mares." That was it. That was when I changed channels and watched the last thirty minutes of *The Horse Whisperer* on ITV.'

While Colin has been talking I've been watching the children through the window playing in the garden with a tent and hose. Now the girls are running into the tent and the boys are firing on them with the hose. They're all wearing swimming costumes and so that's all right. But the noise they generate prevents Aubrey from taking his nap. He sits in his wheelchair beneath a large umbrella with Rose in a plastic garden chair by his side, watching her grandchildren. For the moment her look of rectitude is absent.

My attention flits constantly from the kitchen into the garden. It's as though I don't want to miss a single moment of their childhood, as though I have only a finite amount of time left with them. I see my three-year-old niece, Colin's daughter, climb up the slide and Eliot turn the hose on the slide as she descends, a fast track into the paddling pool. She hits the pool at speed, and being so light, aquaplanes across the surface of the water and out of the pool completely, landing on her bum in the grass.

I am still laughing over that for a long time afterwards. I sprinkle the tea mixture over the foil, cover the pan with another layer of foil and a lid, and place the pan on the heat. When it begins to smoke I remove the lid and sit the chicken breasts on top of the foil. A little cold-pressed olive oil over the meat and a swig of Moretti for me before replacing the lid and the pan on the heat.

'How long's it gotta smoke for?' Colin asks.

'Twelve minutes.'

'Time for another drink for the cooks, I think.' He pulls another three beers from the fridge.

I sauté an onion, stir in slices of chorizo and the rice, add a glass of the ladies' Rioja and bring to boiling point. While that is simmering the children start appearing indoors, their noses up, leaving pools of water on the parquet floor that we had laid three months ago. I have a separate dish in the oven, plain roast chicken and baked sweet potatoes, in case anyone doesn't like the smoked bird and the pilaff. Eliot climbs on to the worktop to reach a beaker inside the wall cabinet, and slips. As he goes down he snatches at the cupboard shelf which collapses after him. Cereals and bags of pasta crash on to the floor. Hearing the noise, Lily races into the kitchen as I am taking the chicken off the heat. Eliot is okay and gets up off the floor. I remove the chicken to the cutting board and the foil into the bin, which smokes out the room. Eliot runs out but Lily sticks around a moment to clear up the floor and inspect what I'm doing. I return her smile with a knowing one of my own. We don't need any music track on the film of our life.

Jerry folds the tinned artichoke into the pilaff and warms it through before seasoning with parsley. He lays the warmed pilaff over a heated dish as I slice and serve the smoked chicken breast on top, drizzling herb oil around the sides. We carry everything outside as Flora is telling her grandmother about the power cut on Friday.

Eliot smirks behind her. 'Flora thought it was Muslims who did it.'

'I said it might be Al Qaeda.'

'Same thing.'

'No it's not, stupid.'

'Good heavens,' Rose sighs. 'What a terrible world we live in today that makes children talk like this.'

'You lived through the Blitz, Mum.'

'Yes I did. And that George Bush is more of a menace than Hitler.'

The hot weather looks set to continue. My sisters-in-law, Julia and Rebecca, have laid the Ikea garden table, where we place the dishes. Julia, who fixes up Aubrey with a bib, is a tall brunette with hazel eyes and mayonnaise complexion. But her beauty is marred by anxiousness, by the fear that it's all going to go any day now. Colin reckons she is the reason why Jerry lacks a sense of humour. His own wife, Rebecca, is less beautiful than Julia, but more sensuous. Her lips are heavy and ripe. Around her I always maintain a certain formality, so as not to give Colin reason for concern. Today she is wearing shorts and blonde downy hairs stand out on her tanned thighs.

The heat is sapping everyone's energy and when Rose insists on us holding hands and saying grace it seems one effort too many. Every Sunday it's the same, and the children sabotage the prayer by giggling. Grace over, we take our plates and sit around the table in the shade of an umbrella. The kids eat seated on the grass. Flora takes her plate into the tent because she claims Eliot is bugging her, and now all the kids want to join her. Eliot decides to eat up in the tree den to be better placed to catch the odd sea breeze that makes it into the garden. I hand him his lunch after he's climbed in.

Rose begins to complain as she always does, about the children not respecting the grace she says before eating, implying they have all been brought up badly. Colin rolls his eyes at me and says loudly, 'Have you seen the papers today, Ray? They've just found water on Mars. Which means there was once life on the planet.

Some species like ours that got wiped out long ago. Looks like the Christians are going to have to rethink the whole creation myth. God didn't invent us after all. We invented him. We're all going to die and that's that. So now we can rape and pillage as much as we like.'

Rose gives him a fierce look and mutters to herself as she hacks Aubrey's chicken into tiny mouthfuls. Then she asks us, the cooks: 'What were you talking about in there?'

'In where?'

'While you were cooking . . . *this*.' She pokes the chicken with a finger. 'I could hear all sorts of noises.'

'We were talking about having sex with horses, Rose.'

'Then that explains why this chicken is so inedible.'

'Oh, and we talked about drugs,' Colin adds. 'Ray was telling us how it's a myth that smoking marijuana turns you on. Might work for the women but when a guy gets stoned, so does his prick.'

'I never said anything of the sort, Rose. Don't believe a word he says.'

'You're all bad men is what I think.' Rose eyes up the pilaff suspiciously. 'What have you done for dessert?'

'Lemon syllabub.'

'What on earth is that?'

'For God's sake, Mum,' Lily says, leaning out of the shadow of the umbrella. 'You haven't even started the chicken.'

'Well I need to know. Your dad can't have too much sugar.'

'What harm can it do? What pleasures has he left?'

'*You* won't have to lift your father if he puts on weight.' She opens the jam jar she brought from home and slams down the four tablets Aubrey has to take with lunch on the table beside a glass of water. Her hands are trembling as she does it. 'What are those flowers in the pot, Lily?'

'Pansies.'

'*That's* a lovely scent.' She looks in another vague direction, her nostrils twitching. 'But I can smell fish. Rotting fish. Coming from the house. Does anyone else smell it?' When no one bothers to reply, she adds: 'Why is it that when men cook they make terrible odours?'

Suffering Rose's litany of complaints ordains me in the eyes of my wife. It's nothing to me, although I've often wondered how Aubrey has put up with her all these years. I guess that's why he went off with another woman, circa 1979. Rose chased her off in the end, but has never relaxed her guard since. Not exactly happy to see him in a wheelchair, she doesn't miss the competition. Aubrey still has an eye for the ladies even now and pinches his nurses on the backside when he gets the chance. One of his old sayings I still remember: 'Hard to get any work done in this city with all these fillies in short skirts running around.'

He is silent much of the time now. A stroke is a mysterious force of nature, randomly killing off some brain cells but not others. So he puts down his fork for a second to adjust his bib, and forgets where it is. And yet he can still name all the walls, steps and wharves on the Thames that disappeared over forty years ago. Before he retired and before this stroke put him out of action, Aubrey was a Customs and Excise officer, Water Rats section, patrolling the Thames.

A couple of years ago I took him to work with me. The crew helped carry him on board and we lashed his chair to the floor of the wheelhouse. As we went upriver he told me stories in a whisper, like the time he boarded a ship from Gdansk in 1940, a small cargo-carrying motor vessel plying between the Baltic and the Thames, crewed by a husband and wife. The Customs launch pulled alongside at Gravesend and Aubrey went aboard with a leather attaché case slung by a strap across his shoulder. He gave out health clearances, inspecting the cargo manifest, their list of bonded goods and other dutiable goods owned by the crew not for landing. He obtained a statement of fuel oil carried, measured the cubic capacity of the deck cargo and assessed the Light dues for Trinity House. In other words, he took a heck of a time. And then he heard a knocking sound from under the stern berth. He removed the mattress, unbolted the empty water tank cover and discovered two Jewish refugee stowaways. The crew had hidden them there. They'd been seasick all the way across the Baltic and were now suffocating in that black hole. Aubrey was very sympathetic but still called in the cops. He thought they ended up quarantined on the Isle of Man while their claim for political asylum was processed at the Home Office, but was never sure of that, and it still plagues him today.

I was a mate when I first started dating Lily and she had some doubts about my inscrutability, as she called it, compounded by her mother's opinion that I was 'common'. It was Aubrey who silenced them. 'A waterman is as solid as a clergyman,' he said. In his book, I needed no further reference. So I owe Aubrey. Lily soon began to accept my inscrutability as being as elemental as the river, with its tides and swell simmering below the surface.

I get up from the table to take some empty plates into the kitchen and smell what might be irritating Rose – the pedal bin reeking of smoke. I tie the ends of the liner and remove it. The dustbin is outside the house. When I open the front door I find the street warped by a strange blue air. Car horns and police sirens bend in the heat. A woman walking past the house stares at me through bloodshot eyes. Two young children trail behind. She admonishes them for being so slow and slaps each child on the back of the legs. It's a ringing rebuke that I sense is for my benefit. So in a half-hearted way I say: 'Respect them a little.'

She tells me to fuck off.

I throw the rubbish into the bin and step back inside the house.

I return to the garden flocked around by the world to find my vexed and unhappy mood replicated in Rose. 'I don't understand what I'm eating,' she says. 'What's this under the chicken?'

From his tree den Eliot is raining down missiles on to the tent, anything that will come away in the hand: strips of timber and six-inch rusty nails. Flora is forced out into the open and he loosens his reserve arsenal of pebbles that have found their way from the riverbank to the flowerbed and latterly up into the tree den. He must surely know what damage he can do with fist-sized stones. It's not just the heat, something's eating him from inside and I don't like it. He stops when I tell him to, but that is not the end of it as far as I'm concerned. Where does this desire for doing harm to his sister come from? It darkens me with worry, for him as much as Flora, for anyone with these impulses.

Rose pushes away her plate in disgust and tells Lily about the mouse in Aubrey's drawer. She even suspects one of the carers of planting it there and nominates her prime suspect. 'She's twenty stone at least and wears a stud in her tongue. Is that meant to be attractive? Every day she's late with an ever more fantastic excuse. Yesterday, you know what she said? "I've been up half the night with my pet iguana shedding its skin."' Despite herself, Rose laughs. Aubrey taps his fork on his plate and diverts her attention. 'What is it, pet?'

But it's me his eyes are locked on to. He spears the

chicken and speaks in such a low whisper I have to place my ear close to his lips. 'Very tender, Ray. Not dry at all.' After forty years keeping his silence on Rose's cooking, that is a very big compliment. But I am careful how I take it, not wanting to rub Rose up the wrong way.

'I didn't make it on my own, Aubrey.' I point to Colin and Jerry, who smile graciously at me.

Lily's brothers like me because I make their sister happy. They never mention that banker who beat her up, but he remains the yardstick for what could go wrong. Like Lily, they love me for what I am not. They have seen me tested by her affair with the widower and not seek revenge. They know I'm unlikely to be running off with some barmaid now or in the future. I have eyes only for Lily and you can't fake something like that.

Their confidence in me took time to earn. I am the only person in the family whose past has to be taken on trust. Everyone else is a local. The landmarks of their childhood are all within walking distance.

So when I was new to this family they'd take me out for a drink and ask questions I swear were rehearsed, about my life hitherto, and I began trading in Tom Reeves' life story as my own for the first time.

You approach this place Oystermouth, I said, from the east along a nexus of heavy industry. Gasworks, iron and steel foundry, oil refinery, carbon blacking, docks. Like the Fall of Eden, belching smoke and fire into the sky. A lot of the town was destroyed by the Luftwaffe, but the Regency Port Authority building was still standing last time I looked, as well as the Customs House and the Chamber of Commerce at the entrance to the docks. I used to go to a nursery near the docks, until my parents discovered the teacher was running a brothel upstairs. After the war they restored the town and you can see the bribes and back-handers in this new architecture; a town rebuilt by criminals. Nothing fits in with anything else, there's no common theme. The shops sell table war games, cheap cutlery, wallpaper and meat pasties. Chapels converted into nightclubs stay open until the early hours, when the streets fill with drunken teenagers. A Scandinavian settlement, Oystermouth is still a town of Viking bastards.

Then, a few miles to the west along the horseshoe bay things start to look up. Past the prison and the law courts are regimented parks and recreation grounds. On the opposite side of the road are the golf links and sand dunes. A little railway runs alongside the sea. Past the Territorial Army drill hall, the youth club, pier and dance-hall, the peninsula opens out on to white sandy beaches that stretch for miles, some empty and windswept, others more commercialised, but in a tasteful way, with green beach huts, cafés and tennis courts. The sea there has terrifying currents and each summer some boy or girl drowned . . .

But my geography lesson began to bore them. Colin and Jerry's eyes glazed over. What they needed was something they could touch.

The breakthrough came one evening in a pub over in Tilbury, on the wrong side of the river. We sensed this pub was a mistake when we started noticing the swingers necking down absinthe in dark recesses. It was heavy weather outside with no respite inside. We were finishing our first and only drinks and planning to move on when a woman of about fifty leant over our table and said to me, 'Weren't you a child actor?' She was sitting with two teenage boys and they were all smoking cigarettes from the same pack.

'No,' I said. 'I must have one of those faces.'

'You've been on the telly then, long time ago. You look like someone.'

She had a clippings file at home, she said, full of television personalities spanning thirty years and asked for my autograph. My refusal made her angry and she accused me of having the arrogance of all famous people. We left the pub, but the woman's comments continued to worry my brothers-in-law.

'Why do you think she thought you looked like someone, Ray?' Jerry said on the passenger ferry home. 'You sure you've never been on the telly?'

'I once got my face in a local paper. But that's it. Period.'

'What was this for, Ray?'

'For stealing a bus.'

When they both started laughing I knew I was winning.

'It was this guy, Janway Davis' idea. He was eighteen going on forty, with a mother on the game. Janway financed his summers by planting young boys to work at the Surfside café, at the ice cream counter, and getting them to rob it. Every hour he'd come by and buy a cone so these boys could stuff a five-pound note into the cornet.

'We stole the bus from a garage in town and I drove. But I was only sixteen. I didn't know how to drive. I was going all over the road until a police car pulled me over and arrested me. Thus the mugshot in the local paper.'

'I think that's what she meant when she said you looked like someone else. You leave the past behind but something of it is retained. If you know what I mean.'

Now they knew I was not so pure, they began owning up to sins of their own: Jerry to the occasional recreational use of cocaine, Colin to having had a one-night stand when he was away from home a few years ago – an infidelity he'd never confessed to his wife, Rebecca.

In the garden, Rose turns her vitriol on to Rebecca.

She knows how to inflict emotional damage there. 'What are you doing these days, Rebecca?'

'Same as I do every day, Rose. Work for solicitors.'

'You're not a lawyer yet?'

'I'm not trying to be a lawyer. I'm a paralegal.'

'You mean secretary?'

'No, Rose. But a secretary will do if it's easier for you to grasp.' Rebecca snatches up a tube of sunblock as she rises from the table and strolls down to the end of the garden where her three-year-old is digging up the flowerbeds with bare hands.

Watching her go, Rose says, 'I suppose you have to be quick with words to be a lawyer.'

Of the five kids in the garden, Alice, who's getting sun-block, and her brother, Max, belong to Rebecca and Colin. Julia and Jerry have just one, Robbie, playing alone with the swing ball. Rose clocks his isolation and, with Rebecca out of range, opens up an old wound in Julia. 'When are you and Jerry going to have another child?' She knows as well as we all do that Robbie was born two months premature, preceded by such nausea that Julia had to be placed on a drip. 'It's not good for Robbie to be an only child, you know.'

'Leave her alone, Mum,' Jerry sighs wearily.

'I was only asking.'

'Well don't.'

She switches her focus again as fast as a snake. 'What did you say that dessert we're having was called?'

'Lemon syllabub,' I say. 'It will take fifteen minutes to make.'

'Give Dad some wine, Ray.'

'Aubrey can't have wine,' Rose snaps at Lily.

'He'd probably prefer a whisky,' Colin says.

'Or a bourbon,' says Jerry. 'Dad used to say that bourbon going down tastes like whisky coming up.'

Aubrey laughs silently, his false teeth slipping out of his mouth. He raises his arm, points down the garden and whispers hoarsely, 'Who is that, which boy?'

'That's not a boy, Dad. It's a sunflower.'

'It's good to have something to aim for,' Rose resumes, as she sees her daughter-in-law return from the bottom of the garden. 'If you *were* a lawyer, Rebecca, it might stop you outrunning the constable.'

'What does that mean?' Flora asks from the awning of her tent. 'Outrunning the constable?'

'It means living beyond your means,' her grandmother replies with heavy emphasis.

'What do you have to aim for, Rose, apart from driving us all mad?'

'Colin, are you going to let your wife talk to me like that?'

He thinks about it for one second. 'Yes.'

'What are you smirking about?' Rose asks me.

I am grimacing, not smirking, at Eliot's Lego city, which I have just noticed crushed and booted into nothing in the grass. And I know by whom, exacting revenge on her brother for hailing missiles down on her head. But Flora has crossed the red line on this one. There is going to be hell to pay when he discovers his city, a month in the making, in ruins – a project he called 'City of Highlights of a Good Time', which I thought was rather marvellous. Every time I inspected it some new element had been added, like a nuclear power plant covered in tinfoil. 'It can provide energy for the whole city,' he explained. 'And uranium for weapons defence.'

'I see nothing to smile about with these damn bugs biting.' Rose gets to her feet and swats both her arms one at a time. 'Those poor children are being eaten alive.'

'Let's get drunk, shall we?' Lily pours Julia another drink. 'Where you going on holiday next year?'

'Back to Italy, fly to Turin and drive to where they grow the wine.'

'They grow wine *everywhere* in Italy,' Rose corrects her.

'Is this the same place you went in December? Where it snowed Christmas day.'

'Robbie'd never seen snow before.'

'Oh dear, not again. We did see the pictures, you know . . . Twice.'

And I made a prison too, Dad. For murderers there's an electric chair . . .

'Why don't you come to Italy with us?' Jerry asks Rose.

She looks at Julia standing in abject silence behind Jerry. 'That would be nice, dear, but I couldn't leave your father.'

'You could put him into respite care for a week.'

'I'll think about it, son.'

'Don't think too long. We'll have to book soon.'

There is one piece of smoked chicken left. Distractedly, I offer it to Lily. 'I'll share it with you,' she says. I cut the chicken breast and give one half to her and take the other half for myself. Rose zeroes in on my plate with forensic eyesight.

'You took the lean half! You gave Lily the *gristle*.'

'Bloody hell!' Jerry puts his arm around my shoulder in solidarity while Rose admonishes him for swearing.

'In front of the children. In front of the children and on Sunday.'

Julia smiles at me. 'Want to know a good mother-in-law joke, Ray? Two old men on a bench, one says, "My mother-in-law is an angel." The other one replies, "You're lucky. Mine's still with us."'

In the kitchen Flora helps me make the dessert by blending flour, caster sugar, butter and egg yolks in the food processor. On a floured surface I roll out the biscuit and let her make rounds with a fluted cutter. I sprinkle the biscuits with sugar, score them and place the tray in the hot oven. While they're cooking I whisk together double cream and caster sugar in a bowl. Flora folds in Greek yoghurt and the juice from three lemons. I divide the mixture in serving glasses and leave in the freezer to chill for five minutes. I make coffee in an espresso pot and remove the biscuits from the oven. Flora garnishes the syllabub with mint sprigs and lemon slices and I lay the biscuits to the side.

Into the kitchen wander Colin and Jerry, on R&R from the garden. Colin says, 'Aren't you grateful you don't have relatives, Ray?'

'That's a real sensitive thing to say, Colin,' Jerry admonishes him.

'I mean relatives like Rose. You understand, don't you, Ray?'

'Why is Grandma so horrible to everyone?' Flora asks.

'I don't know. But she's nice to you.'

'She's not nice to you.'

'I don't take it personally'. And it's true, Rose's criticisms miss the mark completely. She never ruins my Sunday.

Lily's brothers help me carry the desserts into the garden. Flora takes the coffee and as she is placing it on the table, Eliot runs into the arena and punches her as hard as he can on the back. He has just discovered his ruined city. The thump and crack of his fist on Flora's back is sickeningly loud. The pot spills out of her hand on to the table. Scalding coffee runs off the edge of the table and pours into Aubrey's lap. He starts to cry, with real tears in his eyes.

I lash out at Eliot and catch him on the side of the head with the back of my hand. Lily stands frozen in a state of shock, witnessing me hit our son. I am so ashamed I cannot hold her look and stare down at my ringing hand. The air fills with Eliot's piercing outrage. Flora is sobbing and her grandfather is moaning. I struggle not to bolt out of the house, into the street, taking this heinous thing on my back down to the river to drown. The wind shakes the trees above my head. The sun ducks beneath a white cloud, casting a glum shadow. I can't see a single face but my own, reflected in staring eyes.

The garden party has descended into chaos. Lily ushers Eliot into a corner, still beside himself. She throws back at me a look of judgement and I hit rock bottom. I have no power to change everything back to what it was moments ago, cannot restore the order. Rose clucks around Aubrey and holds his head to her bosom. And it is Rose eventually who restores everything to what it was. With her free hand she strokes Flora's head. 'I don't think it really hurt him, you know. It's just that any little thing sets him off. Those antidepressants are only like cling-film over his emotions. It's time we went home anyway. Ray, could you order the taxi?'

Heading towards the house to call a cab I stop beside my son being cradled by his mother. I rest my hand on his stiff shoulder. I want to make amends but feel his rejection through my fingers. We have both lost out, but I should have known better. His violence came out of himself; my violence out of a far more distant self I'd hoped had receded for good. All these years I've lived in new shoes and suddenly and without warning I've trampled on the old ground.

Aubrey wants to use the toilet as we arrive back at their house. A small operation for most of us, but for Aubrey and Rose it's an epic and I volunteer my services. I wheel him into the specially constructed bathroom in the hall, place his limp arm over my shoulder and ease him out of the wheelchair. As he hangs on to me, I loosen his belt with one hand, unzip his trousers and pull them down as far as I can. He helps me by hopping on one leg and together we reverse towards the toilet bowl. He can't stand so has to use the toilet like a woman. As he begins I lean against the wall. His urine seeps out between the toilet seat and the bowl and he stares at me in abject embarrassment. 'It's okay, Aubrey. I'll clean up when you finish.' After giving him another minute I raise him to his feet in the same way as before, lift his trousers and zip him back up. It takes a lot longer loading than unloading and it's particularly hard securing his belt with one hand. He helps with the turn back into the wheelchair. In the lounge/bedroom I move him from the wheelchair to the stiff, hard-backed chair beside his bed. Rose removes his coat and pads him with a cushion behind his back and one down each side, and places a smaller cushion covered with Indian fabric under his dead arm. As she is arranging his table, I clean the urine off the bathroom floor with some toilet roll. The bathroom smells of zinc cream. From the other room I hear Rose gently scold him.

I take a minicab home and from the back seat try to determine, from his eyes in the rear-view mirror, if this African driver is the same one involved in our car accident yesterday. When I get home I understand I've had a premonition. Lily tells me I've just missed the driver of the SUV, who came by to apologise for his behaviour the other day.

'What do you mean, apologise?' It sounds wrong to me, like a man trying to enter a house using false identification.

'I couldn't tell if he was being nice or covering something up. It wasn't his SUV, did you know that? Had it out on trial, on a test drive.'

'But what was he apologising for? You ran into the back of him.'

'He was apologising for being insensitive towards the woman on the bike. He sends his apologies to you too for dumping you at the hospital and not coming in to help. He was putting all this behaviour on his marriage going tits up. I had a busy half-hour with him, that's for sure. In the end I invited him to my seminar, Tuesday night.'

'You did *what*? What seminar's this?'

'I told you about it a month ago, Ray. And you're so bloody coming.'

I scramble all the memory cells and see nothing there but specks of dust.

'Did he say he'd come?' I feel, probably irrationally, that she's trying to punish me for something, for hitting Eliot maybe. 'What's his name?'

'Miles. He doesn't look like a Miles, though. Frank maybe. A Mick or a Jim. Miles seems beyond his reach. Sounds like a name chosen for him by someone who didn't love him.'

How has this come to pass: Miles welcomed into our lives? I don't want anyone I've not fully vetted embraced by this family. Since Friday night everything has gone topsy-turvy.

I take a beer out of the fridge and sit in the garden on my own, at the end of a precipitous weekend. I want to dwell on good things to calm my spirits. I begin considering Rose of all people, doing every day what I've just done once, and forgive her a lot of her trespasses. She still loves Aubrey after he's lost his lustre and sheen, when all that remains of his personality is a lame shadow. That earns my deepest respect, as the account of divorce

I heard from this guy Miles yesterday elicits my deepest fears.

I am having these thoughts when Flora sneaks up behind and catches me off guard. I am too slow in tucking away whatever expression I have on my face. Unlike her brother, Flora can pick up on my disquiet. Worse still, she embodies my disquiet and then becomes ill at ease without knowing why. However hard I try to hide my feelings they seem to get into her anyway. No one else in the family is as susceptible. If I put up a front she picks up on that too and then we both adopt a weird formality as long as the moment lasts. But I don't want her to understand the why. That revelation would be too much for her. In order to break the circuit I buy her something; then Lily accuses me of spoiling her, my little girl. But shopping is the only activity we can share that is guaranteed to bring us back to a natural state of being. It always produces a good result.

But today's Sunday and the shops are closed when Flora catches me deep in these thoughts. 'What's the matter with you?' she asks. It pains me when she adds: 'What have I done?'

'Nothing. You've done nothing. I'm just thinking.'

'Thinking about what?'

At times like this I try and tell her half-truths because with half-truths there is half the shame. I turn my face away. 'I'm thinking how I don't have any relatives to come for Sunday lunch like on your mum's side of the family.'

A long time ago I told Flora and Eliot that I once had a sister who died young. I said my mother and father were also dead. I signed them up to this wretched account and now and then one or the other raises the subject, as Flora does now.

'What did your sister look like?'

'Quite handsome.'

'You mean like a boy?'

'No, not quite. I suppose she was a tomboy, though. As a kid.'

'Did you play with her, or did you fight like me and Eliot?'

'Worse than you and Eliot. I don't remember exactly why. I played with my friends mostly. We never spent much time together. Like we never went on family holidays.'

'Your parents never took you on holiday?'

'No.'

'Well you lived by the sea, didn't you? Mum said you could see it from upstairs in your house. But didn't you want to go somewhere different sometimes?'

'I never went somewhere different, so didn't know that I did. I never flew in a plane until I went to Iceland with your mum.'

'And you didn't like flying, did you? You said you'd prefer to sail by ship and Mum said by the time you got to Iceland on a ship it would be time to come home again.'

'You weren't even born then. Mum told you all that?'

'But you must have done something with your sister?'

I don't want to hide from this, don't want a tense formality to come between us, so continue, 'She used to buy records and play them on the record player. I'd sit on the floor and watch her dance.'

She giggles at this image of her dad. 'What pop groups did she like?'

This is a hard one and I have to stretch back for some sort of answer. 'Duran Duran. Wham!'

'Were they, like, boys and girls?'

'No, all boys. And they played their own instruments. She played the violin, my sister. Quite well, too. I saw her in a concert once, when she was younger than you.'

'Well, Dad, do you feel better now for talking about it?'

'Yes.' My smile gives weight to the reply. 'Yes I do. Thank you.'

'One day will you take me and Eliot to this place by the sea where you grew up?'

'Sure.' I see no harm in that.

And on that promise she skips off into the house, and a minute later I hear her raised voice and Eliot's sharp reply.

Lily comes into the garden without shoes on her feet. I admire her slim calves near my face below the hem of her summer dress. 'Ray, we got to give these two a run before they kill one another.'

I don't want to go anywhere, sacrifice the security of my house and take my chances outside. But how do you explain this? So we head off by bike on an early summer evening for the Cooling Marshes. We slip quietly and quickly through town and glimpse the river from the promenade. I inhale the familiar scent that is half city and half sea. Beyond the tenders leaning in the drying mud the fleet of tugs belonging to my employer squat at their moorings. Two cruise liners at berth outside the docks, the *Astoria* and the *Arion*, wait for their Austrian passengers to return from sightseeing tours of London. The promenade is quite crowded with families enjoying the warm evening. Retired seadogs, still addicted to the water, examine the cruise liners through binoculars. Every so often some boy, but not every boy, breaks away from his family to lean against a dolphin and stare into the main stream. Eliot has the instinct too, wobbling on his bike from staring too far round at a spirit tanker leaving the power station. Eliot, but not Flora, who sits on her saddle bolted to my crossbar. At ten she's overstayed her welcome as a passenger on my bike, but refuses to ride her own; can't ride her own. She stares dead ahead with the wind in her hair, the smell of garden-hose water still in it. Eliot has still not forgiven me for hitting him and cycles close to his mother. I haven't apologised because it seems futile to do so. It really did hurt me more than it hurt him and I wait for him to come round, to trust me again.

Past the Customs House where Aubrey used to work we cycle through a lane of shipyards, copper works, propulsion services, salvagers, divers, excavators, barge repairers. The workshops are closed for business but still emit sighs and whispers that terrify Flora. I hug my arms even tighter around her, locking her between my body and the handlebars. We are forced on to a path two feet wide, enclosed one side by zinc fencing and on the other by a stone wall. Metal doors are rusted into the wall. Brambles heavy with ripened blackberries scrape our heads as we pass. I can't help wondering what ill has happened, *might* happen in this alley.

Via the disused canal we enter the marshes, a flat wilderness intersected by dykes, the grass bleached white by the sun. To our starboard are the firing ranges, silent and forlorn at this time. We go the extra two miles into the Cooling Marshes before laying our bicycles in the grass, and walk around Egypt Bay. We are the only land souls in sight. Two blackened oil tankers chug up the Yantlet Channel on the 14-metre contour, avoiding the foul areas upstream from Chapman Shoal. Scar's Elbow light flashes green every two and a half seconds as steam and smoke from the gasworks drift east across Deadman's Point. Lily and I hold hands as the children run on ahead. We don't talk. We don't say anything at all. It is a lovely moment of peace.

We turn back for home along the Saxon Shoreway as

the last of the light slants across the river, turning it a mulatto brown. A slow, peaceful cycle is disturbed as we draw level with the firing ranges. Red flags are flying on the corners of the perimeter fence and from inside comes a crackle of small arms. A dozen men empty chambers into paper insurrectionists, then stroll up to inspect the group and mean point of impact. Too far away to see their faces, but whoever they are, they notice us too. A couple of gunmen turn in our direction. How casually they could pick us off, one by one, the solitary family on the marshes. They recover spent cartridges and throw them into a black plastic bin. Part of the group walk in one stooped line towards a white van and white Land Rover parked near a green corrugated lock-up. Others remain at the targets and reload.

I feel myself being drawn in by this firing range. What they do – rehearse the taking away of life – has a pornographic attraction. I'm taken by surprise with my reaction, the way it leaves me light-headed. Closer to the fence some of the features of the men become clearer still: their t-shirts and leather jackets and black self-loading rifles. I wonder who they are and where they come from. Who is it that likes to fire guns into a grass bank beside the great river a couple of miles from my house?

6

There is a tension between those who call for rehabilitation and those who call for punishment – who complain that lifers get given treatment they don't deserve. They want to feel safe, wouldn't want us to be a risk. But they never want our pain to end.

I was not looking to end my pain either.

The good guys argued that I would be a burden on society for as long as I lived unless I was helped to become a morally aware citizen.

It's costly, went the counter-argument.

Not as costly as an antisocial adult released into the world.

The death penalty would cancel out this argument.

After they moved me from the young offenders' institution into a prison, the first thing I had to get used to was the pessimism. Repeat offenders/habitual criminals are closed down inside, lost to the world, in many ways as good as dead. Except they are not, and as long as they are alive remain cancers on the vine. The only place for them is prison. They can never be rehabilitated. Such prisoners are also angry people. Anger is their only emotion and goes on for ever. Women's nicks have sex and drugs. Men's nicks have sexual abuse and drugs – tranqs from the medical wing, puff/skunk from the visitors, alcohol from deodorants. Friendships are very hard. You learn never to form attachments to men on short sentences, or those coming to the end of a long one.

From the moment I arrived in prison I started haemorrhaging my personality, reversing my sense of self I'd partially regained while a young offender. Prisons can't afford to accommodate much individuality and all the emotional progress I'd made in the past five years felt a little off the peg in the nick. The therapeutic lingo I'd picked up in offending-behaviour programmes now sounded false. And it didn't relate to anything. It got you nowhere, got you nothing.

Then for a misdemeanour I was given a punishment 'award'. I went down the block. Took the eight o'clock walk. I was given a blanket and linen at 20.00 hours and had them removed at 06.00. Then all day I sat on the rim of the metal-sprung bed under a bright light. After fourteen days 'behind the door' I came out with a new state of mind set on isolation, on being a loner. I worked in the laundry, garden, kitchen, industrial cleaning and recycling unit and in the garment manufacture workshop, but kept my two thoughts to myself. A) How did I get here? B) Where was I going? These were difficult thoughts for someone in my position to resolve. I was too ashamed to remember the past. And I couldn't see the future.

When you are a killer the only way to navigate into the future is by dead reckoning: find out where you're going from where you've just been. Otherwise no one around you will be safe. But I couldn't remember the 'moment of the offence'. In prison I couldn't see further back than my time at the young offenders' institution – called an 'approved school' when I arrived, changed to 'community home' and then to 'young offenders' institution' as I was about to leave five years later. But it made no difference to us what they called it. Always the same place when you woke the next morning.

The day I arrived there is indelibly printed on my memory. After three weeks in court, I came to the approved school just hours after sentence was passed. I still had a blanket over my head as protection from press photographers. The blanket came off inside the gates, and the noise, the obsessive chatter and shouting, was exhilarating. The smoke less so. People know how to roll a thin one inside – more paper than tobacco and the smell clings to everything.

I was stripped, searched and hosed down, given Home Office-issue clothes and then escorted to my cell through double gates, each set locked before the next was opened. My clothes were too big and I had to hold my trousers up with one hand. The bed in my cell was so high I had to take a running leap to get on to it. Out of my window I could see gardens, vegetable plots and trees. I thought that was nice, even though I was locked up there at night.

During the day I mingled with the other boys in the library, sitting room, dining hall and classrooms. I was tutored in a class of three, compared to thirty on the outside. I was given tests and put into an academic working group. I attended lessons from 9 till 12.45 and from 2 till 4. The classrooms were modern and well furnished with good light and fresh air, and warm in winter. There was a pottery kiln, art room, a greenhouse for growing tomatoes, runner beans and some hothouse tulips. We even had a swimming pool. I felt quite free, but was under observation all the time. How I behaved was recorded in my files by the eighteen staff. Even the domestics' opinions were sought.

There is an atmosphere of hope in a YOI because inmates are young and thus not beyond salvation. Many are inside for first offences. And as for the staff, you couldn't hope for better *in loco parentis*. My probation officer was a woman of about forty with thick ankles, who used to smoke throughout our sessions. But she gave me more attention than my mother even did. I was listened to. My most trivial thoughts were given air-time. I was never rejected, never told I was stupid. She gave me all this attention because she wanted me cured of what I had done. She wanted me cured because only then could I be considered safe to send out into the world again.

In particular she wanted to know my thoughts about the past. I could only think as far back as my High Court appearance.

My trial was still a blur to me. I didn't understand what was happening, the judge or the silks or the glum-faced jury. Not for a second did I think I wouldn't be going home again when it was all over. I could remember being told to answer any question honestly, and being told not to drift off. But it was so boring I did drift off quite a lot. Until I heard someone call me cruel. 'A cruel boy who committed this evil act without remorse.' I knew what cruel meant and I understood that to be true in my case because I'd once stoned a tortoise. But evil? I'd heard politicians on TV refer to the IRA as evil. What I didn't know then is when an act of terrorism is called evil, you close down all discussion about why it was committed in the first place. It's comforting I suppose, and convenient, to shout: 'Satan is among us!' But it's not evidence. It can't advance the knowledge.

They wanted me to break down in court, show remorse and shame. They wanted me to cry a river. But I didn't really understand what I'd done, that death meant for ever. Your dog dies, you get another, right? Maybe if I'd been shown the body I'd have been the wiser for it.

The three weeks in court I remembered in terms of being alone. I had to sleep in a children's reception home and was guarded round the clock by two policemen, who were unnaturally hard. To be so alone for so long was the worst part of it. In court I'd look around the gallery for a kind face. But I always avoided looking at my father. And my mother never attended. What I'd do was imagine some couple in the gallery as my parents and smile at them. One woman smiled back at me once. She helped me get through that day.

When the judge addressed the jury at the beginning of the proceedings, he reminded them this was an adult court and instructed them not to consider mitigating circumstances, like childhood or motivation for crime. The judicial process had to be based on evidence only. So either I did it or I didn't. I was either guilty or not. But since I'd admitted it, the prosecution's job was to prove that I knew what I was doing was wrong.

After it was over, the judge set a life sentence, but said it didn't mean I was to be kept in custody for life. Then he repeated: detention would be for life. Then he imposed a tariff of *ten years*! He asked me to look him in the eye and told me that if I wanted to get out on my tariff date, I would have to demonstrate more remorse than I had in his courtroom. He said the position could be assessed from time to time and if it became safe to release me, then I could be released on licence. I didn't understand that at all. I thought he meant I'd be allowed to drive.

At least in the old days they'd have dunked me in the river.

No one in court was interested in my childhood; was allowed to be interested. So it came as a surprise once I began my detention that my probation officer was interested in little else. Even with her guidance, however, and despite her care and kindness, I was unable to revisit the 'moment of my offence'. So her efforts failed.

Some of her efforts.

But at least she tried.

While she tried, I fantasised about crawling into her uterus with my foot sticking out.

7

In the early stage of my marriage, when Lily complained our relationship was founded on entertainment, she made us travel to the cold, eternally lit recesses of Iceland to discover what we were made of.

It was another breach of my Life Licence to travel abroad without the consent of the Probation Office. But by now I was so far out of the loop I didn't really think about it. At the airport all anyone cared about was who had packed our bags.

Several hours after landing in Iceland we picked up a hire car and left Reykjavik shrinking in the rear-view mirror. We headed for the glaciers of the Snaefellsnes peninsula as a late March sun slanted across the sky at eleven at night, tinting the snow-covered mountains a shocking pink. Patches of grass sprouting in rock fissures were pale and limp from ten months under ice. Isolated chapels stood firm beneath the snow line. Near Olafsvik we drove eighty kilometres without sighting another vehicle. Lily was pushing that little Japanese car very hard, skidding on the loose gravel road. The road sheered into ravines and lava beds as sharp as razors. I saw us going over the edge many times, the lava slicing open the car, and the wind and cold killing us.

At our pre-booked accommodation I had to open the car door with both feet against a force ten gale, then swam upstream against the wind to the farmhouse door. In a hall decorated with eagle claws I met the farmer. Wordlessly he showed us to our quarters: a featureless barrack-like building of thirteen rooms in a field of mud. We were its only occupants. The room had a view of a frozen glacier on one side and the whiplashed sea on the other. The wind whistled starkly. What a place to come to test your marriage vows. Even Lily felt the need to draw the curtains on the view.

In the morning, in the house kitchen, the farmer's wife sat with us at the table and watched us eat breakfast: one slice of rye bread and flasked coffee. Her eyes glazed over whenever she looked out of the window to the bleak plains, the drifting cloud, the cruel sea, and she only spoke when Lily asked questions.

'It must be hard getting to Reykjavik in the winter.'

'I don't like Reykjavik.'

'Do you still farm here?'

'We killed all the sheep in 1989. Only tourists now.'

'Fucking hell,' Lily said back in the car again. 'I was waiting for her to get out the chess set.' It was the last time she laughed in Iceland.

The mountains revealed no human endeavour. No flowers or trees grew in the lava fields. In other bleak places in the world, ruins bore testimony to man's failed attempts to harness nature. Here they didn't even try. We left the car and went on foot into a valley. Lily's ankles kept turning on the honeycombed rock. Geysers erupted and frightened her, shooting boiling water and clouds of steam into the air. The valley terminated at a cascading waterfall where hundreds of great black-backed gulls with five-foot wingspans swooped into the water spray on seek-and-destroy missions into small birds' nests. Lily was fighting off a conviction that one of those gulls was going to tear out her eyes and dash them across the rocks. There was no unnatural sound, no mechanical hectoring. We were in God's country. It was His architecture up there and I sensed what it would be like to be dead.

She pointed to one of the smaller snow-capped peaks behind the waterfall and unilaterally announced we were to climb it. I examined her footwear: Adidas trainers that looked about done in. Climbing mountains has never been in my repertoire. It was not my element, and soon I felt the strain in my calf muscles and lungs. There was little pleasure in putting one foot forward of the other on a steep gradient. Maybe it would all be worth it on reaching the top, where Lily hoped our marriage would be validated.

The first signs of her panic set in when the scree crumbled under foot as we climbed around a vertical rock face, and as we forded a fast-running stream of icy water. In the mighty silence of the landscape I felt a distance grow between us. Our footwear worried me. When a few streaks of cloud appeared in an otherwise spotless sky I suggested the summit might be a little too far for a non-stop ascent. But she wanted to get inside that snow line. I tried to talk her out of it, talk her *down*, but she was adamant.

Above that line the snow was antique and crisp, thickening the higher we climbed. Every now and then I heard her sigh, with fear or pleasure I couldn't tell. The sky had completely clouded over by now and the wind had grown much colder. We climbed for another hour and the summit remained as elusive as ever. Then the clouds suddenly collapsed upon us. Frozen needles of rain played tricks with our vision. Visibility decreased from twenty feet to fifteen to ten – until I could no longer see my feet. We took shelter from the wind behind a ledge of rock. Not a thing of the world could we see from this redoubt, and she was shivering and close to caving in to anxiety, a different woman now than just two hours ago.

We could not see the top. The place for crowning our marriage was unreachable. We held each other in a platonic embrace.

If we'd stayed on that mountain any longer we'd have stayed on it for life. I helped her to her feet and began inching my way down. I had no sense of navigation. Visibility was now only three feet. I had to stamp out steps in the snow, aware all the time that the escarpments and sheer drops we'd passed on the way up could no longer be seen. The frozen rain swarmed around my eyes and magnified the smallest event, the slightest gesture. We were in a perfect realm of silence. The mountain seemed asleep, but not dead. Lily sank to her waist in snow and the old snow held fast, only releasing her after a struggle. When she saw she'd lost a shoe she regressed into childhood and became hysterical, as though a limb was missing, all hope lost. I retrieved her trainer and moments later it was I plunging into the snow, twisting my ankle and bringing her down with me. Her whimpering grated on my nerves. I spoke only to tell her not to lean forward. We descended sideways and on our backsides. The smoothness of the snow was threatening.

The snow line began to break up and we gained inches by using our hands. Where smooth exposed granite suddenly fell away in the mist I helped her crawl around the lip. I had no idea how far down the bottom was. We made small advances to the sound of trickling water, feeling the chill breath of the stream on our faces. If there was no solid ground a foot in front of me I retreated, moving her sideways to try again. I felt a lack of density, as if we were cones or husks. Ice in her eyebrows glistened like jewellery and her eyes were black as a sheep's.

We got beneath the ceiling of cloud and the ground below opened up and ordained us. Lily began to sob. Her sobs turned to crazy laughter and then shut off. We reached the road five hundred metres from where we'd parked. Lily was shaking as she sat back in the car and could barely steer or change gears.

She never mentioned Iceland again. She never again asked to test our marriage vows. She began facilitating marriage between strangers instead. Taking care of our children's welfare was life-threatening enough.

At Lily's public seminar on dating and flirting, the object is to put oneself on display. The last seminar of this kind she ran a year ago had felt like an inquisition to me, and my wilful amnesia regarding the date tonight might have succeeded had it not been for Miles, our car-crash buddy, whose invitation prompted Lily to remember mine.

A fair proportion of the sixty people attending the seminar have been through one agency or another. Or they've tried email and speed dating, and amorous lunches. It's a racing certainty they are all single and on the pull, except for me. I get there early to reserve a seat in the back row as these lovelorn individuals slink in. There are no group entries. Everyone comes alone and blushes furiously, embarrassed to be revealing their need like this, on their sleeves. The fact that everyone is in the same boat doesn't help. Deportment goes to hell as they fumble their way to empty chairs, then size up the new arrivals as prospective partners. It's a meaty atmosphere. I look around for, but can't see, Miles in the crowd. Will I even recognise him? Lily is sitting at a table at the front with two female colleagues (all her colleagues are female) and a few minutes later, steps up to the microphone. She is wearing the snow-white cotton dress I bought for her last birthday from Agnes B, her favourite shop. Pearl earrings complete a virginal picture, but a slash of blood-red lipstick gives the lie to her chastity.

She addresses the group by telling them a few home truths about dating. 'The difference between dates that have been organised by our company, as opposed to a chance encounter, is that both parties know too much about what the other wants. If you meet by chance you don't know if he or she is free or not and you flirt cautiously as a way of finding out. An organised date is more businesslike and therein lies the first danger. The mistake many make is to declare their hand too soon. Saying what you don't like in a partner, all in the first few minutes, I'm afraid is not going to win you any beauty contest.' She pauses to allow the knowing guffaws to fade. 'Flirt as if you met by chance. Flirting is a turn-on. Talking about yourself non-stop, on the other hand, is definitely a turn-off. I'm sorry to report that the men are guiltier of this than the women.' She takes a sip of water from a glass standing on the lectern. 'The hardest thing is to know how to balance asking questions with answering them. So try to find some common ground. Do you both like films or books? Do you have knowledge the other person shares? Don't boast or lecture. Just take your time. Don't tell the whole of your life story. This is a first date, remember, not a funeral.'

She pauses again for the air to clear of smirking laughter. 'And don't talk about your children if you have them.'

Next she asks her audience what they look for in a partner – a sweet-shop question really – and as they are volunteering, one of Lily's colleagues writes their replies on a white board. 'Shouldn't be a smoker', 'Mustn't be overweight', 'Better not be wearing cufflinks!' . . . 'Or Sloggi underpants!'

Lily cuts them off. 'These are all *negative* qualities. Come on, think positive.'

I don't know how she does this. Everything I hear is judgemental. Everyone I see is deformed by unrequited needs. The second raft of positive suggestions is slow in coming and just as unimaginative. 'Nice body', 'White teeth', 'Likes salsa dancing'.

A woman from the audience stands up to make her point. 'I think it's important to find the dream guy *before* getting to know him, don't you think? Or you'll start to forgive all his bad habits and settle for less than you deserve.'

Someone else opines that the addictive, compulsive type always gives up early. 'Yeah,' agrees some wag. 'Comes too quickly.'

Lily gets back on the mike to suppress the self-conscious laughter and reiterate that a date is more likely to be successful if one doesn't look for faults. 'Because *you're* going to have faults too, believe me. Looking for faults is a bad habit even in an established relationship. I don't mean you have to put up with extremes like heavy drinking or aggressive behaviour. It's the subtle ways we condemn one another you have to watch. Comments like, "You don't appreciate the effort I'm making", "You don't understand this is a stressful time for me", "I don't think you're giving me any support", "You don't think of my needs, only your own".' She delivers each example with dramatic emphasis and pause, like an evangelical preacher. 'Sound familiar? But is it ever that black and white? You see what you want to see. We only really know ourselves and we see what we want to see. In my view, when you are listing faults in others, you're usually talking about yourself.'

She gets a knowing laugh or two, through which she imparts some advice on good hunting grounds for meeting others. 'The gym, but not in the middle of your workout. Red faces aren't attractive. You're not looking your best. Try to make an approach in the café downstairs. Although the steam room is a good place because you can't see one another blush.' There is more embarrassed laughter, laughter that sounds like a sickness. Lily seems to be the only one in the room who is not mortified by what she is saying.

I begin to notice one or two young and beautiful women, who make me wonder why they need a dating agency. They adopt aloofness as though here on sufferance. Mostly, though, people are almost invalid with shyness. Atrophied men with sloping backs, who keep their eyes off the ball. Badly dressed women whose scent snatches at the throat. Ruined bohemians with nicotine stains in their fringes.

The seminar lasts for an hour, after which everyone is invited to stay for a drink. Tables each side of the room groan with bottles of wine, beer and fruit juice, which the Bliss employees serve. I ask Lily for a beer and whisper that I'm looking forward to our rendezvous afterwards in the Criterion Lounge. Before arriving tonight she ordered me not to tell anyone I'm married to the boss when I'm doing the rounds of the room, and her stern expression serves as a reminder. But the deception comes naturally to me as I join three women nervously huddled together. They are standing near the door for a quick getaway and are dressed in power suits: pinstripes and white blouses. I soon discover their professions are sterile. One is a computer programmer, another a business consultant and the third a securities lawyer. What is also common to all is the stress they seem to be under as I talk to them, flirt with them. If all they really want is a man, they pretend not to care less. This mock casualness distorts their faces.

Lily claims the mating game is a business like any other, with transactions, contracts and returns demanded on investment. She's a heart-hunter. But the mating game is also a dangerous business and I can sense previous on at least two men in my vicinity. And I don't mean divorce. They have convictions for something like fraud, I'd wager, since this is a professional crowd. Lily has files on many of these people, but who's to know what is actually true in their personal statements? There is no law governing the way they fill them in, no watchdog.

Lily once asked me to complete a personal statement, and no one would be any the wiser for reading it. To the question, *Why did you decide to employ an agency?* I answered: 'I've lost touch with my roots. I've lost touch with many people.' To *Who would you like to be in another life?* I wrote: 'Charles Dickens'. *Do you smoke?* Now there's a question to lie about. Lily has a hard time finding partners for smokers. But *Does alcohol play a role in your life?* requires a positive reply. Lily finds it hard to match up teetotallers.

The hardest question to answer was the important one: *What sort of person would you like to meet?* I asked to see what others had written. 'Banker who likes to race cars seeks lady who doesn't mind getting under the bonnet', 'Doctor seeks woman who can read his handwriting', 'Choirmaster seeks a woman more at ease in wellington boots than a cocktail dress' (Lily fixed him up with a PR director who was 'trying her hand at capoeira'), 'Humanitarian aid worker seeks a woman willing to spend weekends with him in country house hotels', 'Finance director who loves *La Dolce Vita* seeks a woman familiar with the phrase, "carpe diem"', and 'Lovely lady with a bigger shoe collection than Imelda Marcos seeks a man who could survive on sushi alone' (she then signed off her form with 'Oh, what the hell. I'd settle for a non-smoker with that indefinable something!').

I catch the eye of a blonde who has spent too much time in the sun. She comes over to me, taking the long journey across the room, and introduces herself with a soft handshake. 'Uh, I've just been sailing for two weeks,' she says in an Estuary accent. Every chance she gets she's on a yacht somewhere. She fiddles with loose strings hanging from her sarong and casually asks if I'm a yachtsman by any chance.

'I don't like water. I can't swim.'

Why do I lie?

Because I am playing the game for fun. Because lying comes easily to me.

She keeps trying, however. 'You don't have to swim to enjoy sailing.'

'I think I'd rather learn to swim first.'

'Well, okay. Let me know how your breaststroke's going.' She turns away from me and edges towards some petrified figure in a grey suit stranded between the traffic lanes. And I hear her say to him: 'Can *you* swim?'

When he replies, 'Yes! *Yes!*' I just know he's faking his orgasm.

I think I recognise Miles on the other side of the room, his shaved head and serpentine back and wide shoulders hunched over a trestle-table. He looks more interested in the free wine than in the free women. He has a glass in his hand as I weave my way through to him. 'Not driving tonight, I hope?'

He turns round. 'This scene's turning me to drink, chief.' The way he looks at me, through me, suggests he hasn't recognised me, and I leave it that way.

'Seen anybody you fancy?'

'I brought my own bird with me. Right behind you.'

I assume he's joking and keep my eyes on him. Then I start to laugh without good cause. Miles' expression changes, studying me as if I've gone insane. And it's true I do feel quite mad in this acting event. The pursuit of love makes fools of us all, even when you're not being sincere.

And tears of laughter blind you to obvious dangers.

It becomes irresistible eventually to look behind and I see a woman trying to hold a steady course as she comes out of the crowd towards us. My head is pulled by her dirty magnetism as she takes up a position by Miles' side and links her arm through his. I avoid looking at the face because I've already identified it, even though much of it has gone. My throat is as dry as wood. I hold the back of a chair and stare at the strip of naked flesh between the rim of her jeans and shirt. Her distended stomach luffs over her belt buckle. I'm holding on to the hope she'll walk away again, and to that end, avoid her eyes. But she's going nowhere. There follows a protracted silence, then I hear her say, 'I've been looking at you for ages. At first I couldn't believe my eyes. Long time no see.'

I step back when her hand touches my arm, ramming the edge of the table and making the bottles rattle. And then I am looking into her face. Her eyes are sleepwalking through all this. Her face is pock-marked and blemished with patches of dead skin. Even so, she is the only live being in a room of mannequins. Horribly, contagiously alive. My heart is beating so fast it's about to burst through my ribs. My emotions spill out into a chaotic black pool. I have no voice to defend myself.

'You know one another?' Miles sounds surprised.

'Long time ago,' she answers in a hoarse caw. 'What about you? How far back do you two go?'

There is no shake in the voice but her hands are trembling. She's aware of it too and grips the table where her fingers become mobile, like spider's legs. I stare at the rings she wears on each finger tapping on wood and at the nails painted blue. My ears are blocked and the air is misty with tiny shards of glass. Her rake-like figure dances in the space in front of me, inhuman and mocking. My senses are all deprived. All I have is memory.

'We met on Saturday,' Miles answers. 'In a car accident.'

'Really. Who went into who?'

'As a matter of fact, his wife rammed me in the arse.'

'You're married, Mark?'

Mark.

'His wife is the one running the seminar.' Miles makes it sound like a boast.

Then I push him hard in the back.

He propels towards the middle of the floor. I am right behind, maintaining the pressure, pushing him out of the door. Without looking back and ignoring his protests going down four flights of steps, I only let go in the street. His eyes are wide with expectation. He has just been overpowered, utterly outclassed.

We are bang in the middle of Piccadilly Circus, stranded in the heavy stream of pedestrians. 'That woman you brought with you . . .' I stall because I don't know what the question should be. We are standing beside Eros. Why is Eros on a plinth here of all places? The very spot in London where nobody knows anyone, in the circus of the lonely.

'You mean Celestine?' He smiles wryly. 'She called you Mark.'

'It's not what you think.'

'How do you know what I think?'

That he told her I am married to Lily plays gravely on my mind. 'We can't go back in there. Do you understand? *You* can't go back in there.'

'Okay, chief. Whatever you say. Relax.'

'You don't know anything.'

'Don't I?'

'You tell my wife and I'm going to come after you.' He holds both hands up in surrender, but with a boyish grin on his face. If he thinks I'm trying to cover up an affair, it'll be easier for me. But I know this isn't over.

* * *

The Criterion lounge bar has a mosaic ceiling that looks so old and heavy I fear it might come crashing down. With my back to the room I nurse a beer and inhale voraciously on a cigar, trying to fill a void. Two tables along sits an American with anchors embossed on the gold buttons of his navy-blue blazer. His companion looks my way, her expression taut as a drum, and makes my heart start thundering with anxiety. She draws my eyes to my hand and I see what is causing her offence is my burning cigar. I quickly hide the cigar in my crotch, communicating an unintentional and unfortunate message back to her.

Lily arrives as high as an actress after the curtain, and I stub out my cigar. She sits down, her eyes flaring. After ordering a vodka tonic from the waiter, she asks, 'So what did you think?'

'Someone invited me sailing.' I glance across at the American.

'Did she!'

'But I told her I couldn't swim.'

'Why did you do that?' But she is laughing. Her question does not require an answer. 'Honestly, what did you make of the evening?'

'Honestly . . . there was an air of fear in the room, I thought.'

'Is that what you thought? But fears end when people make a commitment to one another. I get pleasure from arranging that.'

She seeks pleasure in arranging people's commitment, but seeking pleasure is not happiness. Happiness is more elusive. I have made a commitment to her and renew it every moment of my life. But happiness would be too much to ask for.

I say: 'If there's a prosthetic for a lonely heart, you're the doctor who can prescribe it.'

We toast her seminar's success, that it may bring forth

clients, but it feels like my own wake I'm raising the glass to. I have walked away from trouble but don't know for how long my freedom will last. I'm going to need a miracle, or my life is going to go up in smoke. It's going to reverse.

Probation officers and counsellors who told me that the answers to the future lie in the past don't always know what they're talking about. If the past is a dangerous world, if the ground there is still contaminated, you must erect a lead curtain between your two lives.

Piccadilly is a long way from home. 'We should make a move, Lily. So you can fight another day.' We pay our bill and walk out of the Criterion into the crowded square. Along the way people look at me in what I imagine to be half recognition. Subliminal messages may be passing across their minds. They're not quite sure what they've seen or why they are drawn to it. By the time they may have worked it out, I'm lost in the crowd.

We get on to a bus for Waterloo Station and climb up to the top deck. As we wind our way south, I stare out of the window only to find again people on the pavement looking up and catching my eye. In these faces I see a likeness to all other strangers who have been staring at me since last Friday night in Franco's.

Then what has been obscuring a self-evident truth lifts, and the pattern in a weekend of hostile encounters is unveiled. Miles, whether he was in Franco's that night or not, has been towing behind him the one person I'd hoped never to see again.

We alight from the bus and it is raining for the first time in weeks. And the rain is talking. I have to stop the rain from talking.

8

Around the midway point in my four-year supervision with Tom Reeves, I zeroed in on my father for the first time. The news about him was, he maintained, *sustained*, another family: mother and child – mistress and daughter. Shadows of my mother and sister. I found out about them when this other daughter, Celestine, tailed him to our house in Globe Town. She came back the next day and followed me to school. It was raining hard that morning – the kind of weather that puts a ceiling over memory and contains it. The rain was tossed around by wind and slapped at my face. There was a peach tint in the air from the pollutants rising from nearby Canning Town. I was walking to school down a long Roman road with naked cherry trees that looked vulnerable in the dirty winter light. Such a long road, it did some strange things to one's line of sight, and there were sounds of people's lives drifting into the street from well-lit homes. They were impersonal and soothing, and on the day in question probably masked the footfalls following me.

My secondary school was a silver prefab block at the close of that long Roman road, and at the school gates she stepped in front of me and announced herself. She was soaking. Steam was rising through her hood, a pink sweatshirt hood covering her head. I could sense the danger, like you can with a dog sometimes, some animal presence. Everything about her was hard: a voice of slate, eyes of marble. Anyone could say that of course, 'I'm your half-sister', but I'd never heard it before. She made it sound like a threat, not even a veiled one. What I said to her was crude and obvious, but didn't throw her off. When I came out of school at 3.30 she was there again and dogged my side as I walked home. Her sweater was crumpled and shrunken. I could smell on her a sour odour of greasy water. I began to worry what she would do when I got home. My mother was gone from the house, getting treatment in a Kent psychiatric hospital.

My mother was spending more time in Kent than in London at this time in my life and it made the house feel unsafe. I used to have this constant dread of not being able to lock the doors, or that the bricks and mortar would just crumble if I slammed the door too hard. In Mum's absence Dad made us carry on as normal, appear to the world as though she were still at home.

Outside our house Celestine said, 'Tell yer dad you've seen me, and it's curtains for you.' Maybe not exactly that, but something similar. Her eyes below the hood were lowered to the ground. Oily strands of hair fell across her face.

She asked how old I was. I said, 'Twelve.'

'Twelve what?'

'Twelve and a quarter.'

'Same as me then.'

This I couldn't accept. How could she be the same age *and* my sister? The confusion in my mind wouldn't allow for it, for my mother and her mother to be pregnant at the same time. So I told her she was a fucking liar. She threatened me again with a knife if I breathed a word to my dad, produced a sheath knife to illustrate her intent. It had a bone handle and a serrated edge. 'I've killed before, you know. Lots of boys, floated them down the canal. So keep your trap shut!'

I went in and locked the door and through the curtains watched her standing outside in the rain. My eight-year-old sister Olivia was already in. She'd been off school sick, all on her own. I didn't tell her about our half-sister lurking around outside. And I didn't tell my dad when he came in from work a couple of hours later. I could still see that sheath knife in front of my eyes. We were having our tea when the doorbell rang. Dad went to answer it. When he came back looking a bit puzzled and saying, 'There's no one there,' I knew who it was who'd rung.

Celestine kept appearing so often at my school I started to wonder if she ever went to school herself. But all she had to do if she wanted a day off was to get her mother to write a sick note. Like my mother, it seemed Celestine's mother was also out of her tree. That might have said something about my father, but I was too slow or too stupid at that age to pick it up.

So she would meet me after school and then we'd walk all over the place. Since this was winter it was dark. And she threw down challenges, like, why just walk when there's so much entertainment to gorge upon? She got me to ring doorbells and run away. We tore up flowers from front gardens and stuffed them into postboxes. We scratched cars with the edge of coins. She exerted this power over me from the very beginning. On another occasion she kept a shopkeeper distracted while I stole from the shelves, a mop head, toothpaste – useless stuff. But she was only in it for the rush. *She* was only in it for the rush? Or should I have said *we* were only in it for the rush? But I didn't enjoy it. I was tense in the wrong ways.

I worried about my dad. His future I held in my hands. With my mother off with the fairies in Kent, he was all I had. But the mere presence of this girl implied he was in a whole lot of trouble and I thought about him going mad, like Mum, and then being alone with Olivia in the big old empty house with no food in the fridge. I was scared all the time. I even lost weight. My concentration at school was shot. Even my teacher asked if anything was wrong. Finally my headmaster called my dad, who had to explain about my mother. He was very angry with me because of that. He kept saying, 'These things rub off on my business. Now the headmaster knows, how many more are going to find out through him? He tells the teacher, the teacher tells one of the parents and then it's all round the school gates. It only takes one of those mothers to be married to someone I've got business with and it's all over.'

He didn't seem to notice I'd gone stone cold on him since Celestine came along. She was appearing at the school gates almost every other day now, and things were getting more hair-raising. Once in Victoria Park we discovered a model tepee village that had been built by visiting aborigines from the Yukon territory of northern Canada for the deprived kids of east London. It was her idea to raze it. We burnt it to the ground. And I felt a certain excitement, if I'm honest.

Tom intervened. 'Have you ever heard a theory doing the rounds, about fire-setting having a sexual motive? About arson being part of a triad of sexual deviation, bed-wetting and cruelty to animals.'

'I was no bed-wetter,' I insisted. 'But you could be right about the sexual thing.'

It took a couple of days before they tracked me down. A parent of one of the kids in my school had seen a boy and a girl running away from the park, and identified me. I was interrogated by my headmaster, but didn't grass Celestine up. I didn't snitch – to protect Dad – and for that I was caned six times. I remember the head drawing the curtains in his office and the willow twitching against the ceiling a split second before it came down, a split-second warning that it was on its way. A letter was sent to my dad and he called me into the lounge. He slapped me hard on the face and said, 'This girl, whoever she is, you're not to play with her again. Understand?' My ears were still ringing when I saw Celestine outside the house watching through the window. She was pulling faces at me over Dad's shoulder. Two fingers in her nostrils and two in her eye sockets.

Next day we tore through Mile End, where she spotted some sport in a front garden. I hardly realised what it was before we began hurling bricks at it. Then blood started seeping through its grey armour. A woman came out of her front door and her face collapsed, there was this disbelief in her eyes. I still remember it now and it's how I knew, from her expression, that what we were doing was terribly wrong. It was a tortoise, a family pet, we'd been stoning to death. I felt ashamed, but Celestine was laughing as we ran off. We stopped running in Victoria Park, and then I hit her. But this was no ordinary girl. She was an Apache and came at me biting, scratching and kicking. We exhausted ourselves and lay on the grass in a heap. I must say I liked what I felt then. With my mother absent, no one had been touching me for months. We touched in combat and then with my head in her lap. She stroked my hair as she asked, 'What does our father love most?'

'My younger sister.'

'More than you? More than your mother?' Her eyes closed and opened like a cash register.

'Yes.'

'Then you and me, all we've got is each other.'

We continued to meet after school and each time she'd up the ante, smashing car windows, breaking bottles in the brewery yard, setting fire to fly-tipped waste in back roads. We'd run, get out of range and she'd link her arm in mine as we ambled along. My sense of shame was beginning to disappear. I was feeling stronger with her around.

9

I return home after a twenty-four-hour shift with the river still lapping in my ears. On this occasion, as I open the front door I feel a powerful sense of loss, of abandonment. The house seems funereal. In the kitchen I pour a glass of water and see through the window Lily and the children in the garden. Then I see Celestine with them. It feels like hitting the ground after falling from a high roof. She is out there with my family. A second later I hardly feel anything at all. All is dead inside me. Seconds pass and then the pure light of the future stirs up the dead air as I plan the next move. Celestine sits on one of the two swings on the play centre and dangles her feet, dangling my life before my eyes. She then pushes off and swings high enough for the staples holding the frame into the earth to start lifting. The children are paralysed with morbid fascination. At the same time she holds a conversation with Lily, who is the keeper of two glasses of white wine.

I open the door into the garden and stand where they cannot see me.

'. . . About seeing what you want to see? Like, we only know ourselves?'

'I wasn't thinking about Ray when I said that. Ray's, well, he's unusual – for a guy.' They laugh at my expense. Lily's is benign, but I hear impatience in Celestine's. 'He blushes. Don't you like it when a man does that?'

'What was your maiden name, Lily?'

'Gunther. At school they called me The Grunter. Horrible. Lily Greenland sounds better, don't you think? Especially for someone in my profession.'

'Didn't even have to change your initials.' Celestine jumps off the swing at its highest point and lands next to Lily. Her stiletto heels drill into the lawn. She relieves Lily of one of the glasses of wine. 'Where did you meet him, again?'

'Waterman's Hall, at a Christmas party.'

'The what?'

'It's this place . . . four generations of my family have made a living from the river and I went to this party with my father. Ray was standing on his own in a corner. I introduced myself because he was never going to talk to me or anyone else. Then he said Lily was his favourite flower. I thought it was just a line but he began to blush.'

There is no pleasure in hearing Lily's reminiscence because of the recipient. The pressure builds inside me until I go out on to the lawn and intervene, before my past cancels out my future. Celestine is the first to see me. Lily notices her expression darken, turns and sees me approaching. She raises her glass. 'Ray . . . guess who this is?'

'I know who this is.' But I don't know who Lily thinks she is. Celestine smiles crookedly and folds her arms. I'm secure as long as she wants me to be. It is all in her hands. 'We met at the seminar.'

'Why didn't you tell me! Oh well, I think it's fantastic.'

Celestine explains, for my benefit, how she 'crashed'

the Bliss offices earlier today and introduced herself as my long-lost cousin. She is a canny one.

Lily is beaming. She's so pleased with herself. Only the innocent think all surprises are good surprises.

The party mood slowly deteriorates and then Lily disappears into the house to cook – for she has invited Celestine to dinner. The children follow her, excited that one of my relations has materialised, but not yet at ease in her presence. Alone out in the garden, with the trees sailing high in the wind, Celestine drops her false smile.

'Nice wife and children, nice pad.'

'What do you want?'

'Don't insult me, Mark.'

'Ray.'

'That's right, you're Ray Greenland now. How surreal. But I'm still family whatever your name is. I'm your blood.'

'Not this family.'

'Don't worry, I'm only passing through. Through Greenland . . .' She sniggers, then skips off indoors.

Flora, the more intuitive of the children, stays shy of Celestine. She keeps in the kitchen attached to her mother, while Eliot goes upstairs with Celestine to show off his new computer game, *Midtown Madness*. I leave just enough time for him to get the software loaded and follow them up. In the snake pit of computer cabling and the jungle of discarded clothes they share a single chair in front of the monitor and crash cars all over Chicago.

Celestine has her arm around my son. She turns to me at the door. 'We're getting on like a house on fire, ain't we, Eliot?'

Eliot smiles palely. I am powerless to alter the course of things. I cannot remove her even by force. My legs feel weak beneath me. I look at the Disney clock on the wall. I watch the clock and see the minutes sluicing by.

Lily prepares a fast midweek supper of pasta tossed with chicken, mushrooms and peppers. We use the dining table in the lounge, as befits a special occasion, and from the moment we gather round I can sense Lily dying to ask Celestine questions about our mutual past, but she limits herself for now to the future.

'I'm thinking about writing a book,' Celestine replies to Lily's enquiry. 'About my childhood. Or I might go to law school or business school. I'd like to own a chain of small businesses, shops, launderettes. Places that would employ people no one else would touch with a barge pole. Ex-cons, old people nobody cares for any more. Homeless people. It would have to be on their CV before I'd take a look at them. I'd give them a job. With the money I'd set up a detective agency to work for people wrongly convicted of crimes.'

Lily is a model of restraint. 'Business with a conscience,' she says, serving Celestine out of the Sicilian bowl.

'The thing is, I couldn't just be rich. Why make tons of money just so you can spend it on yourself? There should be a law against it.'

'I totally agree.' Lily searches for me across the table, but I'm not available.

Celestine begins to eat before anyone else has been served. The way she hammers at her pasta and fills her jaws mesmerises Flora and Eliot. They are uncharacteristically quiet, entertained by Celestine's manners and by the way she looks. They detect something wild in her. Flora in particular is fascinated by the woollen gloves she wears at the table with the fingers cut off, her arterial-purple nail varnish and the ten rings, and her eye-shadow like a dark-grey veil.

'Where do you live then, Celestine?' Lily tries to spark up the conversation again.

It takes her a few seconds to swallow the wad before she can reply. 'Silvertown.'

'Did you also live in Oystermouth?'

Celestine looks at me for some help. I say, 'Still drawn to water then?'

'Yeah. Can't get enough of it.'

'Do you have a flat or something?' Lily asks.

'Something . . . Not as nice as this. But cosy enough, I reckon.'

Dinner progresses in staccato fashion. Lily scowls at me in a private aside because I'm not engaging in the conversation and I've hardly touched my plate. I take an olive and nibble the skin.

Lily asks the children to clear the plates to the kitchen and bring in the ice cream from the freezer. We sit in silence until they return with the carton. Celestine tells Flora, 'None of that for me.' Lily serves the kids and soon Eliot is spooning the ice cream into his mouth. Celestine points at his lips, ringed with strawberry. 'You look like you've been shot in the back of the head, mister.'

'I'll make coffee,' Lily announces. She lays her napkin on the table and exits to the kitchen.

'Fucking hell! I don't think I've sat down as long as this in my life. I've got to get off my arse.' The kids react to her expletives as if a cannon has fired off and sit with their mouths open. 'Eliot, fancy another game upstairs?'

Eliot looks at me for permission to leave the table. I nod and he follows her out like he would one of his teachers, without questioning. I cannot contradict her. She has absolute power. I am sick with worry.

'She's a bit strange, Dad,' Flora whispers to me after they've left the room.

Lily returns to the lounge to find the two of us staring at one another. 'Oh. Have we finished dinner then?'

Flora asks, 'Is she really your cousin?'

I struggle, but fail to form some kind of answer.

'She's Daddy's cousin on his father's side.' Lily cups her hand beneath my chin and lifts my head from off the bottom of the dark blue river. 'What's up with you, Ray? You hardly spoke to her. You don't seem pleased she's turned up.'

'My relations are not like yours. I hardly knew her, but I remember she's not a nice person.'

'How long ago was this, Ray? People do change, you know. Sometimes even for the better.'

'I don't think she's changed for the better.'

'Nice or not, you've only got the one. That must be worth some effort.'

I hear Celestine above our heads, walking across the bare polished floorboards in our bedroom. I hear a clink of glass bottles in our bathroom and then her feet move again, wandering around from room to room upstairs. Her presence mocks me, disenfranchises me in my own home. She knows who I really am. She is loaded with deadly munitions of a kind that can destroy my wife and blight the children's lives.

Lily says, 'Hello? Anyone at home?'

'What?'

'Do you want me to welcome her into this family, or not?'

I apply a temporary explanation. 'She's a compulsive liar.' I'm unable to elaborate because Celestine reappears in the lounge.

'My ears were burning,' she says. 'You must have been talking about me.' She pads over to the mantelpiece and juggles a pewter-framed photograph in her hand like a hot potato. 'Who's this?'

'Ray's father . . .' Lily sounds bewildered. 'Your uncle.'

'Yeah, that's the silver-haired old bastard.'

The man in the photograph is as alien to her as he is to me, was a job lot at an auction.

She asks to see more pictures of our family – hers and mine.

'Another time,' I say, and wait to see if she pushes it. She approaches the dinner table, takes the linen napkin from in front of me and blows her nose vigorously. Then she drops the screwed-up napkin back on the table. I can see Lily begin to lose some of her certainties. The veil of goodwill lifts from her eyes.

'Can I order you a taxi?' I ask.

'Are we all going to bed already?'

'I've been up for the past twenty-four hours.'

'Lily said what you do. Well, wave to me when you next pass Silvertown on your vessel.'

When the taxi arrives I walk her outside. I want to make sure she leaves. Standing in the open door of the car she asks me for some money to pay the cabby. I give her thirty pounds from my wallet. 'Well, it's been real . . . Ray.'

I say nothing. I'm already into the next struggle over how I face the family inside, how to get through the rest of the night.

When I do get back indoors Lily is waiting for me. 'I don't know about compulsive liar, Ray, but she's mad as a snake. Has she always been like this? She can't keep still for a moment.'

'I last saw her when she was a child.'

'Is there something you're not telling me, Ray? About her, about the two of you?'

Will there ever be a better opportunity to confess?

I say: 'Like what?'

'I don't know. Did she do something to you? I could have cut the atmosphere with a knife.'

'I never knew her very well. I only remember I didn't like her.'

'Ray, I see lots of people round here I went to school with. One girl – we used to call her Bonehead – used to bully me for years. She now works in Asda behind the tills. Why d'you think I never shop at Asda? All these years pass and yet our feelings don't. We all have unfinished business from childhood, the bruises from when we were . . . I understand how you feel. If you want some time to, I don't know, discover her again, if that's not too cheesy, then that's fine by me.'

'I don't want to see her. But she wants to see me.'

'Then tell her to vamoose. I can't do that for you.'

'I'm not asking you to.'

'Oh, go on, give her some more time. I mean, she's your only relative. The only relative I've met anyway.'

'I'm happy enough without relatives. I've got all I want on your side of the family. I've got you and the kids. That's all I ever want.'

'Whatever. Why don't you sleep on it? You look done in.'

Much later, it is Lily who sleeps while I stroll around in the garden in the dark, considering for a second time in days the preordained pattern of this disaster. Was its origin in the Italian restaurant? Or crashing into the back of Miles? I remember the moment before we drove off from the school fête, expelling hot air from our car and the strange sensation of the sky warping and buckling. Was that the beginning? Was it all in the weather? Has nature conspired against me?

The real disaster of course is easy to mark – that happened when I was twelve.

In the dead of night there comes a momentary windless silence into the garden which helps with my fantasy that I'm dreaming it all up. But then I find something that tells me otherwise. With a knife, Celestine has carved her name into the bark of our plum tree.

10

Before I discovered my dad was a polygamist, I knew him best as a London property developer with a knack for finding old industrial buildings and turning them into restaurant-gym-retail-residential (*resi*) complexes. A sweatshop in Canning Town he transformed into a yoga and writing centre. For people who wanted to write whilst in a lotus position, or for people who wanted to write about the lotus position, I never found out. He didn't know either. That was the vendor's job. All my dad did was put the sites together, then split, selling off units from a great distance with such bullshit lines as: 'The site maintains traditional industrial qualities of cast-iron street furniture and brick paving.' The vendors got a different line in shit: 'The project will show a strong operating cash flow within the first year and a bottom-line profit in year two.' (Remembering these terms he used demonstrates a sort of devotion, Tom suggested.)

My dad said you couldn't fool vendors like you could the punters. Vendors, investors, developers, architects . . . these were his associates, and not one of them lived in the zoos they created. Another of his developments in Bow you could reach by canal barge, passing under a big sign that said: Welcome to Bow*hemia*. That was the vendor's idea. That was the shit they were selling.

My dad was a school-failure success story. Left at sixteen with no qualifications. His headmaster grabbed him on his last day and said, 'I guess we'll be seeing you shortly, Swain, emptying our bins.' He told my dad he'd amount to nothing. But Dad only *started out* with nothing and soon proceeded to make a bundle, buying and selling lock-ups, then resi and later commercial property. Around 1980 he bought the school after it was forced to close – I think after one of those inspector's reports nailed the coffin – and turned it into a sports centre. He sent his old headmaster a ten per cent reduction offer on membership.

My dad was a king. Kings are men who don't make mistakes when they make decisions for our benefit, our betterment. They don't consult but they don't make mistakes. Other kings of the time were Tony Berry, Peter de Savary, Elliot Bernerd and Paul Reichmann . . . later ruined from the effort of building the first Canary Wharf tower. My dad used to say of these men, these *kings*: 'They have built pyramids that will outlive their critics.'

He was small-time compared to these others (but he did keep a private investigator on retainer to snout around for him), who were either toffs or Jews. He used to say, 'Toffs inherit fortunes and Jews inherit tragedy.' The toffs would swagger around town showing off their wealth while the Jews gave half their stash to Zionist charities and Yeshiva schools. He approved of the Jews but not the toffs. Inherited wealth destroys character and is why he didn't intend leaving me a cent. Good enough to support me now, me and my sister, but the moment

I was old enough to work, he was going to cut the life-line.

He used to boast he was wealthy but I don't know if he was or not. One month my mother would get her dream kitchen fitted. Next month someone came along to repossess his Jaguar. But it wasn't money that interested him so much. He loved the game. When I was quite young, ten or eleven, he took me with him on his walks along the Thames towpath. He'd never stop talking about the advantages of developing property on water, explained the meaning of betterment value, Goad's Plan, a Stokes v. Cambridge situation. And yes, the fact I can still remember all these terms suggests devotion on my part. He made me feel special, just him and me, even though it was really only ever him. He might have started the day asking about me but was only waiting on a word to hook his own interest to, and then was away, on his own journey of the river and estuaries. That's what he called the canals – estuaries. Buyers were more seduced by the sound of 'river estuary' than by 'canal'.

One time we were out on one of these walks when he said, 'Mark, I'm going to tell you how to make two mill from nothing . . . all in a day.' Normally you'd need two million – *mill* – to make a couple of mill. But he had a good line in shit. And he delivered the goods. The shit is about getting the credit, and delivering the goods is about honouring the debt. If you didn't honour the debt in those days, you'd end up in the river with your throat slit. He pointed out a block of modern riverside offices. 'That's mine,' he said. 'The development exists. It's there. I delivered. It's empty now but when office space in the City becomes overrun the punters will be moving in.' Originally this was an old chapel with a lot of land but no betterment value . . . because the chapel was listed.

Which meant you couldn't knock it down. But the only way to make a gain was to knock it down. And you could only knock down a listed building by proving it was structurally unsound. 'So here's the thing,' he said. 'I drive all the way up north someplace where they still quarry for slate in the mountains. I find this young bloke in a pub. He's got five young children and a wife with the hump. I ask him what he earns in a year. He says, "Seven grand." I say, "I'll pay you that for a day's work." He comes down to London with me in the car with a small box of high explosives in the boot, purloined from the quarry stores. At the site he sinks a little of the explosives into the foundations, he knows just how much is needed, and it goes off like, *whump!* When the dust settles there's a fourteen-foot crack in the load-bearing wall. I get permission to demolish the chapel the following week.'

He bent the rules because that's what you had to do if you hadn't inherited a stash to start off with, if you weren't a toff. Another property he went out of his way to *get* listed. It had nice art-deco features inside as a selling feature but the brass-inlaid fronts were gone. So he had replicas made on the sly. 'The Heritage can't tell a Michelangelo from a Mickey Mouse cartoon and missed the fake brass-inlaid fronts. They listed the building and I shaved eighty grand off the construction costs by eliminating VAT.'

The happiest man he claimed to have met was a longshoreman from New York who told him to build on water, like some holy prophet of old. 'Like a mother's affection' is how the longshoreman described the Hudson.

And my dad used to say: 'Three rules of property development are: water, water, water.'

This same day we stopped at a little fish restaurant

on Lower Thames Street. He took me in for lunch and the maître d' had to lend me a tie. As we were sitting there, Dad continued the story of how he made two mill in a day. 'Like all big deals in life, Mark, there were several years of plotting and planning behind it. This scheme started off slowly. And sentimentally.' A couple of years beforehand he bought a glue factory where his own father used to work until he died of benzene poisoning. He bought the building and ground lease from British Waterways – the factory was on the canal . . . the *estuary* – but failed to get planning permission from the local council. The factory was one of four buildings on a small industrial estate and the council wanted to offer planning permission on all the buildings, together, as one bag. But when he approached British Waterways again and offered to buy the other three buildings, they sensed a potential gain for themselves. They had the ransom strip that entitled them to fifty per cent of the development gain. So they offered to buy the glue factory back from him. But he was having none of that. Their next trick was to try and smoke him out by putting the other buildings up for auction along with the ground leases.

He was telling me this in the fish restaurant, the only child among the grey suits, and it made me feel grown up, apprenticed to my dad in his business. 'The buildings themselves were worthless. It was the land under them I wanted. Then one day I was sitting in this restaurant, same table, when fate intervened. Luck has a part to play in this game too, son. My private investigator came to have lunch with me. He walked in here with his nose all blistered by the sun, his forehead peeling. And I said, "What the fuck happened to you?"'

'I was on the beach in Spain when Dave Harvey almost falls on top of me.'

'What was he doing out in Spain?'

'That's what I wanted to know.'

'Harvey never takes a holiday.'

'Exactly. "What are you doing out here, Harvey?" "Looking for gold," he says. And he was . . . financing for his Canvey Island shopping city. When Harvey told me *who* he was tapping I nearly fell off my lilo. Only Richard fucking Gower.'

'*Sir* Richard fucking Gower?'

'Apparently he has his yacht moored down there. So Harvey says. But what I also learnt, and this is the thing, old Sir Richard's been nosing into the same auction catalogue as you, vis-à-vis the glue-factory site.'

My dad got very serious at this point. 'I got to know by how much he's interested, Domino.' His snout was called Domino.

We left the restaurant before my dad finished the story, because he had a swimming lesson booked. It seemed odd to me then as it does now that a man of thirty-five couldn't swim. This king of the waterway property deal, builder of liquid dreams, floundered around in the pool, frightened stiff of kids jumping into the water and splashing him. It was very disturbing to watch, seeing him so helpless. His instructor had to support his weight in the pool. It didn't seem right.

When we came out of the pool a parking attendant was giving him a ticket, and my dad was so angry I feared he was going to beat him up. He drove away at speed, going faster and faster all the time, and that was when he continued with the story. We were rocketing through east London, the parking penalty notice flapping under the windscreen wiper as he told me how Domino did the research on Sir Richard. By squirrelling himself into his employ as a temporary chauffeur (his regular driver was off on the sick) he got to overhear Sir

Richard talking to his people in the back of the car. 'His runner was telling Sir Richard how the glue factory's derelict, but the lock-keeper's cottage and the depot buildings are nice. And about the canal as attraction . . .'

'Canal as attraction? How can a canal be an attraction?' Sir Richard replied.

'Attractive for people who settle for less.'

'Has Swain got an anchor in there?'

'Conrad.'

'Has he! That's why BW want to get shot of the rest.'

'They got debts,' his lawyer said.

'What's the reserve?'

'Seven hundred K. The capital value of the buildings with ground leases is eight hundred plus. But with a window for low-density resi and providing the anchor stays in, you could make a nice few mill on this.'

'How do we persuade Swain to sell us the glue factory?'

'He's got a thing about it. His father died there or something. I don't think you'll persuade him. Maybe you could offer to form a consortium, but I doubt he'll go for it.'

'If the reserve is seven hundred, on an eight hundred K capital value . . .'

'You could go twenty per cent higher,' his lawyer advised. 'As high as nine, but no more.'

'How high will Swain go?'

'That we don't know.'

'Say I go above Swain and get the site. I still have to persuade him to sell me the glue factory, or no one can make a move.'

'Something will give. Either he sells it to you or you form a consortium with him.'

'I thought you said he wouldn't do that?'

'Think positive here. Say we do get it all. The site's on a conservation area. We'd have to seek detail design approval from the Heritage, and the bird people, the RSPB, whatever. Who'll want it maintained for navigation.'

'Who, the bird people?'

'Heritage.'

'Navigation . . . what navigation? It's a fucking canal.'

'It's what they're saying, Sir Richard.'

'Any tenants?'

'A few, but we can winkle them out.'

And so it went on, the conversation in the back of Sir Richard Gower's car. Most importantly my dad now knew Sir Richard's highest bid in the auction would be nine hundred K. But we had reached our house by now and he hadn't concluded the story. I had to wait until after he'd finished clucking around my sister, Olivia.

He and I used to walk on water, but he was only showing off his monuments to himself. Coco was his true dear (Coco is what he called Olivia). I might have been my mother's favourite, but she was off her head. And when you have only one parent up and running properly you're going to compete over that parent. I rowed with Olivia because Dad favoured her.

Globe Town, between Bethnal Green and Bow, is a better area now than it was then. Then it used to be a villains' manor. A lot of dead bodies reinforce the concrete foundations of the Royal London Hospital down the road from us, is what my dad used to say, and support the A12 flyover. He could have afforded to move us further west into town, but he was born in the Globe. The good life is about feeling secure and staying lucky. And luck was all in the geography. He knew where all the derelict buildings were, knew everyone, and everyone knew him. When he started making money he got respect and that was important to him, to be a local hero, a king.

A king needs to have a strong family to complete the picture. But the shadow in the picture was my mother, wandering the streets in her nightie, asking passers-by for directions to Paddington Station. She often sat in a darkened room all day without coming out even to eat. So of course my dad had to keep the lid on it, didn't want this to be known among his clan. I think that's why he refused to let her work, yeah definitely. She used to have a job as a shop assistant in a department store when they met, or something similar. But soon after they married he kept her locked up. All she got to do was design our house, top to bottom, from mail-order catalogues. She'd pick up the phone and order furniture, carpets, curtains, and then call carpenters, painters and decorators to do the fit-up. A year later she'd do it all again. No one ever visited us at home. My father's friends, business colleagues, never saw the inside of our house that smelled permanently of fresh paint. I know my mother didn't have any friends. She just had us for company, until I drove her over the edge.

Some mothers are just not cut out for the job, I suppose. The day I drove her over the edge I was playing on the canal. I'd made a raft out of oil drums and timbers and was punting it around. The ropes binding the timbers to the drums came loose and I had to wade back. A canal is not tidal and can't cleanse itself, like the Thames. It runs on the spot. I was rancid and oily when I got home.

My sister and I had our own bedrooms. Territories like bedrooms are for being private in, and for invading. I ran into hers with the muck and skunk of the canal dripping off my clothes. I rolled on her clean bed and pressed myself up against her poster of the original Wham! line-up. My mother heard the screaming and when she came up her face was set, as though she'd planned what she was about to do for months. She dragged my sister out of her territory by the hair. I followed her into the kitchen and I was crying. I knew she'd gone too far. Olivia was thrown out the door into the alleyway. Then Mum turned on me. She locked the kitchen door, opened a cutlery drawer and pinned me to the wall. And made a four-inch incision in my chest with the bread knife . . . a two-inch incision, but four paper stitches. I was thinking of the stitches. Anyway, I went into shock. My sister was rattling the door from the other side. My mum kicked the door, put her foot *through* the frosted glass. Olivia had all these cuts in her face from the flying glass.

I can't remember how I felt at the time, can't recall any of it. But there was something cooking in the kitchen, although nothing you could eat. My mother used to boil dirty handkerchiefs in a big saucepan, a disgusting habit, and I can remember how that sounded – like a car driving on a punctured tyre. She used to boil her knickers too and they'd lie on the radiators for days. She'd take one pair off at a time, when she needed them.

After this incident she went off to Kent and didn't come back. Olivia made a meal of it. She was eight going on twenty-two, accusing me of having driven Mum nuts by dragging the canal into our spotless home. Spotless, apart from the knickers on the radiators.

How did I feel about my mother's absence? It was embarrassing. Everyone was very embarrassed. But I also felt I'd misplaced something. I'm not religious, but I'm sure if you proved beyond doubt that God didn't exist, lots of people would still retain their faith. That was how I felt with my mother gone. She stopped existing for us but I still believed in her. To make it worse I had to pretend she was still at home whenever some neighbour asked after her. And I always had to lie why I and not my mother was collecting my sister from school, until Dad got her a place in an after-school club and then picked her up himself.

Anyway, when my dad got through pampering Olivia that afternoon, he continued telling the story. He was trying to put a deal together with this toff, Sir Richard, in the auction house. In the living room now, he was telling me what an auction looked like, with the corridors crowded by Indians, Hasidic Jews, Arabs, and men like my dad wearing dark suits and hair oil, making private deals. 'People come up to me all the time, Mark,' he said. 'Everyone knows me. Everyone knows I'm a player.' Then he met a colleague whose wife had just given birth to a baby girl. 'Congratulations. Keeping you up at nights?'

'Sure, with colic.'

'Oh too bad. Poor baby.' He told me this man's family name, the guy with the baby. It meant nothing to me at the time. 'As big a name as Guinness. He inherits a fortune and sits at home all day with the baby. Might as well be dead,' is what my dad said.

But the real point was, they knew my dad, knew he was a player. And that meant he knew who might be interested, apart from Sir Richard, in the glue-factory site, and went around asking and broadcasting his intention to outbid anyone who tried to get it. This was sheer bluff of course. He intended to get it for the reserve price. In the event Sir Richard was the only other potential bidder, and thanks to Domino's intelligence, he knew Sir Richard's bid would be no higher than nine hundred K.

The auction was like a theatre, the auctioneer spending millions of pounds of other people's money in minutes, while Dad was in a private room with Sir Richard and their lawyers half an hour before his lot would be going under the hammer. The catalogue was on the table, along with a briefcase belonging to my dad. They were laughing and smoking Cubans.

Dad said: 'Is there any way we can avoid running for the same lot, Sir Richard?'

'What do you propose?'

'A consortium won't work for me. Not this time. I don't know what you intend to bid, Sir Richard, and I can't afford to bid for ever. But I'll tell you what my top bid will be. It'll be one mill. If that's higher than you intend to go, that's between you and the butler. But if it's not, not higher, then maybe you'll take twenty K in cash, on the table. If you agree not to go against me and subject to me successfully acquiring the other properties.'

'If it means something to you, it means something to you.'

'It does mean something to me.'

'Can you draw up a letter of agreement, Charles?'

Charles was Sir Richard's lawyer. The said document was drawn up. Sir Richard and my dad shook hands. Then he handed over his briefcase with the cash inside. Sir Richard had just made £20,000 for doing nothing.

In the auction room the auctioneer started taking bids for the lot. His assistant took bids from a single customer on the telephone. 'Five hundred and two . . . five hundred and four . . . five hundred and five . . . anybody . . . you sir?' He was not asking my dad. The auctioneer knew him and knew he was not someone you prodded. 'The gentleman on the phone . . .' He got a nod from his assistant. 'Six hundred even . . . to the gent on the phone. This is getting interesting. You sir . . . care to bid six-five? If the gent on the phone could see the whites of your eyes . . . Yes? Six-five. I have six hundred and five . . . and six-seven even from the gent on the phone.' Then my dad came in with seven. The reserve price. There was a shuffle and a whisper in the air. 'I have seven. Any advance on seven? Seven once, seven twice . . . Sold for seven hundred thousand pounds.'

Sir Richard Gower was staggering all over the place. He didn't understand what had happened. He had been prepared to go as high as nine. That briefcase full of cash he was holding began to feel rather light.

Now my dad had all four buildings on the site and all the ground leases. What he didn't have was the £700,000 to pay the auction house. So he offered the whole site to . . . Sir Richard, the same day he bought it. 'Four parcels of land with ninety-nine-year leases. Planning consent on use more valuable than current.'

'It's not exactly Chelsea Harbour, is it?'

'No, but water resi for people who can't afford Chelsea Harbour.'

'Who wants to see a canal? I could do two and two. I can't really do more than that.'

'It's off the main route, no important buildings. But it's going to bring in interest from people in that neck of the woods who'd like to invest in something a little bit special. Who like to be reminded, in pursuit of modern goals, that some things stay the same. I can see my way forward with three and two.'

'But the canal . . . It's never going to be the Thames however hard you dress it up.'

'Think of it as an estuary of the river. A little sibling if you like. It's got historical links . . .'

'It doesn't move. Doesn't go anywhere . . .'

'We're not talking of a thirty-mill betterment value, I grant you. We're talking about six mill, realisable in two to three years. People will buy here who are upwardly mobile but not in the salary bracket of say, city bankers. They are good people. Like doctors and university people.'

'Is two seven oh all right, as a way forward?'

'I can live with two seven oh.'

So my dad sold the entire kit and caboodle for two million seven hundred thousand to the noble Sir Richard – the toff – who did make his six million eventually, but not for years to come. While my father, after paying the auctioneer the £700,000, made not only two million, two *mill* . . . he made two *mill* in a single day.

11

There's a tension in water, but no tension in me. It's seven in the morning and I'm flush with the tidal streams. Eliot is sitting happily beside me in the wheelhouse. My transgression from Sunday finally seems to have been forgiven.

He has shipped out with me on a day off from school. I wish I had Flora along too, but she wouldn't step on a boat for a king's ransom. A pity, because no one can find us out here, or chase us down the stream. Whether he cares to listen or not I tell Eliot how the river never changes. It's meant to be a comforting remark. It comforts me, at least, that some things in nature stay the same. The Thames is still fed by the same arteries and drains, the same five thousand square miles of southern England. Winter rains recharge the water table in the Cotswold limestone and the Berkshire Downs, same as they always have. Thousands of tons of silt and gravel continue to form shoals. And what I do each working day is what fishermen, fowlers, reed cutters and bargemen have done for centuries: glide along the Thames' course, married not to the ever-changing shore life but to the eternal river. Once my shift begins I never get off this ship. My responsibility begins and ends in the wheelhouse.

The air is cold rising off the river. A mist that was clinging stubbornly to the water an hour ago is burning off. The early-morning sun glancing across the earth turns the surface black and oily. Eliot helps me start the day with navigation routines. We study the Admiralty's *Notice to Mariners* for any changes on the river – to lights, buoyage or construction. He turns the radio on to Channel 68 and we listen to Port of London Radio's hourly broadcast, announcing heavy vessels working in our vicinity, the weather forecast for the next twelve hours and the tide at Tilbury (three and a half metres above chart datum).

We are travelling down-river at twelve knots. 'Twelve knots against a two-knot tide . . . what's that over the ground?'

'Ten knots.'

'That's right. Why are we running stern first?'

'To reduce the wash.'

'To reduce the wash . . .' I ask him to switch on the radar, which he does with intense concentration, then confirms the order back to me.

'Radar on, Dad.'

I can never tire of hearing that word, *Dad*. It swells my heart. It's mine. I legitimately own it, even if I don't deserve to. He tears off the Navtex weather fax and palms it to me. The forecast is in my veins, but I read it for his sake.

I say the river never changes, but it does have one volatile characteristic that may yet be its epitaph: it keeps rising. Long before the Thames Barrier was erected, traders sank vertical revetments between their premises and the water, back-filled with spoil . . . actually building *into* the river. There are ten metres of these accumulated deposits over the original Roman water levels. Now the technology is available, it's conceivable that a system of locks and weirs above and below London could be installed, which would turn the Thames into a clear, freshwater pool with no tides. In his lifetime, I tell Eliot, he could see London become a city on a lake, like Geneva or Chicago.

This is a sentimental education I'm giving him, because as any man knows who works on the Thames today, its glory is in the past. Not so long ago really, forty thousand men serviced two thousand sailing ships and five hundred colliers on the river. Now there are fewer than a hundred men working. The only likely job you'll get, after five years' apprenticeship, is on the tourist boats: impoverished successors to the ornate ceremonial barges of the nobility and the city livery companies with their flared raking bows, half covered by carved and gilded cabins and orchestras playing on the upper deck.

Despite this, despite all I know to be true, I can't resist tempting my boy with forbidden, shrivelled fruit. Even the mate, Noel, is at it: 'You going to work on the river when you grow up?' he asks Eliot. A fourth-generation waterman, Noel does not want to see any of his own children making it a fifth, for all the same reasons. His eldest son is a twenty-eight-year-old gynaecologist at St Thomas' Hospital, and that's the trend he wants to see go down the line.

But my boy is fair game.

'Yes I am,' Eliot replies, even though he and I have never discussed this. Even though he may suspect it's not true.

Where did this politeness come from? I worry, but not too seriously, that he may become a priest when he grows up. He has not got his sister's acerbic humour as defence against the world.

'Then whatever you do,' Noel continues, 'don't be an engineer. Be a pilot like your dad.'

Say I: 'Noel, I had to step into a dead man's shoes to get this job.'

His shoulders shake in his overalls as he laughs at me. 'Don't want the boy getting excited by the river, best leave him at home, Ray.' A broad and swarthy man of great strength, his sagging eyeballs and broken veins attest to a lifetime of smoking and heavy drinking. He also has a gambling habit, to which he has sacrificed a home and a marriage. But whatever his vices are on land he never brings them on to the river.

I don't want Eliot following me on to the river but I still want him to be intimate with it. So, yes, it pleases me sensing Eliot share my euphoria. We all need something bigger than ourselves to worship. We no longer throw African slaves overboard as offerings to the river god, but there still is a river god. And he requires a human sacrifice now and again. Forty suicides a year jump off the London bridges, sometimes two by two. Recently, a West Indian torso floated down-river from Richmond to Bermondsey in a suitcase. In the year I started my apprenticeship, the *Bowbelle* dredger struck the passenger vessel *Marchioness* with the loss of fifty-one lives, a hundred years after seven hundred were drowned when the *Princess Anne* was sunk in Galleon's Reach.

Eliot is overwhelmed by his father's 'office' – a class 9F tug, 30 metres long with a draft of 4.6 metres, powered by twin Voith Schneider propulsion engines delivering 3860 brake horsepower. He is aroused by the vessel vibrating beneath him and by the river running sleekly as an Arab horse. With the look of the stowaway he peers through my binoculars as large as his face, locating the Royal Navy frigate at Sea Reach Six. Having sailed in last night from Portsmouth, we are to assist her up-river to the Pool. Battleships may rule the oceans but in this river they are nothing much without me. For a couple of hours I'm going to be their daddy too.

As he is looking through the binoculars Noel remembers to tell me something. 'Oh yeah, you got visitors in your cabin.'

'What visitors?' I make a wish (for Lily and Flora). But that is a wish too far.

'Woman says she's your cousin. And a bloke.'

I over-correct by four degrees of leeway on the compass, against the hard tide pushing towards the drying flats. 'When did they come on board?'

'Ten minutes before you.'

'You let them on?'

He can hear the accusation in my voice. 'They came down from the office, Ray. They signed an insurance waiver. I guessed it was all right.'

I cannot afford to betray any more emotion to Noel. He has been in the dark all the years we've known each other. 'Take the helm, would you.'

I descend alone into the bowels of the ship. I check the heads and the galley and find Celestine lying counterwise on my cabin bunk. Miles lies beside her with his feet in dirty trainers on the pillow and his hand under her skirt, between her bare legs. They are watching breakfast television with the volume off. 'This is great,' she says on seeing me. 'Don't have TV where I live.' At 07.30 Miles has a beer on the go. She drinks tea from my mug with a picture of Eliot and Flora burnt into the side.

I don't understand how they came to be here. On what grounds did management let them on? Does someone there know the score?

I don't know how much Miles knows either, whether he knows the score.

'You got to get off this ship,' I stammer with emotion. 'I'm going to go ashore and put you down.'

'Be nice, Ray. Like your mate, Noel, who made me the tea.'

'I have a ship to run. I can't be entertaining visitors.'

'Don't need to entertain us,' Miles says, slurring slightly. 'We're happy enough right here.' He raises his can to me. This must be his own dynamite. There is never any alcohol on board.

'Drinking's not allowed on board.'

'I'm not driving the fucking ship, chief. You're the one who needs to stay sober.' He takes his eyes off me, signalling the end of this conversation, and welds them back on to the television screen.

HMS *Marlborough* is waiting for us on the Zulu anchorage. Noel has allowed Eliot to steer us in while I've been gone but now I can see the whites of the *Marlborough*'s eyes, I regain the wheel. This is a delicate business and for the next couple of minutes play has to stop. I manoeuvre stern-first to within a few metres of their bow and stem the tide. The second engineer leaves the humid heat of the engine room for the chill of early morning on deck. He throws a line to a rating on board the *Marlborough*. The rating hauls in the heavier towrope attached to the line, securing it to a cleat. By remote control in the wheelhouse, Noel tightens the towrope around the winch and I gently lift the *Marlborough* off her mooring.

The minute we are under way I say, 'Did you make her tea, Noel?'

'Sure.'

'In my mug? The one with the picture of the kids?'

'I was trying to make her feel welcome, Ray.'

'Well don't. They shouldn't be here. Management had no right to put them on board.'

'Christ, what's that woman done to you?'

I don't know where they might be right now, but Celestine and Miles' absence carols throughout the boat. 'All right. Go and make her another one. Keep them below. I don't want them up here. And watch that guy. He's on the piss.'

'Aye, aye, skipper.' Noel gives me a mock salute and disappears below.

We've been under way less than fifty minutes when an alarm goes off with a shrill ring in the wheelhouse. Eliot stiffens, but not as much as I do. I break the circuit and explain how this often happens when towing heavy ships. The engine overloads and the alarm goes off. But this is not true. The engine is not straining. The alarm tripped too easily.

I have lost my confidence.

As we make fourteen knots up-river with the tide, I wonder about sabotage.

We have four hours' sailing ahead of us to get through.

Noel returns to the wheelhouse with two mugs of sweet tea, a hot chocolate for Eliot and a plate of steaming sausage sandwiches. 'I checked on Hansel and Gretel below,' he says, offering Eliot a sandwich. 'They're watching *Big Brother* highlights on your TV.'

'Is he still drinking?'

'He's had a couple of cans.'

I try to concentrate on towing this warship up-river while Noel keeps my son entertained, pointing out of the window to a church spire on the south shore. 'If you want to work with me and your dad, Eliot, first thing you got to know is you can't get off for twenty-four hours. So if you want to get off . . .'

'I don't want to get off.' Eliot is adamant.

Eliot doesn't want to get off but I wish he'd never come on board, now I've seen our cargo manifest. Can't get off for twenty-four hours? Yes, you damn well can in some instances. Before this shift is over I'm going to dump them on the shore.

After rounding the bend at Broadness Saltings yet another alarm rings on the bulkhead. This time it's the fire alarm. Noel runs below and shouts up to me that someone has left the oven door open in the galley. Another reason to like the river: in any struggle between the forces of fire and water, water will always win.

Eliot begins to shows signs of restlessness. There is nothing much for him to do for the next few hours but I can't leave my watch to entertain him. When he charges down the perpendicular steps to rummage around, I start to worry. He's been thoroughly schooled in what he can't do, where the hot zones are, but now I cave in to different anxieties. There is a new poison down below. I'm torn between my responsibility as a father and my responsibility as a skipper.

He reappears ten minutes later and I order him to stay put, at least until we cut the *Marlborough* loose. Because I want him here I try and distract him, to prevent him going somewhere else. Passing beneath the Queen Elizabeth Bridge, I point out the Ro-Ro ferries bringing Vauxhall cars from Belgium.

How interesting is this to an eight-year-old?

I do my best. 'Ro-Ros have bow and stern thrusters, but they can't always cope with strong winds.' Noel's liver-spotted head rises up the companionway and he hears me say, 'On days when there's a powerful northerly blowing, they can't get on to the moorings.'

'And we sit on the bank over there and wait for them to call,' Noel adds. 'Like vultures, aren't we, Ray, waiting for a job.'

My senior by fifteen years, in a more just world Noel would have been skipper of this craft instead of me, but he couldn't pass his STCW 95 navigation exam. The river is in his head, but he can't seem to match that with what is on the charts. Navigation's an oral thing with Noel, a chain of words across the water.

For Eliot's benefit he points out the old Erith paper-mill, now a promenade, and a wharf that takes lead from Australian ships. He shows him the aggregates we sometimes discharge into barges and tow upstream to White Mountain Wharf. Near Thunderer Jetty that is swollen with Ford Focuses from Germany I hear him chant: 'Copper Jetty . . . Horseshoe Corner . . . Cross Ness . . . False Point. Good names, eh? This reach was once called the Guzzard, itself perhaps a corruption of Buzzards Bush from many centuries ago.'

I wonder how much of this Eliot's taking in, if he'll remember the language as a demonstration of devotion to his father. But his eyes look glazed over.

On the bend between Jenningtree Point and Old Man's Head I feel the tide setting across the river at peculiar angles, going in two different directions at once. In deference to my load, I reduce speed and take it easy into Halfway Reach.

Then Noel announces he's going below to see the engineers. I know it's just an excuse to escape all the talking. Neither he nor I venture into the engineers' territory from one month to the next. We don't like the heat and noise. I don't know how it all works and fits together. The engineers feel similarly about the wheelhouse.

Now Eliot and I are alone again he confesses, 'I feel a bit sick when I look through the binoculars.'

'Like reading in a car.'

'Do you ever feel sick?'

'No, not really.'

'I bet Flora would be.'

'Flora gets seasick in the bath.'

Eliot laughs at that and for a moment the world is all

right, and I have just enough juice in the tank to remember taking them to see Nelson's flagship, *Victory,* in Portsmouth. How Flora ran out of a simulated battle scene at Trafalgar. 'There were real sparks coming out of the guns!' she cried, her eyes wild and staring. 'I was shaking so much.' On board the *Victory* itself, of all the things that might have fascinated her, it was the plastic rats in the galley and the fake weevil holes in the rubber biscuits that she seized upon. And the story of how, before battle, officers' furniture was lowered over the side in tenders for safekeeping. All those red velvet armchairs floating around in the blue Mediterranean appealed to her imagination more than the gun decks and the hammocks that Eliot liked, where five hundred pressed men slept off their daily quota of sixteen pints of ale.

Something about having the two kids together dilutes the overbearing intensity of my feelings towards each of them. On their own they make my soul swoon, every few minutes. Like any parent, I fear for them in every way possible. But unlike other parents, I have to stay vigilant over those fears in case I crush them.

A dark shadow passes over us, creating a slight melancholic cooling of the air. I look back to see the frigate looming behind. I tap Eliot on the shoulder. He cranes his neck round and appreciates this grey cathedral attached to us by an umbilical cord and blacking out the sun. For one happy sliding moment I feel he and I are part of a big extended family of smiling ratings, deckhands and officers in starched blue uniforms milling around on their deck.

Then Celestine appears. Following her up the stairs into the wheelhouse is Miles, looking green. 'Miles is feeling sick downstairs,' she says. 'Mind if we join you?' Celestine ruffles my son's hair. 'All right, Eliot? Having a good laugh with your dad?'

Eliot doesn't know how to reply. He smiles at her instead.

I see an advantage and go after Miles. 'You're not off the ships yourself then, Miles?'

Nausea has defused him. He has little to say for himself. 'Not down there.'

'Stop being a Wendy,' Celestine ridicules him. 'This is not exactly Cape Horn.' She seeks out Eliot, ruffles his hair for a second time. 'Lovers' tiff,' she says. Through the window she points at the pale edifices of the Millennium Mills in King George Dock. 'I thought you said you never come up this far?'

'What's in 'em?' Miles makes an effort not to seem weak. 'Why didn't they knock them down like the rest of the docks?'

I don't know why these warehouses survive but not the docks, or if they symbolise a great Empire or the history of forceful acquisition of animal and mineral resources from overseas. And I don't know what's in 'em, only what they once stored: gums, hides, skins, tallow, spices and elephant tusks; wheat, oats, barley, rye, maize from Nebraska and the plains of Canada; Virginia tobacco; Malay rubber; tea from India and Ceylon; Colombian coffee.

But all I say to Miles is, 'They used to be policed by armed men.'

Low-flying aircraft taking off from City Airport strafe the skies above the defunct Harland and Wolff shipbuilders, Woolwich Arsenal and the ruins of Barking power station, and set off a twitch in the *Marlborough*'s VHF mast. From the shore at Silvertown a tug sheers into the river towing two swim-head lighters. The skipper turns the whole load around 180 degrees in midstream and backs on to Angerstein Wharf on the opposite bank. He negotiates the bight and makes a good fetch against a mooring dolphin. Two men in safety-yellow oilskins balance precariously on the gunwales and lash on another two lighters. The popping of polypropylene ropes tightening around dollies echoes in the hulls. The skipper eases off the dolphin, now with four refuse barges in tow, and marshals the tide to help get back into the channel.

Whenever I witness such a nice piece of work I am always moved to sing a praise song. But today is a different day. I am inhibited from being myself. I collapse under the load. Even so I manage to whisper to Eliot, 'An over-correction of a few degrees on the wheel with that kind of length, and five minutes later your tail swings off course.'

Celestine overhears me initiating the next generation, catching me red-handed doing what our father, in his line of work, once did to me.

The river swells and bucks and leaps into the wheelhouse as I wrestle an unwelcome memory: my father getting that parking ticket after we came out of the swimming pool. He couldn't swim and now he'd got a parking ticket to make him feel even more aggrieved. The attendant was still writing out the penalty notice. My father appealed that we were only two minutes late and showed the mute attendant his ticket, but he still got the penalty. So my father called him a cunt, then added, 'And your mother's a cunt too. Go on,' he snarled, 'take a swing at me, make my day.' Then: 'Why don't you do a man's job?' The attendant wandered off dizzily but unprovoked and we piled into the car. Dad kept accelerating, pushing the car faster and faster. He took a right-hand turn and his wing mirror flew off as he hit a bus waiting at the junction. I pleaded with him: 'Put on the brakes!' He swore, he shouted, but didn't stop, and continued telling me how to make two mill off the river.

I don't want Eliot apprenticing himself to me. I don't want him to emulate me at all, want him to be his own man. If he learns things about his father he doesn't like, he'll need plenty of his own character in storage to survive the blow. Isn't this the responsibility of all parents?

Some acrid smell brings me round. Miles, looking more disabled the further we've ploughed up-river, has found the furthest corner of the wheelhouse to throw up in. The stench fills the cabin. And then I notice we are alone in here. Celestine and Eliot have gone. Where have they gone?

At the same moment the wake from a passing vessel shudders through the hull and I feel her stall beneath me. Miles stumbles, snatches at the chart table and rips the paper charts in his fist.

Eliot reappears outside the wheelhouse, on his own on the rear deck. No one goes on deck when we are sailing. How did he get so far out of bounds? How did I not notice? Who is responsible for this?

I see Eliot snatching the towrope in his hand and taking up the slack while we are stalled. A terrible mistake which I'm helpless to avert. Glass makes a mockery of my fear. I have nothing to say that he'll hear. We are in two different worlds in a critical moment. Eliot is in the dangerous one.

I throw the engine into reverse. But the momentum of thirty metres of steel cannot be quickly checked. This is not my father's car. There are no brakes to apply. We are at the mercy of the running tide and Eliot's hand gets caught between the towrope and the steel gunwale. I leave my watch, putting all lives at risk and take the stairs three at a time. I leap past the cabins on to the deck, and that's when I hear him scream. A terrible thing to live through.

What can one man do against the gravitas of a warship? But then Noel appears, my great ally in a crisis. Eliot's screams are arrows. I shout at the *Marlborough* like a fool. Noel starts to pump the towrope and I help him. We release Eliot's hand and he slides on to his backside.

The tug is blind, drifting on the tide. Celestine has reappeared in the wheelhouse. Through the window I see her pushing her tongue into Miles' sour mouth. He lies against the chart table, destroying our navigation, the order of things.

Noel goes to take over the watch as I cradle my son in my arms. His sobs ease as I gently massage his hand. He's going to be all right. But I am not going to be all right. Something has snapped in me. He belongs to me by blood and genes, when I do not deserve such privileges. It was my father who possessed me for those few seconds on my watch, when I should have been looking out for my own son. Love is so corrupt. We can never be free of our past, its influence. It seeps into your actions in unguarded moments. We are not our own people.

Subdued, Eliot sits beside me in the wheelhouse. Every few seconds he removes the ice pack on his hand to inspect for damage and I synchronise with my condolences. He will have a bruise, it will hurt for a few days, but he shall live. It's a drag for him more than anything. He was happy a while ago and now he's not. There is no virtue in being unhappy when you are eight.

I let him steer with the other hand. He over-corrects like a lorry driver, but this is what he's been waiting for, and he cheers up a little. Noel is below containing our stowaways and no one disturbs us. For this one hour I'm overwhelmed by the emotion running from me to Eliot; so poisonous compared to the pure line of emotion from him out on to the river that excites him. He takes us past the brave new universe on the Isle of Dogs, his little blond head level with my stomach, his knees and shins scraped and bruised from other adventures in the physical world.

As we near our destination in the Lower Pool, where the *Marlborough* is to raft alongside HMS *Belfast*, I take back the wheel. The captain radios me and asks to go in stern first. For this operation another one of our tugs, *Jamie Green*, comes to meet us to give support. Her skipper talks to Eliot on the radio and tells him a joke. It goes something like this: a man buys a centipede for a pet. That night he invites the centipede out for a drink. The centipede doesn't reply and so the man repeats the offer. The centipede says, 'I heard you the first time! I'm putting on my shoes.'

At Limehouse Reach heads appear out of the windows in brownstone housing as we screw the *Marlborough* through 180 degrees. Pedestrians on Tower Bridge wave to the Royal Navy crew standing to attention on deck as we pass under the opened bascules.

It's a carnival – everything around us is operatic and nothing seems quite real. My Eliot forgets his recent trauma and listens to the architecture singing the great ideas. He watches boulevardiers wave their little Union Jacks. Secretaries imprisoned behind plate-glass windows wave sensuously to the sailors, and buried in the Tower, royal skeletons shake their fists. What none of them can do is run after us. We are the only ones going anywhere.

A couple of police launches block the river traffic from both directions and from the shore an inflatable buzzes into the picture. The four-man crew is dressed in black oilskins, balaclavas, and carry self-loading rifles. This is the armed unit of the river police, and they *can* run after us. Presently called SO19, they will be renamed again when Security decides it. From the skies a helicopter offers air cover. This is a show of force in an age of paranoia and the crowds on the bridge applaud. I fight the sensation they are hunting me. Every few minutes I reach out and touch Eliot while shunting the *Marlborough* closer to the *Belfast*.

With the *Belfast* within her grasp, the *Marlborough* swaps allegiances. She leaves me for one of her own kind. The two warships raft up with springs and lines at bow and stern. Ratings detach our towrope, which Noel winds in by remote. We are free to go. But before we sail off I want to do one last thing, and trust the ship and my son into Noel's care.

Down in my cabin Miles is still looking pale. His shaved head glistens with sweat. He is suppressing his sickness with beer, squeezing the can in his hand. Celestine has gone limp in front of my TV.

'You can get off now, Miles. Last chance,' I say.

Miles starts to get to his feet. But Celestine is not going to be overlooked. 'Where you going? I want to go back down the river. How often do I get the chance to watch TV?'

'You can have the TV.' I unplug it from the step-down transformer. 'Here, take it.'

'If we stay, can I still have it?'

'No.'

'Well, Miles, looks like we're being bought off.'

Miles is too incapacitated to reply. He completes the move to his feet and I help him on to the aft deck. From there it is comparatively easy to access the deck of the *Marlborough*. Celestine follows, carrying the small TV by its handle, and together they cross the decks like stones in a pond until they reach the riverbank.

Tower Bridge recedes to the stern. Eliot's ice pack lies melting on the floor. The wheel is all his. I am ecstatic from survival. 'Take us home, son, on this beautiful summer's day.'

He clutches the wheel with so much excitement the knuckles on his hand grow white. This experience today will be scorched into his memory. Maybe when we are both gone from this world, those memories will combine with my own and telegraph into the same blue sky.

When Noel next comes up I let him supervise Eliot and go below to heat a pre-cooked shepherd's pie. While it warms in the oven I attend to some paperwork. In a while Eliot joins me. We sit around the table in the galley, blowing on the steaming shepherd's pie. I study tonight's worksheet as he completes his maths and English homework, his strapped hand resting on the table like a war trophy. A while later he calls his mother on the mobile phone to relate the adventures of the day. I hear him say he 'crunched' his hand, but that it's all right now, even though it still hurts. I take the phone and chat to Lily, who asks what really happened. Eliot tells me he's off to my cabin to watch cartoons. I forget to tell him I've given the TV away and then hear the cry of indignation when he discovers that for himself. I try to close the account with Lily and her voice sounds agitated. 'What a strange week we're having, Ray. So many accidents. So many surprises. I hope our luck isn't changing.' She puts Flora on the phone. Still excited after shopping with her mother on her day off from school, she describes the green trousers she bought from Gap with sequins on the bell-bottoms. I tell her how beautiful that sounds, which serves as a description of how I am feeling towards her.

Eliot returns to the galley with a pack of cards. There is nothing on the worksheet until later tonight and we moor up so I can play cards with him. We play pontoon and three-card brag and poker. Later in the evening I purloin Noel's TV and we watch a video together – *Parent Trap* – until it's time for him to go to sleep.

I watch him sleep until we are due in Tilbury docks.

The joy of it is immense: the way you can assess a child's contentment by how he lies in bed, the sound he makes. I remember when he was torn from his mother's belly, the first sound he made was to cry. Such a traumatic experience to breathe in oxygen after nine months in amniotic fluid. But now, eight years later, he's calm and easy once more, curled up in a foetal ball with water lapping around him. He'll sleep like this until seven, when the next crew comes on. I'll make him a hot breakfast before leaving by taxi and drop him off at school on my way home.

We complete our tasks in Tilbury. At 02.00 I turn in and hear a change in him. I hear him moaning in his sleep. His wounded hand twitches on the side of the bed. He is held captive by some nightmare in a world beyond my reach.

12

My father used to burn her. I'll say that again. He used to burn Celestine. Set her hair on fire. Stub cigarettes out on her foot. Drip candle wax on her arms. Heat a fork on the gas stove and stab her in the hand.

He burned her and doused her in water. Pain and pain relief. He supplied both, like a god. He liked to inhale the smell of burning flesh. She said he used to go very tense and have spasms.

Tom raised the stakes a little higher: 'If it was sexually motivated for your father, it's possible his deviancy transferred to Celestine, who was at a psychologically impressionable age.'

But why did he do this, keep one conventional family and another to abuse? I know some men lead this kind of parallel life with prostitutes – pay for violent liaisons in a cheap hotel, then go home to help the kids with their trigonometry homework.

How did he get away with it? He put money into a bank account for them – the price of a London house – and told Celestine's mother it would be hers when Celestine reached eighteen. Even though this account existed, he was never going to pay up. It was just a way to control them, keep them where he wanted them, on a barge one mile from where we lived. One mile separated our two families.

Celestine took me to the barge once, when her mother was out, out for the count. She took me into the bosun's cabin and showed me her vagina, in a frame of short black hairs. She prised open her legs and told me to smell her. I went down on my hands and knees. It smelled like the canal. I didn't understand it. I didn't understand what she was showing me any more than what she was telling me about my father, our father. I do now. He was a bad man. He was a very, very nasty piece of work.

There were no signs of playfulness on that barge, no sense of it being a home. It was a shell, airless and stuffy. Forty feet of hollow rusting steel full up with timbers, paints, and piles of old clothes that Celestine used as a bed. There was a sink, Calor gas cooker and a couple of car seats. In the aft was the boatman's cabin with a Torglow solid-fuel stove and back boiler. The cabin was five feet by four with no standing headroom. Everything was in reach from a sitting position. A cupboard door doubled as a hinged table. This is where she showed me her muff. And where my father fucked her mother, presumably. The engine was a Russell Newbery DM2 but was only ever used to charge the batteries. The lights and water pump ran off the batteries. There was no mains electricity. A sea toilet drew water for flushing from the canal. Bulkheads had been cut from recycled timbers. The walls were lagged with Rockwall. Half a ton of paving stones had been swiped from a building site for ballast.

This is where Celestine was raised. Where she was *born* . . . I wouldn't call it raised, because her mother was tranqed up all the time. When I saw her that first time she was slumped into one of the car seats, deathly pale and skinny as a pole, her eyes chimped out. I don't think she even noticed us. Her skirt was hitched up around her waist and her knickers were showing and I could just see my father coming on board, fucking her, then leaving again without expending a single word. She had a great ball of bleached blonde hair entwined on top of her head. Celestine was more or less her mother's carer. Each morning she got her up from bed and dressed her. She did all the cooking and the shopping. My father paid for that too, the groceries.

It appeared the reason why she and her mother slipped through the welfare safety net is because they were never dependent upon the state. My father's patronage saw to that. Celestine's school might have picked up on her situation, but her school was a fucking shambles with ninety per cent Afro-Caribbean and Asian pupils, and teachers just trying to survive the day. Because she didn't bring weapons into class, they thought her pretty classy. And when she didn't show up at all, she always produced that sick note from her mother the next day.

She told me her earliest memory of our father was the time he pushed her into the canal while she was strapped into a pushchair. She was three years old. Her mother jumped into the canal and dragged out the pushchair. She'd been inside the barge when she heard the splash.

Tom asked, 'How would she know her mother heard the splash? How would she know any of this, at three? If it's true at all, her mother must have told her. Celestine remembered not the experience but her mother's account of it. What that implies is her mother had an understanding of the dangers, of the risks to her daughter posed by your father from when Celestine was three. So why didn't she do something to protect her?'

'Money.'

'Can you explain that?'

'Nothing to explain. Money is the answer, my father's money. Money was more important than a daughter's welfare.'

'And who could she tell, Social Services? They'd have placed a care order on Celestine.'

'As they did finally, when I went down.'

Tom asked, 'How do you feel about that?'

'About going down?'

'About her getting off.'

She didn't go down because the powers in the land pitied her. They could see she was the one with the deprived childhood, with no running water or electricity, and I was the one with the privileged childhood, relatively speaking. My father playing Guy Fawkes with her didn't emerge in the trial. It was recorded in the CATS interview but couldn't be used as evidence in an adult court.

And I didn't grass her up to the silks or the judge that it had been her idea all along.

'How could my father love Coco *and* do what he did to Celestine?'

Tom replied: 'One needs a capacity for being good in order to commit evil.'

'That's like something my father used to say. A good nature is a limited nature. Nobody admires it. People exploit it.'

Then Tom pointed out I'd stopped calling him 'my dad'. He was now 'my father'. I said, 'My dad was the king who took me on walks along the Thames, whose name was synonymous with civic pride and responsibility. My dad looked after Olivia and me when Mum was on the bench. But it was my father who burnt a young girl on the canal, where no one could see what was going on.'

The canal, the 'estuary', is where the king removed his crown.

When I found out what my father was, I wanted to hurt him. I wanted to call up Sir Richard Gower and tell him his one-time business partner liked to press flaring matches between a little girl's bare knees. But Celestine said, 'That would be too good for him.' She suggested we should 'do' Olivia instead.

I said, 'Why Olivia?'

'Because he only loves her. Even death's too good for that bastard. Doing her would hurt him for ever more.'

I came round to her way of thinking . . . I don't know when I came round to her way of thinking. All I had was Celestine and she was older than her years. But my father was the provider, I thought about that, and if we did Olivia he would still be able to provide. And I was always quarrelling with her, of course, with Olivia.

I asked Celestine, 'How do you want to do her?'

And she said, 'We got to burn her, of course. Like he burns me.'

13

Wednesday is yoga club night: while the wives are at their Pilates class I meet my brothers-in-law to play snooker. All babysitters are on retainers for Wednesdays.

Lights fall like curtains over the six tables in an air-conditioned basement, where the protocol is not to stare when someone is stretched over the felt in case you disturb his concentration. Players stand in the shadows, dazed by cigarette smoke, earthed by their cues. You'll never see a man's face all night long and that is why snooker is my game.

Jerry and I arrive at the same time and set up the balls. Colin comes in five minutes later dressed in a suit and black tie, fresh from a colleague's funeral. 'Big Irish wake,' he begins telling us. 'So many people I got left behind at the crematorium. I had to hitch a ride to the reception in the hearse. The driver kept saying things like: "Not many people get to ride in one of these more than once. Breaks the ice, though, don't it?" His widow gave everybody a tiny box of the ashes to take away with us. Like party bags.' Colin laughs at the memory. 'They were still warm when I scattered them out of the taxi window. A little bit of Ireland spread over the Old Jamaica Road.' Then he turns on me a harsh and sudden spotlight. 'Were your folks buried or cremated, Ray?'

I've never been asked this before. No one in the family has enquired this deep. For twelve years I've kept Lily and her brothers at bay with terrible lies about terrible deaths, and out of courtesy they've left the subject alone.

'They were cremated,' I say.

'What about your sister?'

'Cremated. Everyone was cremated.'

Jerry says, 'Stop being bloody morbid.'

Colin leans towards me as Jerry goes to take a shot at the far end of the table. 'I don't think we should let the bastard win tonight, agreed?'

Jerry misses his shot. Colin examines all the angles on the remaining reds and says, 'Must have been tough, though, losing them all.'

Jerry overhears this and complains from the shadows, 'Are we playing snooker or what?'

Celestine's disembodied face flips up in front of me, her hair dissolving in a mist of split ends, earrings cheap and garish. I rub her out by squeezing shut my eyes. 'I can't remember much of how I felt.'

'Then don't describe the grief. Describe the coffin.'

'Describe the coffin?' Jerry repeats.

'Yeah, you know . . . the scene.'

'Why are you pursuing this, Colin?' Jerry is now sounding cross.

I begin to describe the 'coffin' in the cool darkness of the snooker hall, but it soon becomes a description of the grief. 'When my mother was close to the end, my father and I sort of lived in her bedroom. She was shrivelled up and ghostly white. The last thing she said to me was "Look after yourself, son." To my father she said, "I'll see our little girl soon." When I looked again she was gone. My father gave up after that and died about six months later.'

It's my turn to cue up and I miss the red completely. Four points away. None of us is very good at snooker. The biggest break anyone has made is thirty-four (Colin). My top break is twenty-seven. To be any better would be a sign of a misspent youth. We'd probably be good-for-nothings.

'Ray can't concentrate with you asking about bloody funerals, Colin.'

'I only asked him to describe the coffin. What's wrong with that?'

'What I can remember is collecting my father's ashes from the funeral home and the undertaker telling me about a salmon he'd caught the night before. I was clutching the urn with my father's ashes and this guy was bragging about a fish. I walked out in a daze and sat on a wall, wondering what to do next. There was a football ground on the other side of the road and in the end I scattered the ashes over the pitch. For a couple of months afterwards I'd go back there and watch school kids playing soccer.'

'Your sister was killed in a car accident, right?'

I take a deep breath. 'Yes.'

'Something I've always wanted to ask, Ray, I hope you don't mind, but who was driving the car, your mother or father?'

'They couldn't remember.'

'I don't understand.'

'They said they couldn't remember who was driving.'

'They forgot?'

'Either they forgot because of the trauma, or it was a pact they entered into to share the burden of responsibility.'

'Which do you think it was?'

'I think they decided to share the burden of responsibility.'

Colin's questions keep coming. Finally Jerry stops objecting and joins in. Our game is momentarily suspended. There is only the click of balls colliding on the other tables. I can no longer determine who's asking what, for they have both taken refuge in the darkness.

'Why weren't you in the car?'

'I was at home in bed with the flu.'

'They didn't have seat belts in those days, I suppose.'

'Is this why you don't drive, Ray?'

'Most watermen don't drive. No one in my crew. The river is the only highway we understand.'

'But your sister's funeral . . . that must have been awful.'

'I didn't go to my sister's funeral. They said it . . . they said it would be too much for me. But it was harder for them than me. Parents aren't meant to outlive their children, are they?'

'They didn't for long. Your parents, I mean.'

The coloured snooker balls go blurred and only then do I realise I'm crying. I'm crying over a counterfeit grief, over a phantom coffin. But the tears are real and sting my eyes. Colin and Jerry go deathly quiet. I excuse myself, and in the toilets gush water from the tap into my face.

Returning to the table I hear Colin say, 'Do you want to stop playing, Ray? Let's stop playing. I need a fucking drink.'

An hour later we are sitting in a window nook at the Ship and Lobster, overlooking the river where it is broad and solitary. I go to the bar and when I return with a round, Colin is telling Jerry, 'Twenty-seven thousand in one borough and three thousand in another. Why is that? Talking about Ghanaians, Ray . . . Twenty-seven thousand live in the London borough of Haringey and only three thousand in Fulham. Why is that? Do the councils get a quota or something? Fourteen thousand Iraqi Kurds in Islington, I can understand. But what's gone wrong in Ghana?'

'There's a hundred and fifty thousand Bangladeshis in Tower Hamlets.'

'I tell you why it is. Haringey's trying to cover its debt by taking in Ghanaians.'

I lose the drift of their conversation to wrestle with Celestine's image. She's flipped up again, that head of hair, the charcoal eyelids, and ear lobes distended with chains.

'Immigrants coming in now, you don't know who they are or what they've done, the places they've run away from.' Colin lands an arm on my shoulder. 'Like our Ray here, from Oystermouth. We don't know where that is, do we? Or what you've run away from.'

'No, it's true, London's full of people who used to be somewhere else,' Jerry picks up Colin's drift. 'There are big tribes of them. And if they didn't get on in their old countries, they're not going to get on now. We're going to have a Sarajevo one day, on our own doorstep.'

'Yeah, that's right,' says Colin. 'Ask any kid on the street what it means to be English and they say, "Stop kidding around." They don't know what you're talking about.'

My brothers-in-law move the conversation on to computers. As Colin is explaining to Jerry what a neural network is – a self-learning computer program that simulates the way the brain works – I look up at the picture of Charles Dickens above our heads. This pub claims to be the inn in his book, *Great Expectations*, from where Pip and Magwitch set out to hitch a ride on a foreign steamer bound for Hamburg or Rotterdam, so desperate are they to get out of England. As I am looking up at the picture, Celestine's head replaces Dickens' in the frame. I push her out of my mind, out of the pub and into the dark and sullen water outside. Her hair floats in a frenzy of air bubbles as her head goes under the surface.

That night I dream of the dead running along the towpath and disturb Lily with my moans. She shakes me awake and for a moment seems a great distance away, like a woman on the shore seen from a ship setting keel for open sea. 'I was dreaming of dead people,' I say and because that sounds macabre, add, 'Jerry and Colin were asking me about my parents tonight.'

'You've never really talked to me about your parents.'

'Yes I have.'

'Not for a long time. Not for years.'

'I've never felt the need,' I say weakly.

'Talk to me, Ray, about your dream.'

'It's very late.'

'Well I'm awake now. Talk to me about your mum and dad.'

I feel cornered and the only way out is to satisfy her curiosity a little. 'I can just about remember us doing family things when I was very young. But then it all went to hell after my sister died. They couldn't stand one another and gave up, going off in opposite directions. I was abandoned to survive the best I could, while they rowed in the hall, in the bedroom, in the kitchen.'

'Is that why you cherish us, because your family fell apart?'

'I cherish you, yes, and it's got nothing to do with my family.'

'Must do. But it's usually only people who've been cherished themselves that can do it.'

'I don't know.'

'You've even cherished me when I haven't deserved it.'

This veiled reference to her affair makes me fear she's

going to raise the subject. The form I prefer is for me to remember it and for her to forget.

I do not want to go any further with this wolf-hour conversation and tell her to go back to sleep. She does as I suggest at the speed of light, the speed of a clear conscience.

A night of telling lies has over-exhausted me and I can't get back to sleep. When I think about those tales I told Colin and Jerry, and Lily too, I realise how much I've blended my own childhood with that of Tom Reeves. My parents didn't kill their daughter in a car crash, but they did fight in the hall, in the bedroom and in the kitchen.

Although it was the lies that made me cry in the snooker hall.

Around 04.00 the telephone rings in sharp rebuke and I lean to pick it up before it wakes Lily. Then with my wife snoring beside me I listen to Celestine speaking from a payphone. She wants to meet me in town later, on Oxford Street, and tells me to come alone. Her voice seems to affect the clock on the bedside table, making it tick louder. Outside the window through a gap in the curtains I see clouds accelerate and their shadows run across the street.

I spend the rest of the night waiting for light to break. At 06.00 I call in to work sick. My line manager is sympathetic to a fault. He reminds me this is the first day's work I've missed and when he orders me to get well before I show my face again, I am almost moved to tears. Everyone is still asleep as I leave the house twenty minutes later.

14

The hot weather has broken as I emerge on to Oxford Street. Rain clouds are massing as I find her sitting outside Starbucks, stirring sugar into a cappuccino and staring up at the sky. Dressed in a short leather skirt and red ankle boots, a t-shirt with *NORF LONDON* emblazoned across the chest, she looks set for a good time. I am reminded of how thin she is. Her hair looks thin also and when I call her name she greets me with a thin smile.

'All right, Mark? Looks like it's going to rain at last.'

'Stop calling me that. It's Ray.'

'Sorry, going to take me a bit of time to get used to it. How can I remember to call you Ray? Ray of sunshine, perhaps. Ray of hope.'

'You won't need to get used to it. I don't want to see you again after today.'

'Is that a threat?'

'It's a statement.'

'But I need you . . . Ray,' she says. 'I want what your wife has got. What your children have got. I want some security.'

'Stay away from my family.'

'You're not in any position to tell me what to do.' She

lights up a cigarette and throws the match into her coffee. It dies with a hiss. 'Wouldn't you agree?'

'You contradict me, in front of my family.'

'Then tell me the lies you've fed them and I won't. For instance, this place Oystermouth we're meant to come from, where the fuck is that? Does it even exist?'

'What do you want from me?'

'You mean, what do I want to go away?'

'If you prefer.'

'That's not nice. I'm a very sensitive person, you know.'

'That why you're not selling your story to a newspaper?' I assume she knows the embargo lifted years ago.

'Who says I won't?'

'Because they'll make a monster out of you too.'

'You seem to be forgetting, I was acquitted of all charges.'

'And I've paid my debt. There's nothing you can do to me except hurt my family and I won't let you do that.'

She sighs, exhales on a stream of smoke. 'Let's not get the gloves off, Mark. *Ray*. I'm your flesh and blood.' Her face does a U-turn and she beams at me. 'I've got things to do. Like buy a new jacket. Come and help me choose.'

I follow because I do not have the security to pass in the opposite direction. She is more dangerous out of my sight than within it. So we walk in the direction of Marble Arch with her arm linked inside mine like a married couple. London is still blighted by the long drought. Dry bodies collide and crackle – strangers grinding one another down, creating a kelp-like darkness. Their mass turns the air warmer along the nexus of shops – shops but no churches; just the Salvation Army. The wind has no trees to shake and runs along the street turning it into a roaring thoroughfare of ghost-like noises. I can't make sense of anything. These currents and bights are hard to navigate. It hardly seems human at all, like a place to go when you are finished with the business of this earth.

We enter the swing doors of Selfridges and I follow her around the designer stalls in the women's department. She tries on a white leather jacket still attached to the rail by a wire. A shop assistant unlocks it for her and she takes the jacket and two Joseph sweaters into the changing rooms. When she emerges a minute later, modelling a sweater and jacket for me, I feel like I'm betraying Lily. Whatever new clothes she tries on does nothing to change what I know of her. Her character cannot be altered by the likes of Joseph. She cannot choose between the two sweaters and decides to have them both. Passing along the floor she lifts a handful of lingerie off a table. I stand behind her at the tills as she hands over the sweaters, leather jacket, and assorted lingerie to the cashier. When the total comes out at £1200, she turns around and offers me a crooked wordless smile. I pay the bill with my Visa card. When she tries to show her gratitude by kissing me I step backwards into an abandoned baby in her buggy.

Outside Selfridges she says she wants to take a boat home to Silvertown, with me as her guide. I don't know if passenger boats go that far, but in any event, we end up at Westminster Pier with her purchases. Shortly after boarding a cruiser the wind stops, the heavens dump on the endless summer and the river sizzles with falling rain, like bees in a hive. There are about a dozen passengers who shelter from the storm inside the ship. Celestine wants to be in the open stern, wants the total experience. We leave our mooring and ease out into the stream. In the blanket rain visibility is eight to ten feet. We can't even see the House of Commons, where the politicians have less navigation than us.

It makes little difference to me that we cannot see the

bankside architecture. I am in spirit with the skipper anyway, running his ship on the radar screen. It's a very strange sensation, being driven by someone else on the Thames. I feel vulnerable against the tide. We make an advance downstream to the sound of tumbling water and the chill breath of the river on my face. Rain pours down my neck. Floating past on the smooth surface to foul the propellers are frayed hawsers, lost buoys, tree trunks, two-by-fours, bricks of anthracite. When you have killed once, you cross a line and can never return to a state of innocence. You're a virgin no more.

In the Upper Pool, London Bridge evolves out of the rain. There has always been a bridge at this point; the first built by the Romans, and its successor by Peter of Colechurch. It was to last for six hundred years, the only bridge on the tidal Thames until the eighteenth century. The tide makes Sunday music as it lips against the hull. I start to conceive of Celestine at the bottom of this river. The tide would take her out to sea. She would not even show on the radar.

In those six hundred years so many buildings were added it came to resemble a street more than a bridge, with water closets hanging straight over the river. A draw-bridge was cut in, but as ships grew fatter and too big to pass through, their cargoes had to be unloaded at Billingsgate and taken upstream by lighters, passing under the bridge at slack tide with their masts, set in tabernacles, dropped. But I see the possibility of her swimming to safety and my ruin.

The last ship to pass below London Bridge was an accident. A West-Indiaman broke free of its moorings in the Pool and was driven upstream by the tide. It hit the central arch of the bridge and all masts were broken off at deck level. The ship continued up-river as far as Somerset House.

Out there is Billingsgate. It dates from AD 1000 and fish was its principal merchandise even then. But the 5 a.m. ritual of unloading from boats moored at the old quay is no more. Fish from the coast now arrives by road and rail. How do river traditions that stay the same for a millennium change completely in the space of forty years? Why do things have to change at all? London has an elusive quality, full of places that were one thing and are now something else. Like the Royal Festival Hall, its lights blazing through the sheeting rain, built over the ruins of the Lion Brewery. Or the Coal Exchange in Lower Thames Street – an early-Victorian revival of the Bibliothèque in Paris – sacrificed to the motor car. Queenhithe, the first wharf to be recorded by name in AD 889, was demolished in 1971 to make way for a hotel.

I calculate we are making six knots, reduced from twelve to reduce our wash as we pass HMS *Marlborough* rafted alongside the *Belfast*. It seems a lifetime ago when I towed that frigate up-river, instead of six tides.

As there are two tides per day, we can have two lives. I've always understood this about London: you live one life, then move a dozen miles away and never will the two worlds collide. Londoners are tribal. They are villagers.

That is what I chose to believe until now; now I know that it takes only one person to roam from one village into the other and ruin you.

'Look! Greenland Docks . . .' Celestine reads the name off a sign hanging over a lock gate. 'Is that where you got your name? But Greenland's not green, is it? It's frozen in ice. Named by someone trying to trick people into going there.'

I turn my back on her, to rub her out. The wind picks up, visibility improves and we are given a brief glimpse of the vast, disorderly buildings on both shores. Transit sheds, chemical works, processing plants, pubs, seamen's missions. Orchard, Delta, Follyhouse, Enderby, Lovello and Oliver's wharves, where the old petermen once lived, who baited for salmon, flatfish, whitebait, mackerel, eels, oysters and lobsters on this river. I am in despair.

Onboard engines and pumps rumble. From the shore cranes groan and scream. The odours on this stretch of river are as ripe as they ever were. Liquor burning off at the Golden Syrup plant, molasses at Tate & Lyle, gasoline nectar from the refinery, yeast from the brewery, animal bones smelting in Castles soap – that smells like roasting coffee. This is Celestine's destination and the boat sheers across to pick up passengers from City Airport. Before the rest of the world arrived by plane, they arrived by ship. Sailors from China, West Indies, India, West Africa settled alongside the French, Russians, Irish, Poles, Serbs, Croats, Cypriots, Turkish and Greeks off the immigrant ships. They became shipbuilders, ropemakers, chandlers, carpenters, engineers, stevedores, timekeepers, tally clerks, wharfsmen, welders, publicans and cooks. All the old people lived in this history that the younger generation wants to shake off; maybe because it made their parents violent, drunk and insane.

I watch as Celestine alights from the boat. She raises her Selfridges bag on the jetty, whether to show her gratitude or to indicate there is more owing to her, I don't know. The mate stands on the jetty holding one end of the rope that is turned around a cleat, waiting for the order to cast off.

There will be no relaxation for me, not any more. I try to look away from her, towards the south shore, at the Victorian gasholder on Blackwall Point. It was originally one of two – the other was blown up when the chemical works on the opposite shore, manufacturing

TNT for the First World War effort and using side products from the soap factory, exploded and took out the smaller one. Nitroglycerine is a powerful substance. Violent changes can be made, to bring things back on line as they were. Things from the past do not always survive. Nothing needs to stay the same.

I get off the boat and walk with her towards Silvertown.

Celestine breaks open an air rifle, feeds a .177 lead shot from an Ox Power tin into the barrel and snaps it shut. Out of her porthole window she takes aim at a small gathering of homosexuals cottaging on the towpath. Their raw hides are luminescent in the darkness. The crack of the rifle is succeeded by a shout from the other side of the canal. She laughs as she pulls the rifle back into the barge. 'That'll make him come like a bull.'

It's been twenty-six years since I last saw the inside of this barge and very little has changed. There are still the old car seats propped up on timbers, everything in a state of chaos, with no running water, telephone or electricity supply. Only the location has changed: two or three miles out of Silvertown close to Mill Meads, beneath gasholders and pumping stations. Industry but no residential . . . *resi*.

I feel incoherent in this Third World pocket of the First World, lulled into a childlike state of mind.

'When did you move the barge here?'

'Couple of years ago, when the old girl died. Looks like I'm going to have to move it again. Now these queers are gentrifying the place.'

'I didn't know your mother died.'

'Stone-cold dead. It's just you and me now, Mark . . .'

'Ray . . .'

'Ray . . . You and me are orphans.'

'Our father's still alive.'

That gets her attention. 'Where is he?'

'Last I heard he went to live in Eastern Europe. Somewhere like Georgia.'

'Hope the Russian Mafia kill him then.'

'He sent me a letter when I was inside. One miserable letter without a return address, about how he was making so much money in the old Russian states.'

Celestine's Selfridges bag sits in the stainless steel sink on top of a pile of dirty plates.

'How do you make ends meet?'

'I'm on the social, and on the banjo – moonlighting as a waitress in a casino.'

I don't believe her. Experience warns against it. 'Doesn't the casino dock your wages, for tax and National Insurance?'

She doesn't answer me and flops into a car seat, nursing the air rifle to her bosom, the wooden stock between her legs. When she was a child she used to fight like a wild animal – kicking, biting and howling. That rifle suggests her potential has been retained.

I am experiencing an oddly comforting sensation being here again, and that's the first thing that surprises me. All my adult life has been lived with the fear of disclosure. And now it's gone. For the first time I can be myself and the state of release is very heady. In that clock-stopping moment I start to project wildly: if everything goes wrong I'll move in here. My destiny will come full circle. I'll eke out an existence with her until one of us dies. I will live in hell with her, but hell will no longer live in me. Even bad blood is thicker than water. We could take the barge out of this gay industrial enclave and vanish on the waterways. Canals run all the way into Scotland. We could keep travelling, redefining ourselves in slow motion, never staying in any one place long enough for some local to see a resemblance in my face to the pictures of a twelve-year-old boy stuffed away in some press clippings album.

My band of high-pressure euphoria does not last long. It is undermined by concerns for Eliot and Flora. There is no telling what great harm it would do to them, to lose their father into a void. I go stand in the companionway to sober up. A light breeze carries with it the stench of burnt caramel, gasoline and salt. The earlier rain clouds have cleared, and the stars wink in a raw, feral sky. I feel yet another switch of emotion, into something less than human and capable of much wrong. I have killing on my mind.

Maybe this is all Celestine can do for me – resurrect the cruel instincts and destroy the edifice of good faith I've earned for myself.

It is time for me to try to leave.

I go back inside the barge. 'So,' I say. 'You know where I live. And now I know where you live.'

'What's mine is yours, Mark . . . Ray. Fuck, I'll never get used to this.'

'I don't want what's yours.' I stare at the rifle between her legs. 'I don't know who you are. Don't know if you're married, anything.'

'Me, married? Why do you think I went to your wife's seminar on dating? Not for the free wine, I can tell you.'

'You went with Miles. You took your own date.' I still don't understand why.

'But I only had eyes for you, Mark.'

'How did you meet him anyhow?'

'Miles? Oh you know, in one of those places where the lonely hearts congregate.'

'I see too much coincidence in all this.'

'Everything is coincidence. Don't forget how I found you when we were kids.'

'That wasn't coincidence.'

‘Perhaps we can go out on a double date, with you and Lily.’

‘I’m not going to tell you again. We’ve done enough damage, don’t you think?’

‘I ain’t gonna kill them, Mark, for fuck’s sake. I got dissed hardcore too, you know. And nothing to show for it, like you.’

‘You could kill them, and then I’ll kill you.’

‘Don’t be mean, Mark. You’re the only person I have in the world.’

What momentary lapse of sanity gave me to believe I could live there with Celestine? We knew one another for less than two months when I was twelve. I consider the way we used to play, play and kill, with no thought of consequence, knowing only the action itself. Yet this bond, that seems made more from rusting steel than blood, betrothes us in an intangible way. It could sever the leaps of faith I’ve made with Lily in a second.

There is nothing more I can say. I leave this hole in the black earth for the air above. As I begin to walk along the crumbling towpath in the dark she shouts after me, ‘Where are you going?’

‘I’m going home,’ I say, and the sound of the word comforts me.

15

I will never sneer at teachers, detectives and bereaved parents who refer to a lost child as 'very popular with her classmates' . . . 'a beautiful child' . . . 'happy all the time'. They may sound like clichés but my sister Olivia was all of the above. Her character was well formed. Time would have polished and sophisticated her, but the bulk of her personality was in the bag. She was witty, and a bit of an actress. I think she was probably intuitive. I thought she was graceful. I saw her play her first and final school recital. There were ten kids in all, giving short recitals on piano, cello or violin, from a clumsy two-finger 'Run My Pony, Run' to a scratchy *Bach Concerto for Two Violins*. Olivia performed a couple of short violin solos: 'Song of the Wind' and 'Long Long Ago'. She stood in front of thirty adults and children and played the pieces I'd heard her rehearse at home for weeks. But only now, in performance, did they really exist for me as music. When she reached the final, drawn-out chord I heard her sigh and saw her legs buckle. When she came to sit beside me and Dad, I heard her say to him, 'I didn't think I'd get through that.' But she did. That was Coco for you.

Tom said I had to talk about the moment of the offence. It was time. Or we'd still be here when hell freezes over.

I didn't know how to begin. The thing just happened, I said. It just went off.

Tom replied, 'You *thought* the thing just happened. Just went off.'

Could I remember any warning signs – buried and burning emotions that might have alerted me to what happened later, to what went off?

I went over some details, from different angles, starting from the beginning. The beginning was simple to mark. There was a woollen sweater soaked in cigarette lighter fuel. I put a match to the dripping sleeve.

'That's not the beginning,' Tom interrupted. 'There are three stages: before, during and after. Motivation, action and effect.'

We had already discussed the effect stage, the effect on the victims. And I really tried hard to consider the feelings of the victims, such as the relatives. But I always ended up in a cul-de-sac. Because I was a victim too, but with none of the privileges victims are entitled to. For years I'd waited for divine help with this conundrum, for some kind of message that I'd been forgiven. No message has ever been flown to date.

I tried reconstructing the scene before, and during, but it felt as much a taxation on my imagination as anything else.

Tom did not lose patience. He wanted to know instead if I recalled feeling that it was wrong, what we were planning to do.

I did think it wrong. But also I didn't. Conscience exists in children but hasn't reached full maturity. Besides, knowing the difference between right and wrong at that time was connected to another logic. If my father burned Celestine, then by burning Olivia we'd show him that such a thing hurts. And burning someone he loved, well that would *really* hurt. Was it not also true that Celestine was living proof you could survive fire? Survive the burning thing. She was a salamander.

So I never thought Olivia wouldn't survive. Not once did Celestine tell me it actually hurt her *physically.* I only understood how upset she was, how emotionally hurt and angry it made her.

'You must have heard or been told by one of your counsellors inside that arson can provide an effective means of changing difficult-to-tolerate circumstances?'

'Really? Well actually, no, I haven't heard the likes of that.'

'You release all your stress through fire, such as the stress of losing your mother to a mental institution. Fire-setting produced sexual arousal in your father, but for you it was a defence mechanism.'

'That's too much psychobabble for one day, Tom.'

16

At the swing buoy opposite St Katharine's Dock I notice the tramp barges still moored alongside the new apartment quays. The residents here paid over a million, *mill*, for a view of the river, and now these scruffy barges, one with a Portakabin clamped to its deck, are getting the same view for zilch. A week ago lawyers were appointed and eviction notices served, but so far the trampers have ignored them. A week ago I was siding with the trampers. Now I feel my allegiance shifting.

The bascules are raised on Tower Bridge so we can enter the Pool and nudge up against HMS *Marlborough*'s stern. Something holds us back from getting under way, however, some problem on their deck. The ratings can't loosen the springs they tied to the *Belfast*. The delay stretches on as other ratings coil ropes on the helicopter deck, feigning meaningful employment. A couple of sailors keep watch with self-loading rifles that hang from their shoulders. Security is still active from yesterday, when they had a hell of a visitor: the President of the United States, on board the *Marlborough* for lunch.

The Royal Navy finally frees the springs. I see a pair of gloved hands waving from a hole below the stern deck of the *Marlborough* as my second engineer passes him the line. The rating pulls the towrope in and secures it. Noel winds the slack in the towrope round the winch and I drive into the starboard quarter, lifting the *Marlborough* away from the *Belfast*. My sister tug, *Jamie Green*, is attached to the bow of the warship and together we pull her into mid-stream. A rating comes out of the helicopter shed with a Hoover and begins vacuuming the rear deck. The crowds watching from Tower Bridge don't like this domestic image. It de-sexes the Navy and that makes the spectators agitated.

The police SO19 inflatable once again skitters across the surface of the water. The crew is nothing but masculine, carrying small arms to prove it. They look up at me, straight into my eyes. Their faces are hidden inside balaclavas like burkas, their eyes raging through the slits. They seem agitated too. The long delay in getting under way has been a tense moment for them. *Sitting ducks*. Now the President has gone it's me they want to keep under surveillance. In this modern war, these men have developed hunches about who is and who is not hiding under a false identity.

When you are guilty of one crime you feel guilty of them all.

We're on the border between night and day on the old King's Highway. I switch on the navigational lights as Noel chats to me in the wheelhouse. But I don't listen. I don't hear. Even the drone of the engines seems five days away. I watch the warship on the silky river, waiting for me to cut her free so she can run out to sea. I have a warship on a leash but can't shake off my half-sister's collar from around my neck. Darkness slowly falls with her on my mind. And with her on my mind I soon have Olivia on my conscience again, and my flesh aches with guilt.

This renewed force of sorrow spills like blood from an old wound. I cannot stem it. Now has to be the time to tell Lily, before she learns the truth from Celestine. But Lily has been disappointed in love before and I don't know if she'll survive another disaster. She's quite frail. The only thing standing between her and debilitating insecurity is that business she runs; a business founded on the belief that she is a good judge of character. She can broker connections between strangers in search of love because she believes she's in possession of it herself. Even though I'd try to explain that my love is stronger because of what I did when I was young, I can hear her dark laughter now. She'd go into orbit. She might spiral into madness like my mother and live out her days on the edge of a Kent orchard, watching the apple blossom drift to the ground and thinking it's snow.

The SO19 inflatable buzzing around my hull serves to remind us these are dangerous times. I see children filing out of the Tower, fuelling up on 'family-size' bags of crisps. In the Castle carrion crows gather against the coming of the night. Any one of these visitors – to the Tower, St Paul's, Canary Wharf – may now be in someone's cross hairs. But what can one do? You have to carry on living until the moment comes when some stranger with a rucksack stands shoulder to shoulder with you on a crowded train.

At least you are the man your family trusts to be who you say you are.

The darkness drops over the river. The river by day and the river by night are different animals. At night the familiar rippled surface becomes an uneven floor between uncertain shores. All landmarks go dark. White mast lights blend with window lights blazing on the banks. Green starboard and red port lights are indistinguishable from traffic lights. I have the radio on and talk to masters of ships I can't even see. I talk to these strangers as intimately as I talk to my wife and children.

By day the river engages the intellect, by night the imagination, and I rake over the damage a disclosure about my past could do to the children. My condition, if it is a condition, might be genetic. Certainly I have inherited some of my father's passions. But isn't this the desired state – that our children emulate us? Even when they are grown up we want them still to be in our control, like pension funds – rather unstable of late, but in principle only a phone call away. Having children is an act of self-love and it goes on and on.

Yet this cannot be for me. I am a danger to Flora and Eliot. What is good for them is to be rid of me . . . But then my permanent absence would echo constantly in their heads. Isn't that also dangerous, for them to be wondering where their dad is, *what* their dad is, all the days of their life?

In Limehouse Reach we screw the ship around then release the towropes. The *Marlborough*'s going down on her own steam from here on in. *Jamie Green* heads back up the trail to rendezvous with a floating restaurant. The *Marlborough* looks innocuous, her lethal munitions not apparent as her grey hulk blends with the river. I stow away my fears on her deck as I watch her make headway for the open sea. My last glimpse of this distant gunship comes as she snakes round the bend on the Isle of Dogs, cutting quite a figure as she passes the bold towers of Canary Wharf.

Now I am alone again. The hours of my shift trickle through me like water. I pass the time thinking about the *Marlborough* out there in the dark with my sorrow and fears stowed away on the ordnance deck. I want to open fire on Celestine, because I want her dead. She is the enemy, surely. Remove her and I remove the obstacle to my children reaching a place of safety. Ten more years and they will be autonomous. They will have made it to shore.

But removing Celestine will only bring forward new combatants. And there will always be some dark figure in a restaurant, asking if we've been to school together. It's history I need to remove. My real enemy is the past, the one enemy that will always be beyond reach, that can never be destroyed.

Why does this river have to end?

17

Tom wanted to know if I ever tried forgiving *myself*? I never wanted to forgive myself. I wanted to hold on to the shame. Shame was all I had left of her, and it was just. I intended going to the grave with it. If I didn't understand what I did then, at twelve, I do now. Then is a different county to now.

An exhibit at my trial was a list I'd written on the back of an envelope of the things I thought we needed before setting off that day. It read: *Matches, lighter fuel, woolly jumper (Olivia's)*. To this day I cannot remember making that list. So what I felt when I wrote it is also beyond recall.

I did remember where I got the matches: a box of Swan Vestas – my father's supply – from the kitchen drawer. I bought lighter fuel, four cans of it, from a shop. It had a rather pleasant sweet smell. The same benzene, I suppose, that killed my grandfather in the glue factory.

I tried but failed time and again to remember beyond this, beyond the last minutes. Tom kept referring to the CPS Bundle, where the last minutes of Olivia's life are recorded by those who saw her and at what time. He tried to jog my memory by reading out witness statements. The teaching assistant at Olivia's after-school club said on oath that I'd told her my father had asked me to collect her, which wasn't true. Olivia and I were seen again at 15.50 by the lollipop lady, walking along Bancroft Road in the direction of Mile End. Then again at 16.05 by a cyclist on the towpath of Regent's Canal.

I couldn't remember any of them, only the two of us walking along the canal. But was it the experience itself, or the prosecution's reconstruction? Tom told me to remember through my senses. So I struggled, through my senses, to recall another part of that day, until another setting beyond the canal came into focus, a place we called 'The Club'. It was the overgrown land belonging to a run-down social club; acres of woods, tracks and corrugated iron garages – World War 2 lock-ups. We used to play in these grounds.

On the day, Celestine was already there, waiting for us to appear, sitting on the roof of one of the iron garages, her legs dangling over the edge, drinking a can of orange Fanta.

The weather I remembered like it was yesterday. It was raining, and Olivia was wearing her yellow PVC mackintosh. I was worried because I didn't want the rain to put out the matches. I told her there was something I wanted to show her, a secret place. It was . . . she was . . . running around.

Tom told me to say the first words that came into my head, to jerk them out.

Running around with thorns in her bare legs, making muffled screams, her head in flames.

Deep burns are relatively pain-free because the nerves are damaged.

Blackberry bushes. There's wild rhubarb.

The rain talking. Who'll stop the rain talking?

Heat. Not fire, but inside me, a sensation of heat.
Like desire, but not sexual desire.
Some deep emotion with no name that feeds off itself.

18

From the front door and through the hall I recognise Miles standing in the kitchen. His arms are held behind his back in the handcuffs position, his fingers splayed across a workspace and he's talking to someone. I can't see who it is but hear Eliot laughing in there. He should not be home for another half-hour and this man should not be here at all. It was my detail to collect the children from their after-school club. I'm halfway down the hall, a few more steps short of an answer, when Miles spots me, and without missing a beat he turns his head back on whatever the subject is in there. I complete the walk into the kitchen with the front-door keys gripped tightly in my hand. Blood rushes to my eyes on finding Celestine sitting with Eliot and Flora at the table.

I'm tripping over several unformed explanations all at once. Did Lily leave work early? Did she collect the children? But she's nowhere to be seen. It's four in the afternoon and the children's school uniforms are covered in white flour. The table is covered in flour. The three of them roll dough-balls flat with milk bottles. On a sheet of tinfoil are a dozen pastry triangles and heart shapes, sprinkled with sugar and ready for the oven. Such a domestic scene that would normally hearten me crushes me to the floor. Flora looks up too casually for my tastes, and without even saying hello – so easily has she swapped allegiances – turns her attention back to a jam turnover she's constructing. Eliot peels his rolled pastry off the table and inspects its undercarriage. No gesture of welcome from him either.

There are words strung out in the air – I can almost see them framed, but not who's saying what.

I'm over-conscious of this man leaning against the workspace. I'm keeping calm for the kids' benefit, while zeroing in on him and eyeing up the carving knives pinned to a magnet on the wall. My heart pumps so hard it sends the blood fizzling around my chest.

'Where's Lily?' I manage an octave higher than usual.

'Don't you know?' replies Celestine. 'Probably breast-feeding some lonely heart, wouldn't you say?'

'Why's he here?' I point to Miles who has yet to say a word to me. He seems different every time I meet him. He looks older than I first figured, due to the three-day beard, the same hue as his grey suit. The trousers are too long and billow around his ankles. His shirt is frayed at the collar. Miles is not quite the man he once portrayed in his borrowed SUV.

'Miles' mother was half Italian,' Celestine says, apropos nothing.

'Now you know I don't talk about that, Cel.'

'Why not? I think it makes you mysterious.'

'I don't talk about it nonetheless.'

'Saying that only makes you more mysterious, Miles, I'm telling you.'

'Don't care if it does. There's no way I'm going to talk about my half-Italian mother.'

'How did they get here?' I nod at the children.

'We picked them up from school.' Her words trickle through my veins like ice water.

'Who's we?'

'Me and Miles.'

'You had no authority to do that. Who told you to pick up my kids?'

'*My kids*,' she mimics me. 'Your kids . . . what does it matter? Children belong to everyone.'

'No they don't. They do not . . .'

'Like when kids show these talents and stuff for maths or art and the parents don't have either. Isn't that saying, you know, isn't that saying, they belong to us all?'

'Did the teacher allow you to take them out?'

'Keep your hair on, Daddy-oh. I called up Lily for permission and she rang the school.'

But she didn't ring me. Conspiracy is hard to resist.

I watch Flora shaking sugar from a jar on to her dough shapes. 'Didn't you go to the dentist this morning?' I remember to ask, amidst this crisis of possession.

'The dentist said I got to have four teeth out.'

'What! Which four?'

She opens her mouth and prises her gum off the front teeth. 'Theth four baby teef.'

'You were only meant to be going to have them cleaned.'

She pops out her fingers. 'He said they're pushing on the new teeth and will disturb the roots and my new teeth won't grow straight.' Her face brightens as she concludes, 'I can still have a brace though.'

'This a private dentist?' Celestine asks.

'No,' I say. 'NHS. But she goes private there.'

'That explains why he's pulling her teeth.' She rubs her thumb and fingers together. 'I went to a dentist a few years ago. He asked me, "Do you want this done on the NHS or private?" I said, "Like what's the difference? Brad Pitt coming in to fit me a crown? Gonna show me a wine list?" '

'If you have four baby teeth pulled, why do you still need a brace?' I ask.

'Because Annabel has one, and Fenella . . .'

In the short time I've been here I've sensed Miles trying to find some way of talking to me, and now he hits upon a subject. 'Ferrari can never be beat,' he says, 'not because of the drivers, but the car itself. Damon Hill was committing suicide when he moved to Arrows. Like Skoda, that is!' I fail to respond and he switches subjects, but still on the theme of cars. 'That's a Lexus outside your house, isn't it?' he says, and names the model.

If he thinks it's mine, I don't enlighten him. 'What happened to that SUV you were driving when we met in dramatic fashion? Did you have to pay for the damage?'

'I didn't wait for the guy to look at it. Just took it back and split. It's something I do all the time, borrow a Merc or Beema twenty-four hours, they lend you anything providing you got a suit on. Car salesmen'll lend you their wives for a test drive.'

These remarks give me a better impression of what he wants; something for nothing. His eyes roam over the contents of the kitchen. He touches my wife's Greek vase full of large daisies and makes it wobble on the stand.

Eliot says, 'Joel in my class has lost *twelve* first teeth. He says it's a world record.'

'How does he know that?' Flora asks.

Eliot pauses. 'It's in the *Guinness World Records*.'

'Oh, yeah *right*!'

'Sprinkle any more sugar on that biscuit,' Celestine says, 'and you're going to be needing dentures in a couple of years, never mind a brace. Ain't that right, Daddy?'

But I am still seeking answers to different questions. 'How did you get in here?'

'We picked the lock.' Celestine laughs. 'Just kidding. Your neighbour, the one where your babysitter lives?'

'I know who you mean.'

'Lily said she'll be home about five, by the way. Gonna make us all supper.' She seems to notice for the first time my optional Navy uniform, the blue NATO sweater with epaulettes, and smiles sardonically at my disguise.

Miles' voice starts up again. 'I put a bet on Schumacher winning the championship by a clear fifty points.' Celestine raises one leg and lowers it audaciously upon Flora's knee. On her bare ankle I see a tattoo of a snake. Her hair is tied in childish pigtails and there is glitter on her eyelids.

She pulls down the hem of her t-shirt over an exposed pierced navel as she reaches for and lights up a cigarette. 'Lily doesn't allow smoking in the house,' I say.

'She's not here, is she?'

'Put it out now.'

From her own experience, Flora recognises the signal in my tone of voice, knows that I'm feeling less than a hundred per cent and fixes her gaze on me. She only switches it to follow Celestine's hand dropping the cigarette into a cold mug of tea.

What seems a long time later, Lily arrives home. She is wearing a thin blue cashmere sweater and I'm struck by the loveliness of it on her. When she says, 'Hello . . . hello, everybody,' I have to resist falling into her arms. 'Look at you two,' she says to the kids. 'A fine mess you've made.'

'Sorry,' says Celestine. 'It was my idea.'

'That's all right.' She touches the edge of the tinfoil. 'These look lovely.'

'We made them for dessert,' Eliot explains, his eyes on Celestine with a look of infatuation. Lily smiles at them both.

My family trusts these strangers because they have faith in human nature. They expect everyone to be as benign as they are. My sense of pride in them is corrupted by the knowledge of these same strangers as people who can ruin us. It would take less than the two minutes Lily announces will be needed to cook the mushroom ravioli she's brought in from an Italian deli. She lights the gas under a deep pan of water, and as Flora and Eliot take themselves out of the kitchen, wipes the flour off the table. She frowns on seeing a cigarette butt floating in the mug of cold tea but says nothing.

I'm waiting for Celestine to ruin our lives. I can hear the seconds crashing. I'm waiting on the big fall. But she's in no hurry to play her trump card and when she does start talking again, it's an account of how she met Miles speed dating.

'You pay eighteen quid and then you have like three minutes with each guy. Twenty dates, less than a quid each. You get three minutes to ask questions on all sorts of stuff. Like what's your favourite TV programme? What would you do if your holiday got cancelled at the last moment? I don't have a TV where I live and the last holiday I took was a day trip to Canvey Island. So I wasn't sure this was going to work for me. But when I got to Miles he said, to the TV question, that one day it's going to be compulsory for everyone to appear on *Big Brother*. Like jury service. We had a right laugh. We didn't even need three minutes to know this was it, did we Miles? And here we are now in no time at all, like a married couple with two kids. Sorry Ray, *your* two kids.' She slaps her hand on Lily's arm, feeling the soft texture of her cashmere sweater, a gesture that turns my stomach. 'Do you believe in love at first sight, Lily?'

'I don't rule it out, put it that way.'

'What about Ray . . .' She extends her half-cocked

smile to me. 'Does he believe in love at first sight?'

I'm not sure whom this question is for, whether Lily should answer or me. What *I'd* like to know is why did they go to the seminar on dating and flirting if they were already a couple. And who of the two had the first sight of me? I consider all possibilities, including the one where they both engineer the events of the past few days to trap me. But Lily driving into the back of Miles' test-driven vehicle cancels out at least one of these possibilities. Unless of course, she is in on their scheme. Whatever the truth, the dating industry has got me boxed in.

'Ray and I met the old-fashioned way. But organised dating has no stigma any more,' Lily says. 'It's so mainstream now.'

'Like VD clinics,' Miles considers thoughtfully.

'Miles has two kids, did you know that?' Celestine announces.

Lily asks her, 'Have you met them?'

'Well, you know, all in good time.'

'What are their names?' Lily smiles at Miles.

He takes a little time as if to remember, and says, 'They still know who their daddy is.'

Lily takes the pasta off the heat, removes the biscuits from the oven. She orders me to set the kitchen table for six, puts her head round the door and shouts to the kids. I hear their feet stampeding down the stairs and seconds later they are thawing out the kitchen once again. 'Look at your biscuits' – Lily points to the tray on the oven hob. 'Aren't they lovely?' When Eliot tries to take one, she removes his hand from the hob. 'Not yet. Wait till after dinner.'

'The jam turnover's mine,' Flora says.

'It's got your name on it,' says Celestine.

'Has it?' Eliot already believes everything this woman is telling him.

We sit down in the kitchen to eat. The lunatics have taken over the asylum. The world has turned upside down. Lily serves our guests first and puts the cheese grater in my hand. I grate Parmesan on to Miles and Celestine's plates as Miles reaches for the bottle of red wine and pours himself a glass to the rim. I file some skin off the end of my finger. I think it goes into Celestine's pasta. The nervous system responds late. I lower my hand and watch the blood blossoming on my finger.

Lily asks Miles, 'What is it you do?'

She has to wait for him to drain the entire contents of his glass. 'I'm in between things at the moment. You know how it is.' He wipes his mouth with his sleeve. 'Lot of money out there to make.'

Lots of money out there to make. You know how it is. I wait for combat to begin. I want to know how much he knows about me. Celestine can't talk. She requires a full stomach first. I look at my children and wonder how long it will be before I see them again, if ever I do. But combat doesn't start. Halfway through supper and nothing happens. When Lily explains to our guests that she and I have arranged to go out tonight, to yoga class and snooker, I feel the beginnings of a great relief. But then Celestine raises her arm like a schoolgirl. 'Oh, I forgot, your neighbour said she can't babysit for you tonight.'

'Oh, did she?' says Lily.

'No problems. We'll babysit for you. Miles loves kids, don't you, babes?'

'I don't mind staying in tonight, Lily,' I tell her.

'No,' she replies. 'Let them babysit. That's generous of you, Celestine. We accept.'

'That's sorted then.'

Lily accepts her offer to please me and I feel powerless now to contradict her. She is trying to bridge the family divide. What she can't see is Celestine's damage. If she could, then she would see mine. This turn of events cannot be reversed without consequence, and so it is that I leave my children in the care of two explosive characters for a few hours, for the greater good of self-preservation. Never have I felt so weak or wretched.

I like the dark halls of snooker for giving protection against things coming from behind. But that darkness is beside the point, now the danger is in my home. All these years I've been lying low, I've been lying low from her. She might be priming my children for when we return. I'm caught up here when I should be there.

To help me get through this night I suggest we play for money. Five pounds a pocket . . . thirty quid a game.

'We've never played for money before,' Jerry protests. 'What's up, Ray, stripping assets or something?'

But Colin enters into the spirit of the thing. 'Thirty quid might give us some focus.'

We rotate on the table, with one staying out to play the winner. Colin and I play the first frame and I lose. Then Colin beats Jerry. I play Colin again and win. I play Jerry and beat him too. Colin and I play the fifth frame and I lose. I have my hand in my pocket when he says, 'Just buy the drinks tonight, Ray.'

I palm thirty pounds out on to the felt. 'Take it. And you buy the drinks.'

'You're not really going to take Ray's money?' Jerry asks.

'Yes he fucking is,' I say with such aggression I startle them both. 'And you owe us thirty quid each, Jerry.'

'Yeah, cough up,' says Colin.

'What about if I buy the drinks?'

'Or play another frame. Double or quits?'

'Not on your life,' says Jerry.

We go to meet the wives after their Pilates class, at a bar called The Sirens. They are already there as we arrive, seated around the counter. We pull up stools and Colin orders a bottle of Côtes du Rhône. The Australian barman pours him a glass, which Colin holds to his nose. 'It's off,' he says. 'Corked.'

The barman takes a sip from Colin's glass. 'Yeah, you're right.' He removes the bottle and takes a new one from the rack.

'How did you know that was off,' Julia asks, 'from just smelling it?'

'How's this bar going to make a profit,' Rebecca comments, 'if you keep sending them back?'

The barman seems to have similar doubts and asks if we are going to pay now or run up a tab. But Jerry is there with the money, our wager. 'What if I buy this and give you the change, Colin?' Jerry suggests. 'Will that make us quits?'

'You lost sixty quid. This wine's only sixteen-fifty a bottle.'

'What are you boys talking about?' Lily asks.

'We had a little flutter tonight.'

We settle into the counter and for once I do not bother looking anonymous, nor hang my head in the shadows. I just want to get out of here and begin what has to be done. It's a real effort to avoid poring over my watch and so I mark time in millimetres of wine sliding down the glasses. Then as bad luck would have it, our conversation turns to the strange case of Celestine and time starts to roar in my ears.

'Lily says she's seen a bit of life in the fast lane. Been round the block a few times.'

'Don't be rude, Colin,' Rebecca scolds him. 'She's your cousin on your father's side, right, Ray?'

Julia asks, 'He was a tax inspector, wasn't he?'

'It's a longer story than that,' says Lily, who thinks she knows it. 'Ray's dad went from mining into selling life insurance before Ray was born. In the war he was seconded into military intelligence, intercepting mail from Germany. Haven't I ever told you this? He got into the I. Corps because he *was* intelligent and now wanted more from life than he was getting before the war started. So he went into local government, as a civil servant, tax or something. When he retired he went to university to do a degree in politics, but died before finishing the course.'

As she is telling the story, my nose starts to bleed. At the sight of blood dripping on to my glass Lily produces a tissue from her bag and makes a joke. 'He always gets a nosebleed when I talk about his father.'

'It's probably high blood pressure,' I say.

'Oh, don't say that.' Lily stares at me with concerned understanding, while understanding absolutely nothing at all.

'Have a fresh glass, Ray. Unless you want to drink your own blood.' Colin calls over the barman.

I see my chance and shake my head, nose pinched between two fingers. 'I'd better be getting home. But you don't have to.'

I step outside and the sky is full of stars. A light breeze, sharp with salt, travels up-river from the sea and cauterises my nose. Then I start to run. Five minutes later I'm home, which doesn't feel like home any more. It has acquired a soiled, primitive odour. It is also deathly quiet. I climb upstairs to find the children still awake, but in the same bunk-bed. They do this when they are feeling insecure and their eyes stare at me through the dark. Then I hear a dull thudding sound from down the hall.

I go the distance from the children's room to our bedroom. The door is closed and from inside unfolds that thudding noise. I open the door and it takes me a moment to understand what I'm looking at. In the full glare of the overhead light and with the curtains wide open, Celestine is kneeling on the floor with her torso flat against the bed. Her face is pressed hard into a pillow and her arms are outstretched. Miles is on his knees behind her. They are both naked. The wooden bed frame bangs against the wall from the force of his hard, fast action. There is no sound coming from either of their mouths.

Celestine does not notice me, but Miles does, whose trousers are hanging from one foot. 'Get dressed,' I say. 'Then get out of my house.'

I wait at the top of the stairs, blocking off the rest of the bedrooms. When they appear a few minutes later flushed and pleased, I escort them downstairs. At the front door Celestine says, 'Any time you want us to babysit, don't hesitate to call.' I hold the door wide open but she stands her ground. 'What about Lily? I want to say goodnight.'

'I'll give her your regards.'

Her voice grows hard and businesslike. 'We need some taxi fare.'

I reach into my pocket and give her a fistful of notes. 'This is all I've got.'

'All you've got is all I want.'

19

Three tides later she hunts me down again. Wants to gamble at the casino that allegedly employs her as a waitress. 'How much is this going to cost?'

'A couple of thou.'

'I'm not giving you a couple of thousand pounds!'

'You'll get it back. I've got a scam on the blackjack.' I don't believe this for a minute. She sees me hesitate. 'Why do you think I work there, because I love being a waitress? To get to know the scams, man. All I've been waiting for is the sponsorship. Miles is coming with me.'

'Why does Miles have to go?'

'For muscle, when I leave the joint with six grand, or more.'

'I can do that.'

'You don't need to come at all.'

'It's a condition of the loan.'

'Okay, but Miles is coming too.'

There is no question that I have to find this money and as soon as I'm able, raid the joint account I share with Lily. My withdrawal leaves the account in the red.

We rendezvous the following evening in central London. With pockets swollen I sit between them in the back seat of a taxi. Celestine is priming herself as we travel west along the Embankment, singing the words to Michael Jackson's 'Thriller', while Miles stares out into the night like a kid on a school outing. The river at the turn is going in the opposite direction.

The casino does indeed allow Celestine plus two guests inside. I'm still trying to understand that, in the thickened atmosphere of the gaming floor. Like a snooker hall the room is in a gloaming while the table lights burn sharp and hot. I sense guilt all around me, democratically distributed, feel myself being silently welcomed by this anonymous company of players.

I exchange £2000 for chips and ration Celestine to half. She protests loudly and I remind her I'm not going anywhere and that I'm not gambling. She drifts off to one of the blackjack tables and Miles makes for the bar in the suit he wore the day we crashed cars. I wander around the £30-minimum-bet tables, soaking up worry so much weaker than my own. My life is a gamble and helps me understand this place. Despair and avarice are the only emotions on show. There is wealth here, but no intelligence. They rarely go together anyway.

After thirty minutes Celestine finds me again to ask for the rest of the chips. 'The croupier was too fucking quick. I'm going to try another table.'

I let her have the chips then join Miles at the bar, where he is nursing a bottle of Budweiser. I want to know what he knows. 'Looks like my cousin's losing,' I begin.

'Your cousin?'

'Celestine.'

'She said you were her brother.'

'She said that, did she?'

His face cracks open with a dirty smile. 'I know all about you. So you'd better buy me another beer.'

I buy another beer for him, a very cheap price for such

24-carat information. Now I know finally where I stand. My enemy has doubled in strength, but so have I.

'I don't care much for casinos,' he says, taking the bottle by the neck. 'Formula One's my game. This place is full of losers, chief.' He sits at the bar staring at the wall of liquors. His moroseness is palpable.

'You want to get out of here?'

'What about Cel?'

'She's got all the money I have.'

'Where to then?'

'We're about a half-hour's walk from the river.'

'I want a drink, not a fucking swim.'

'My office is there. I buy a few bottles, we go drink it there.'

'Thought you said Cel had all your money?'

'I've got a reserve . . .'

'All *right*! I'd better tell her, though.'

'You might screw up her luck telling her we're leaving.'

'She's losing, you said.'

'Then maybe we're the ones bringing her down. Let's just go, Miles.'

I am thinking several moves ahead, although I'm not clear at all about the last of them. But separating him from Celestine is the crucial first step. The second of the moves is to get him drunk, so I buy a bottle of Scotch from the bar at a hugely inflated price and five minutes later we walk out into the street with ten knots of wind behind our backs. I twist open the neck and offer the bottle to him. With his head back and throat open his feet shuffle along the dry, cracked pavements, following me blindly towards the Thames. There are quite a few people out at this hour and all of them drunk. I encourage him to feel inspired and work on the whisky some more.

We enter the old city of ceremony. A few minutes later we are standing on Lambeth Bridge, dazzled by the lights of Westminster Palace burning on the surface of the water. Miles guzzles the whisky. He doesn't know where he is. The tide races out to sea at eight knots, running the ancient course, sucking at the buttresses of the bridge.

Some communality with this man has to be found. If you ever have the misfortune to spend time in prison, finding communality is a matter of survival. Sharing your cell twenty-four hours a day with some psycho turns you into a psychologist. I take a sideways glance at him working on that bottle and doubt very much if life affords him much pleasure. He doesn't exercise the kind of knowledge that generates strong emotional ties. He had a family and lost them. That's more than carelessness. He's going to live a short life as anyone does who lives only inside himself. Such men are suggestible.

In this zone of political ideas, I begin the search for communality. 'Okay here, Miles?'

'Where's this office you said you had?'

'You're in it. Office with no walls, no roof.'

'Really? What's the rent like?'

His humour worries me because it demonstrates intelligence. I seek out a wound to work on. 'Do you ever bring your kids down here?'

'My kids? I see them twice a year. Wife's solicitor called that an arrangement. I call it a fucking ambush.'

'They're growing up without you, Miles. You're not going to make a dent.'

'Don't rub it in, chief.'

'Without your kids you get kicked off the bus. The world rolls on by while you're left wondering what it's all about. What are their names?'

'Tony and Liam. My boys . . .'

'Must be hard, not being part of their lives.'

'Yeah. Fuck me, why are you bringing this up?'

'It's bad to bury them. You bury the dead, not your kids.'

'Sometimes I'm the one who feels dead.'

'Because they're your only shot at immortality.'

'Eh? Like what, you mean?'

'We live through our children when we die. Between now and then they keep you sane. But only if you have them. And you don't.'

'I can't work out nothing like that. But that's . . . true.' He takes a long ponderous swig from the bottle. The deeper his thoughts, the further down that bottle he needs to drink.

'I did ten years inside. That's plenty of time to work things out . . . in your peter twenty-three hours a day.'

'What's a peter?'

'A cell, after St Peter, a jailer who held the keys to heaven.'

'It's all fucking chaos, that's what I know.'

'Chaos, yes.' I point at the glistening water. 'The only order is that river. River knows what it's doing. Comes in and out twice a day for all eternity.' Further along on the bridge two lovers embrace, leaning against a Mazda sports convertible. 'That's why I love my job, Miles. I go on to the river to escape the chaos of life. Out there feels so good it's got to be right. Not like getting religion or anything. This religion's all around. That's what I believe. It's in that water below. The order.'

For the first time he looks straight at me without side or hostility and we lock eyes like antlers. He's no longer grasping, demanding. He doesn't think I'm a mad fool and is compelled to keep listening. His resistance is breaking down. With a little more work on the communality, I'll be able to persuade him to do anything.

'You don't have to be Nelson or Christopher Columbus

to be great. All you have to do is step off the shore on to the river and you'll know what they knew. You'll never feel grief again. The end of the blues is waiting for you on that water. You live in some crummy little bedsit with a Baby Belling and a pile of filthy washing in the corner. Dirty plates in the sink. You're even too ashamed to take Celestine there.'

'Not quite, but close. Very close.'

'Have another drink.' I grab his wrist and raise the bottle to this mouth. Miles sucks at the teat. 'Not many people know this, but the river's being oxygenated by a little barge that goes up and down here every day. That water is now fresher than a spa. It's got minerals that could make you feel two hundred per cent.'

Miles steps up to the four-foot wall. The sweethearts sitting on the bonnet of their red sports car are kissing and not watching this, the moment when Miles climbs on to the wall and gets to his feet. He looks down, swaying a little. 'These minerals . . . what they do again?'

'Make you live for a long, long time.'

'You're having me on, chief.'

'The politicians over there in the Palace, they know it. Don't they know how to outstay their welcome?'

'Would it be dangerous to jump down there?'

I say: 'In this dark, the river looks further away than it is.'

His face contorts with the effort of comprehension. He's not sure if I've properly answered his question. 'So if I jump in there the worst that can happen is I get wet.'

'That's about it, I guess.'

'Okay, chief. Put your money where your mouth is. Come up here and jump with me.'

I step up to the wall and climb on next to him. It is late at night with no one around to witness what we are doing, apart from the two sweethearts who have yet to break from their long kiss. Miles laughs, takes another pop of the whisky and hurls the bottle into the water. It's because that bottle isn't empty that I know he's going to go in.

He bellows like a horse and disturbs the lovers' interlude. They notice us for the first time, see two men acting independently. They can see no one is pushing anyone, that there is no crime being committed. What I said to him . . . that's a matter for the birds.

'You ready, Miles?'

'Ready as I'll ever be.'

'One. Two. Three . . .'

I've never jumped off a bridge before and the ten-metre descent is a short death of sorts. I'm marginally aware of Miles plummeting alongside but not a lot else until the impact with the water – with a mother's affection, as my father once called it, quoting someone else. My arms and legs are pulled apart with terrible violence and my body goes into a spasm of shock from the cold. I sink deeper into the black recesses with my eyes open and see the water effervescent with imprisoned sodium light in a million air particles. I have never been *in* the Thames before and it's . . . *interesting*. The drift of the tide claims me immediately, turning me over and rushing me down-river under the thick, leathery surface.

You cannot beat this current, cannot win against the drift. You have to submit to the order of things. There is a snap as I break the surface and I hear my own colossal intake of breath, like a balloon being inflated. Taking snacks of oxygen when I get the chance, I travel with the current rushing in my ears. I catch one glimpse of Miles trying to swim against the tide. One glimpse before the night comes between us.

It's a bumpy ride over the bights and eddies in the middle of the stream. Lying on my back affords an

Arcadian view of the city. The traffic leaves thin trails of light on the Embankment. There is St Thomas' Hospital where my first mate Noel's gynaecologist son is probably right now laying his hands on women in the maternity ward. There is the old County Hall, London Eye . . . static at this hour, the RAF memorial, the *Tattershall* Castle, the *Hispaniola*. I sweep under Hungerford Bridge where the river bends and the tide pushes me towards the north shore. A buttress of Waterloo Bridge obscures my view of Cleopatra's Needle for a moment. When I emerge I have the light of the city in my eyes again. And shortly after that I feel my knees ploughing up mud below Temple Pier.

Moments later, dripping on the steps of Somerset House, that once held records of every birth and death, I scan the black river with my naked eye. I'm looking to see if Miles is hanging to a buoy and needing my help. I'm hoping he survived the fall, but appreciate the convenience if he hasn't. I have gone beyond myself while Miles might be well on his way to Cap Gris Nez.

20

In one of the books I studied in prison I found this quotation: 'All our Creeks seek to one River, all our Rivers run to one Port, all our Ports join to one Town, all our Towns make but one City, and all our Cities and Suburbs to one vast, unyieldy and disorderly Babel of buildings, which the world calls London.' These are the words of Thomas Milles, Customer of the Port of Sandwich way back in 1604.

In the same book I learnt there are two historic cities: City of London and Westminster, but only one river. Ten thousand years ago, people were poling or paddling up the Thames on skin-hide boats. Bronze Age seafarers threw offerings of tools, spears and swords to the water gods. The Romans established a supply base on the banks and built the first bridge. In its pre-natal state the city survived sackings by Vikings, whose clinker-built, flat-bottomed boats would be run up on the sloping beaches at low tide. These Norsemen attacked, but did not stop trade between London and the Baltic, which increased so much that larger ships were built, with wide beams and square-rigged sails they called cogs. Elizabethan voyages of discovery opened up new trade routes and now there were thousands of sailing ships from all over the world at berth in the two-mile stretch of river between Wapping and Limehouse. The waterfront became packed with granaries, warehouses, shops, taverns, fishmongers, brewers, dyers, coppers, carpenters and metalworkers. Prevented by London Bridge from going further upstream, these ships lay at anchor while their cargoes were removed into flat-bottomed barges or lighters. During the reign of Elizabeth I, lightermen's families formed the largest part of a tight-knit riverside community. On the north shore they were all Protestants; Catholics on the south shore. At night, in the grog shops, the gin palaces, they would fight like dogs. But come the next day and back on the river, northsiders and southsiders became onesiders, because that river could take your life. Dangerous though it was and is, a life on the river was deemed the real prize among the working communities. By the turn of the twentieth century London was choking on its own noxious fumes, but out on the Silver Mile you could breathe fresh oxygen.

My book said these lighters could go wherever a seagull could swim and some of the spritsail barges made Atlantic crossings, although not many made it back. In 1914 they were deployed to transport munitions and in 1940 used during the evacuation of Dunkirk. When the first docks were sunk and cargoes craned straight out of ships' holds into five-storey warehouses, there still remained plenty of work for lighters further upstream in the Pool, taking freight from ship to shore as before. But the writing was on the wall. Ships got too big and fat to make it up as far as the Pool. They all had to be unloaded in the docks and a two-thousand-year-old quay game came to an end. And then the docks started closing too. The former traffic of East India, Millwall, West Indies and the Victoria, Albert and King George V stopped at Tilbury.

Moss and lichen grew over the gantries in the abandoned docks, until new kings – the property developers – saw dollar signs reflected in the imprisoned water. They inherited the old palaces and turned them around, then sold them to the City people, to Westminster people, for fortunes in flying money.

21

Leave the house at 02.00. There must be no witnesses to where I'm going and taking Lily's car is a good ruse because I'm meant to be a non-driver. I take it round to a marsh-land road and run double-sided Sellotape along the edges of the roof and around the number plates. A white bed sheet from the boot I pull tightly across the roof. Ours is a green car – but not any more! I stretch black bin-liners over the number plates and drive off. I make headway but the wind is so strong it tears a corner of the sheet off the roof. I stop again. As I'm securing the sheet in a built-up street, the wind dislodges a tile from a house. It crashes onto the pavement and moments later a woman's face stares out of a window. I stay still until she vanishes. It's possible she's seen me. As I am driving away it starts to rain heavily. On this stormy night the roads run with excess rainwater. It comes off the North Sea where ships are diving into harbours. Hailstones play timpani on the car bonnet and announce my progress. I feel pursued by the rain, slamming upon the car.

At 03.00 I leave the car under the shadow of a Victorian gasholder and walk to the canal with a carrier bag under my arm. At the barge I check the opposite towpath for homosexuals but everyone over there seems asleep. I remove the two washboards to open up the bosun's cabin and place them flat on deck. From inside the carrier bag I remove a bottle filled with petrol and put a light to a soaking rag jammed in the neck. The bright yellow flame illuminates the interior of the bosun's cabin and Celestine's head sleeping upon a rolled-up trench coat. I throw the bottle at the Torglow. It smashes against the cast-iron stove and the flying petrol ignites, putting down fire into all corners of the little cabin, and consumes Celestine sleeping in her bed.

I cane it on the way back home, foot to the boards. The wind and the rain rip the sheet off the roof and through the windscreen I see it lift into the night sky like an unanchored and ghostly kite. A few streets from home I stop the car to remove the plastic bags from around the number plates. I get back to the house just before 04.00. Lily is asleep as I slip into bed beside her.

Well that's the plan, anyway. Each night I run the drill through my head to help me fall asleep, like counting sheep.

Lily discovers the hard way that our joint account has gone into the red when she tries to draw money from a cashpoint. She walks in through the front door after work in a state of high anxiety. 'Last time I looked there was over a thousand in that account. I had to borrow my train fare home.' If the car hadn't been out of action, she'd have driven to work. And I'd have survived another day. 'Do you know anything about this, Ray?'

I tell her the truth. 'I gave it to Celestine.'

'You did? How much?'

'Two thousand.'

'Jesus, Ray, what are your priorities?'

'I'm sorry.'

'You're sorry? Something's going on here and I don't like it.'

I can't say anything to allay her fears. All I can say is, 'I'll pay the money back.'

'That's not the point. You're missing the point. You could have told me first. How long have you lent it for?'

'I didn't give it to her as a loan.'

'What do you mean!'

'I mean I'll pay it back if she doesn't.'

'Then you'd better start booking some overtime, Ray. Two thousand's not nothing. Two thousand's a lot of money. What's she want it for?'

'I didn't ask.'

'No one gives two thousand pounds without asking what it's for. Not even a bank. Does she think we're made of money? You're taking food out of the children's mouths.'

The children are within hearing. Eliot emerges into the hall where Lily is berating me and asks in a trembling voice: 'Are we bankrupt?'

'No, Eliot, we're not. Go and play.'

'You see . . .' Lily fires back when Eliot has gone. 'Your generosity affects us all.'

Flora is next to emerge, picking up the signal that not all is well. 'I can give you my twenty-pound savings.'

'No, darling, that's not necessary. But thank you.'

'Can I still go shopping then, with Dad?'

Lily knows nothing of this. 'You're going shopping? When was this decided?'

'I promised Flora I'd take her to a shopping mall. She wants to spend her tooth-fairy money.'

'You've got a few more baby teeth to come out, Flora. If your father continues with his generosity, we may have to give you a few IOUs.' She looks at me through tired, red-rimmed eyes.

* * *

Riding on the top deck of the bus an hour later, Flora asks me why her mother is mad with me. 'For good reason,' I say. 'But it needn't concern you.'

'Oh, grown-ups always say that.'

'When have I said that before?'

'You never tell us anything.'

The truth of this cuts me deeply. Children do not know their parents as a rule, other than as providers, and in my case I'm happy to maintain that distance. But Flora, as I've said before, knows something is up without knowing what she knows. And now she's hurt because I'm hurt. I'm hurt for reasons far too big to ever explain.

We need to reach that shopping mall to break this deadlock. Shopping will get us back on track.

At the top of the bus her attentions flit from the family to life outside the windows, to thoughts about the extended family. 'Alice is three now, Dad, and Aunt Rebecca still dresses her in a Babygro.' She takes her twenty pounds out of her jeans and inspects it, making sure it's still there. 'My friend Emma gets five pounds a week pocket money. That's twenty pounds every month. And when there's five weeks in a month she gets twenty-five pounds.'

'When are there five weeks in a month?'

'We just had one. Thirty-one days, that's five weeks. Twenty-five pounds.'

I'm unable to challenge her maths. In the state I'm in there may well be five weeks in a month.

'I want to stop playing the flute and take up the piano. Laura has one and she's really good . . . Isn't that where we went skating?' She points to the sports centre.

It's been some time since we went ice-skating but I still remember that strange tension I felt on the ice, between me and other skaters and one old memory. The old memory was of walking round and round in circles in a prison yard. In the ice rink I was skating in the same anticlockwise direction.

'If you want to be a physiotherapist, you need to be good at PE. But say you wanted to be a physiotherapist and you're no good at PE, what do you do then?'

'You want to be a physiotherapist?'

'I want to help people who have problems with their brains, but I'm no good at PE.'

'You mean a psychiatrist.'

'Is that different from physiotherapist?'

'Yes.'

She thinks about this. 'Does a psychiatrist have to be good at PE?'

We get off the bus and walk across a bridge straddling the dual carriageway and into the shopping mall. Flora, who has a summer cold, takes a small menthol inhaler from her jeans' pocket and jams it up her nostril.

Inside, the mall is a treadmill for glazed-eyed and listless people to sleepwalk. We join the stream, going in and out of Computer Games for a look at their CD-ROM collection, in and out of the Gadget Shop, which Flora claims is only for boys, and in and out of Gap who don't have the shirt she desires in her size. I feel a debilitating lethargy creep up on me. John Lewis is a somnambulant experience. By the time we reach Television and Hi-fi on the third floor I no longer understand anything, how we got here and how we get out. I am overwhelmed by a whole floor of flickering, gel-screen, high-definition sets. I have what an epileptic might recognise as a *petit mal* as my arms shake and my tongue expands in my mouth. Over the story of Niagara Falls told a dozen times with a supersonic soundtrack, I superimpose an image of Miles on the riverbed.

I am in Domestic Appliances before I come to my senses, and the first realisation is the worst: I no longer have Flora with me. I spin through 360 degrees but can't see her. I've never done this before and never have I been so scared, running past displays of kettles, pans and lamps, straight out of the shop on to the mezzanine floor. I take the escalator down one flight and re-enter the department store at the level of cosmetics. I ask the first sales assistant I find if she's seen a girl. I try to describe Flora but can't remember what she's wearing. The appeal is lost on this woman anyway. She's French, with very little English. I canter through the floor, looking each way, then run up the escalator back to the second floor. Eventually I resort to shouting her name, drawing fearful looks from everyone in the store. I don't have emotion, because I don't have Flora. All I have is adrenaline that crimsons everything in my line of vision – the rows of men's trousers and the hanging shirts. There are bars in front of my eyes too, as I cry out like an animal. I am filled with limitless strength. At the top floor I howl and howl. Flora is still lost in this place.

Running once more to the escalator and trying to think, an assistant in blue uniform waves at me. It's like a flag. In a second I am by her side and on my knees, and staring into Flora's sobbing face. When I try to take her hand she refuses me.

Without a word we march out of the mall and in the car park she punches me in the lower back. She punches me as hard as she can and then screams with all her might.

Lily is running down the hall as I am opening the front door. Ignoring Flora she rams into me and beats my chest with the sides of clenched fists. I am undone. It is going off. Then I see what looks like a ribbon hanging out of one of her fists. What it is in fact is a paper receipt –

discovered in the pocket of the trousers I'd flung into the laundry basket and with which she now confronts me.

'Victoria's Secrets lingerie!'

'I bought those things for Celestine.'

'Is that meant to make me feel better? *Why* are you buying her lingerie?'

Flora gets caught in the crossfire; the turbulence buffets her. She chooses this moment to announce that I lost her in John Lewis. If it wasn't for that sales assistant who saw her crying she'd probably still be there now. Or abducted, dead . . .

'Flora, please . . .'

'Are you having an affair with her?'

'I know what an affair is,' Flora smiles wryly.

'Go and play. *Vamoose!*' says Lily.

'I'm not having an affair,' I say for both sets of ears.

'Do you swear it? And remember what I do for a living, Ray. I'll *know* if you're lying.'

'I swear it. Celestine is my problem and I'll deal with it.'

'Then don't take too long. And remember, I'm watching you, Ray.' That was what her mother said to me on our wedding day. *I'll be watching you, Ray.*

And now that family closes ranks, freezing me out after Lily raises the hue and cry. On yoga club night Jerry informs me he can't play snooker and Colin elects for a night in. But when I telephone both their houses later I get only their respective babysitters.

I call Rose and try to hide the hysteria in my voice as I ask why I'm being cold-shouldered. 'Well, Ray, you tell me,' she says. 'I don't want to interfere, but Lily is very unhappy about this cousin of yours.'

'I'm upset about this cousin of mine too, Rose. Can you understand that?'

'I understand blood is thicker than water,' she replies coldly.

But it's water, not blood, that flows in my veins. It's a relief to return to work on a twenty-four-hour shift, where I go through the motions in an automatic frame of mind. The routines, the drills, are all in my head as I log on and let the ship follow a time-worn course. At the docks I take ferries in and take them out. I escort a spirit tanker with a fouled propeller into Tilbury, speaking to the master on the radiophone with a thick and heavy emphasis. I hardly say a word to Noel. My mobile phone is quiet all day. Even Jerry neglects to make his routine call.

Then I am off for three days and find everyone still withdrawn behind the line of blood. I feel the chill standing on the other side. I'm hurt and lonely but can't find the courage to do what I'd like to do, fall into their arms and weep, confess and beg forgiveness. I fear telling them the truth and yet am so tired of lying.

I do my best with the children. They *are* my blood and don't close ranks. Eliot seems immune to my distress, but Flora is watchful and tearful. There is a depression hanging over her and a formality creeps into our conversations. I can't even afford to take her shopping, and would be too scared of losing her if I did.

Lily, her brothers and their wives may have sent me to Coventry, but what they don't realise is how well I know Coventry. I've lived there for a very long time. And I know that if you wait long enough you can be sure someone else will break the silence first. Silence is too powerful for most people.

The silence is broken by Celestine, arriving at the house like a banshee. 'I've fucking had enough of men!' she shouts. I run to close the doors of the kitchen, cordoning off the children in the lounge where they are watching *Newsround* on children's BBC. She looks different from when I last saw her, as she was different then from other times. Mercurial as an addict, she paces from the table to the window. Staring out into the garden with her arms folded across her chest, she begins again, 'Where could he be? When I find him I'll kill him.'

'You mean Miles?'

'No, Santa Claus. Of course I mean Miles.'

'I think I know where he is.'

My declaration puts a crease in her forehead. 'You do?'

'He's diving.'

'Diving? What you mean, diving?'

'He's gone sub-aqua diving in the sea.'

'Sub-what?'

'You don't need to shout. I can hear you without shouting.'

'Don't tell me what to do!'

I hear the scrape of tiny feet in the hall. 'Come into the garden,' I tell her.

Out in the garden under the tree where she carved her initials, I invent a scenario as carefully as I can, while formulating another unveiled plan as I go. 'He's gone to Sheppey. There's a shipwreck there, the *Richard Montgomery*. He's diving on an historical wreck.'

'He never said anything about this.'

'How long have you known him? How long do you think it takes to know all there is to know about someone?'

'But he told you.'

'I have an interest in maritime things.'

'Diving . . . what's the point of that?'

'Salvage.'

'Like gold and stuff?'

'Something like that. Brass, copper, and maybe gold, yes.'

'Now that makes more sense.'

Eliot tears into the garden shouting excitedly about something he's heard on television. 'Dad! They found piranhas in the Thames.'

When Celestine bursts out laughing his face crumples, and registers even more hurt as I tell him to go away. I tell him again. I turn my own son away and it's hard to forgive myself. But I can't allow him to witness what I'm conspiring to do, my thoughts are poisonous spores. He bolts out of the garden and into the house, leaving the back door flapping.

'He's off the north shore not far from Sheerness.'

She smiles for the first time. 'Can we drive to this place?'

'I don't drive, Celestine. And even if I did, our car's in the garage being repaired.'

'Then how do we get there?'

'I don't think he'd appreciate it if I tagged along. You should go alone. Get a train to Sheerness. I'll give you the money. I can call you on your mobile when you get there and tell you where to go.'

'What mobile? I live on a barge, Ray, remember? I've got no electricity to charge up a mobile phone.'

'Then I'll tell you now. Walk east along the footpath from the station until the groynes run out and you'll be looking out at Cheyney Spit. Miles will be diving just off there.'

'I thought he was a fit bloke, but never did I imagine this. Buried treasure! Ain't he the romantic.'

'The romantic bit is seeing you on the shore.'

Staring at the unbroken surface of the grey sea.

22

My last chance to extend the future and protect the family for a few more years is waiting for me to take it. I'll follow her to Sheerness and persuade her to join Miles in his underwater adventure. If I can't persuade her, I'll force her. Someday I may be called to account if their bloated bodies float back to the surface, arm over arm, their eyes pecked out by gulls, and for that reason I must leave no tracks in the sand. And no trail from London and back again. At times like these it would be useful to have a car, instead of having to rely upon South-Eastern Trains to get me to Sheerness without drawing attention to myself.

On the morning she sets off to find Miles, I escort her to the station, give her cash for the ticket and watch her board the Sheerness train on platform 4. Someone can't fail to notice the way she has prepared herself for this reunion. She wears silver chains around her waist like a gunslinger's belt. There is a nine-inch gap between the top of her knee-high boots and the hem of her pink tulle skirt. Her bare legs are streaked with instant tan. Her earrings look punitive.

After her train leaves I buy another ticket for cash, a

newspaper and a large tea from the Croissant Shop and catch the next train to Sheerness. I am grey on the outside and grey on the inside, sliding into an empty seat. As I wait for the train to leave I keep my head lowered over a newspaper. The carriage is about a quarter full. The guard's whistle blows, the train begins to roll and a man comes into the carriage and sits directly opposite, when there are several empty tables. I summon all my powers of invisibility. He is dressed in a suit and tie, and places a hard hat on the table beside my polystyrene cup of tea. A civil engineer, and so drunk so early in the day, his presence may not be the disaster it could have been. Within minutes of the journey beginning his mobile phone fires off. He checks his pockets but can't find the phone and the caller rings off. He has better luck locating it with his eyes closed, and places the phone on the table. His face sags and grows whiter as the train picks up speed. With effort he hauls himself out of the seat and staggers towards the toilets. He's gone two minutes. When he returns I can smell a sour odour of vomit. I listen to his breathing lengthen, just like I listen to my children when they fall asleep. I am doing this for my children.

As he begins to snore I pick up my tea for the first time. But I take it by the lid and the cup falls out of my hand. The inevitability of what then happens disables me, and all I can do is watch the steaming tea spread along the table, pour off the edge and into this man's lap. His bloodshot eyes spring open and register the pain. He takes a few more seconds to focus, recover where he last was.

'That woke me up,' he says, not nicely, without looking at me.

I run to the toilets where he has just been. The pan is smeared in vomit. I roll out a wedge of toilet roll and return to my seat to find him in the same stiff position.

I offer him the toilet paper, which he snatches greedily and begins to wipe his trousers. He dabs his legs and with escalating violence, throws each parcel of sodden toilet roll into my empty cup. I watch him helplessly until it becomes irresistible to apologise. 'Is there anything else I can do?' I ask.

His bloodshot eyes rest upon me for the first time. 'What I want is to throw a cup of hot tea in your face.' I look at the light winking on his mobile phone, the yellow hard hat. 'You're not offering to pay for my suit to be cleaned, are you? So I don't accept your apology.' Drunk or not, he will always remember this train journey, and me. There can be no killing C. It's over, the opportunity has passed.

I take a quick abject look out of the window. The train cuts through open country, the Kent farms. My mother's saddened face appears in front of me for the first time in years and I fancy I can hear apple blossom falling in the orchards, even though the season for that has passed.

I turn my attention back to him. 'I'll pay for your suit to be cleaned. Ten pounds. Is that acceptable?' I remove a ten-pound note from the wallet in my jacket pocket and pass it across the table.

He looks at me again and I see that his eyes are rusting away with age. Taking the money, he says, 'Not many people would do that. You're a gentleman,' and offers me his hand.

We shake hands across the table. 'Then it's closed?' I ask. 'It's settled?'

'I will get it cleaned, you know.'

'Good,' I say. 'I hope it comes up well.'

His phone rings a second time as we reach the coast. With his head against the window, the sea in agitated mood behind him, he makes arrangements with the caller to have a few pints later. Then he adds, 'I'm having a bad journey. Just had scalding tea poured into my lap.' And then I hear nothing more but the sea in my ears.

From a hundred metres' distance I see Celestine on the beach, in relief against the water. In her chains and pink tulle skirt she stands on the last sea-polished groyne in a row, to get a better view of the empty sea; an abandoned lover trying to rule the tides with her sorrow. Offshore, the wreck of the *Richard Montgomery* is marked by a ring of yellow cardinals. But there's no diving vessel out there. Low white clouds drift towards the lee shore, darkening the surface of the water. There is no one else around and slowly she grows alert to my presence, the shingle crunching beneath my feet. She jumps off the groyne and begins in my direction.

The wind pushes in from the sea and makes a rolling noise, like a visitation. It pulls her hair over her face and for that moment she looks like the little girl who followed me to school. I can sense her longing for something far more elemental than Miles and as soon as I am close enough to touch, she transfers it on to me. We converge where the sea meets land, between two states of mind. With our heads close we maintain a thick silence. Then without premeditation she kisses me on the mouth.

For ten seconds I am lost to the world.

She takes one step back and wobbles on the heels of her boots. 'What are you playing at?'

'What am *I* playing at?'

'You kissed me.'

'Then I think someone else was pulling the strings.'

She straightens her skirt, more a symbolic gesture than a practical one. 'Where the fuck is Miles, then?'

'He isn't here?'

Her eyes narrow into pin-holes. 'You knew he wouldn't be here, didn't you?'

Shimmering six miles across the water are the artillery ranges on the Black Grounds. There are stakes and posts in those drying sands marked by Beacons of No Significance. If only they were six feet away instead of six miles, I would take her there and sink her. To the east at the Warp, the Shivering Sands lightship flashes white every five seconds. Lightships are paradoxical things. Their enchantment is irresistible but something best avoided.

'This island's where I did my time,' I say, 'in the young offenders' institution. Five years on this island and never once saw the sea.'

'If you just wanted to come out here to remember the good old days, why drag me along?'

'Miles could have been here. Or maybe he's in Dover, France. Can you ever trust someone you've only known a week?'

'I've known him longer than a week.'

'You don't have much luck with men, do you?'

'How would you know?'

'I know you'll never get over our father, what he did to you. You'll carry those burns to the end of your days.'

'I've got no marks on me, don't you fucking fret.'

'Then why are you trying to hurt me?'

'I ain't doing anything to you.'

'You're practically stalking me, demanding money.'

'There was meant to be money in a bank for me. To make it better. But I never got a penny. You kill your own sister, man, and it's like you get a fucking reward. Nice house, wife, family. It's not fair.'

A cormorant dives into the sea and comes back out with a tiny fish in its beak. The sea hisses and the air is ruptured by screaming gulls on the wing. 'You think taking me down will make it better for you?'

'Next to justice, best thing is revenge.'

'You keep coming after me and my family and I'll eliminate you.'

'Well you've certainly had the practice, Mark.'

'Then you know I mean it.'

'You're all mouth. I'll kill you before you kill me. Then I'll go get your children and garrotte them.'

My arm springs out and unleashes a hard slap against her face. She reacts instantly and slams into me, her knee finding my groin, her lips peeled back. Her ferocity pushes me off balance and locked together we roll into the water. Her teeth sink into my cheek and she pulls at my hair, digs her nails into my eyes. I try with all my strength to prise her off but can't. She's winning *again*. I feel the edge of the sea lipping against our forms. There's just enough water to drown in and I pull both our heads under. She unclamps her teeth from my face and rears her head back. As my own face explodes out of the water I see her head firing down. Everything goes black as she head-butts me on the bridge of my nose. I have life insurance. My debts shall be cleared.

This beach is so shallow you can walk half a mile out to sea and it still won't come higher than your chest.

I am wrapped in her arms, all violence spent. My head on the shingle, feet in the sea, I weep into her breast. She strokes my wet hair out of my face and her eyes come into focus. We are those two children again and the air is full of cinders and ash. Her tulle skirt is hitched up round her waist and I stare mesmerised by the line where her fake tan ends and the white mottled flesh of her thighs begins.

We lie there for a long time. What brings me round like ammonia salts are a couple of swans standing sentinel an arm's length away, their heads cocked to one side and waiting for an explanation.

23

Rose and Aubrey's ruby wedding anniversary falls into my schedule like lead. It's all aboard the charter *Jason Goddjin*; an ordeal I must get through with a false face. Lily, Julia and Rebecca went on board earlier this afternoon to prepare the buffet and my detail is to travel with Rose and Aubrey in a taxi. Aubrey, dressed by Rose in a suit and tie, sleeps in his wheelchair. 'Lucky him,' Rose observes. 'That's what I feel like doing.' She removes a vanity mirror from her bag and complains as she tries to check her make-up: 'This party could have been much smaller and cheaper if we'd had it at home.' I glimpse my own face in the driver's mirror, the discolouring under both eyes. The motion of the taxi makes it difficult for Rose to hold her mirror steady and she gives up. 'I'm not complaining, but it is very inconvenient. For instance, will there be any toilets on this boat he can use?'

At Gravesend Pier I pay the taxi fare and wheel Aubrey out backwards on to the jetty. A uniform sheet of grey cloud covers the sky and the air is humid. He is still asleep as we get him stowed into the lower deck where the tables are swollen with the buffet food. Two bar staff uncork bottles of wine behind the counter. Lily is looking lovely in a floral dress and with her hair pinned up. She turns and gives me a wide smile before she remembers I'm on probation in her book and closes down the goodwill. Rebecca lays napkins and cutlery at regular intervals on the tables, her thin and sinewy arms in a sleeveless dress. Flora and Eliot are here too, lighting the candles under Julia's supervision and fighting over their quota. Flora drops a lighted match on the floor as it burns too close to her fingers.

Eliot clocks me at the companionway. 'Tell her, Dad! She's going to set the boat alight.' But I don't know how to tell her. Flora runs across the deck and clings to me, saying that she's nervous. We almost had to change this venue because of her water phobia until Lily persuaded her that with me on board, the pilot, it would be safer than houses. I wouldn't let it sink. She only really took the bait when she was promised a new red dress, which she now wears. Eliot is stuffed into a starched shirt and chinos and runs past me, up the companionway.

I follow Eliot up to the top deck that has been stripped down for dancing and where a four-piece covers band from Tilbury is setting up their equipment: a bass saxophone, two guitars and drum kit, two Orange amplifiers and speakers, microphones on stands, an AC/DC transformer. Lily booked the band to play a range of songs covering all forty years of her parents' married life. Yet none of the musicians looks over thirty. Eliot drifts over to the window and within seconds is in deep meditation upon the surface of the water.

The guests pour in: distant family, friends of family, Aubrey's old colleagues in the Customs and Excise. Rose breaks into tears each time she receives their gifts – a silver tea tray, cut-glass fruit bowl, porcelain vase, silk tablecloth. 'Oh you shouldn't have done this,' she says to one and all.

Lily stands above Rose in her chair, with her hands on her mother's shoulders, and laughs. 'Just like a new wedding, isn't it?' Aubrey gets poked in the ribs by Rose, who wants him awake and to shake hands with the men. His forehead is already smeared in various coloured lipsticks. I meet members of Lily's distant family for the first time; like Aubrey's two sisters who long ago married a Welshman and a Scotsman, and have travelled all this way from the Celtic fringes with their children and grandchildren – who clearly don't get on so well. Conversations about football rivalries go in different directions. They mock each other's accents. When my brother-in-law Colin appears, Rebecca tells him *sotto voce* about this rivalry that threatens to sink the party, and he in turn explains how the Scots have never forgiven the Welsh for joining the English invading armies. 'They're only kids, Colin. They wouldn't know anything about that.' But he persists with his idea by suggesting this ancient antagonism entered the genes at some point.

Guests rock the boat and lower it deeper into the water. Two of Lily's colleagues from Bliss materialise and are so self-consciously feminine they put their husbands on edge. The love business is a funny business and these women do not stop laughing. Lily is laughing herself as she asks me to chaperone the husbands. I lead them to the bar and relay orders for beer to the bar staff. They entangle me in a back-slapping conversation about what it's like to be married to madams. On the jetty the mate is about to cast off. I am about to take offence with these two jokers for calling my wife a brothel keeper, but a sound of jangling tin, like a jailer's keys, distracts me. Then I witness Celestine descend the companionway steps, chains bunched on her wrists and around her neck. Violet sequins sparkle on the bodice of her tight black chiffon dress. Her dress is cut low and reveals a lot of dry cleavage

Who invited her? Once again it's impossible not to think of Lily and Celestine combining forces to punish me.

She has made it on board with seconds to spare. My thoughts are already bloody before the vessel sheers into the stream to begin our journey into darkness. We have it booked for two hours up and two hours down. No one gets off until midnight.

As she approaches me I bark at her, 'Who invited you? Every time I step on board a boat you seem to be behind me.'

'What happened to your face, walk into a door?' She grins, waiting for my retort. 'Come on then, introduce me to some of these people.'

I am mechanically obeying her command when I realise I don't know the names of Lily's colleagues' husbands. They introduce themselves but even then their names go straight through me. Celestine dismisses them anyway. Her attention has already moved on. She asks to be introduced to the ruby anniversary couple.

'All right?' Celestine says to Rose, looking down upon her head.

'Yes, I'm all right . . .' Rose looks at me for an explanation.

'This is Celestine.'

I watch Rose calculating, but she restrains herself. 'I hope you enjoy the party,' she says.

'I intend to, so long as Ray here doesn't throw me overboard.'

'Why would he do that?'

'Oh, Ray has many reasons for doing all sorts of things. International man of mystery is our Ray.' She wanders away from us through the guests to the bar.

'So that's the infamous cousin, is it?' Rose asks. 'I must say she lives up to her reputation.'

I begin to count the minutes, watching Celestine raiding the free bar, snatching mini-quiches, sausage rolls and a vol-au-vent before anyone else has started. She engages with the warring cousins from Wales and Scotland and I hear her advice drift over to me on how to settle their Celtic differences: 'Feck off to Ireland.'

When the band begins to play she follows its lure to the top deck. Joining her is irresistible, in order to protect the young children running around in circles. From there I can see the skipper and his mate encased in the wheelhouse. I understand what they're doing, if nothing else. Jerry appears at my side and asks, 'How's it feel, Ray, not driving the ship?' The first thing he's said to me for days.

Keen to find my children, I abandon Jerry and go below where my little girl is sitting on her mother's lap. Flora catches my eye and grows very serious.

Then: 'The name's Bond,' she jests, raising one eyebrow. '*James* Bond.'

Because I don't laugh her expression quickly grows insecure as she taps into the murky sources of her dad's anxiety.

'Where's Eliot?' I ask Lily.

'What's the matter with you, Ray? Up and down between the floors like a fireman on a pole.'

'Did you invite Celestine?'

'She's here?'

'Did you invite her?'

'No, of course not. Why would I do that? I hardly know her.'

'You invited Miles to your seminar and you hardly knew him.'

'Calm down, Ray. What's the matter with you?'

'How did she even know about this party?'

Lily's eyes narrow. 'Maybe I talked to her about it, I can't remember. Sorry. But I wouldn't have invited her without asking you. And I certainly wouldn't have wanted her to come after the way you two have been behaving. But since she's here now I suggest you let it drop. One more won't sink us.'

'I'm going to look for Eliot.'

But I can't find him. How big can a river launch be? With fifty passengers we ride low in the water. The surface is just an arm's length away through the open porthole windows. I am still bothered by the memory of Eliot on the deck of the tug with his hand caught between the towrope and gunwale. When I do locate him, in the heads, he tells me as he shakes himself off at the urinal how Celestine swears. 'She called that boy from Scotland a fucking prick.'

'Keep away from her, do you hear?' My voice alarms him. 'Stay where I can see you.'

Upstairs Celestine has coerced Colin into dancing. Jerry is their sole witness. 'She's a right little minx, your cousin.'

Rebecca appears and overhears this. 'She'd better stop pawing my old man or she'll be a dead minx. Any more like her in your family, Ray? One look at her and I begin to understand why you come with no relatives. I mean, look at that dress. She's coming apart at the seams.'

'Who's coming apart at the seams?' Eliot materialises. He looks at my face, the rectitude. 'You said to stay where you can see me.'

'What do you think of your new cousin, Eliot?' Jerry asks.

'She gave me a penknife.'

'She did what?'

He thrusts his hand into his trouser pocket and produces the gift. I snatch it out of his hand and he begins to brood, sensing his possession slipping permanently from his grasp. I press a chrome button on the black handle and the blade flicks out of the side.

'Oh my God,' says Rebecca.

'You can't have this, Eliot.'

'Why not?'

'It's illegal.' I close the blade and put the knife into my pocket. 'When did she give it to you?'

'Just now.'

Celestine waltzes with Colin on the dance floor as the band plays 'I Saw Her Standing There'. Rebecca looks winded as she observes Celestine lock her hand on to her husband's backside. Jerry is saying something completely unrelated, adding to my tension when I try to follow it. 'I mean, is this fair? Dragging us off to Venice and Paris and Florence, around museums and art galleries, demanding the kids appreciate the Botticellis, who've got their heads down a drain hole after they saw a rat run into it. It's always so bloody hot when we go. Forty degrees in the shade and thirty mosquito bites a night. Everyone gets sick except Julia. Nothing touches her. And then she brings back all these blue and yellow plates and won't let us eat off them, hangs them on the wall. Next year we're going to Dorset, I'm telling you.'

The band finishes and Celestine swaps Colin for me. At the changeover Colin glances at me, then takes a longer second look at my bruised cheekbones and black eye. He whistles and says to Celestine, 'I ought to see the other guy, right?'

The music starts up again and I hardly move. But I do maintain an iron grip round her back. She sees Lily appear, and as she passes, shouts loud enough for her to hear, 'Christ, Ray! You trying to dance with me, or fuck me?' Buildings sigh as they slide out of view. The river slaps the hull in the growing darkness. Fairy lights are switched on along the edges of the deck and give the lie to this event. More people come upstairs to the top deck, watching us, the only dancers. Celestine whispers in my ear, 'Looks like we're the entertainment tonight.'

I feel a chronic fatigue, the years of duplicity suddenly catching up with me. 'Why can't you leave us alone?'

'You can't sack a sister, Ray. Divorce a wife, but you can never get rid of me.'

'Don't bet on that.'

She steps back but maintains contact through the hands. 'You want me to tell these good people what you just said?' Then she storms off the dance floor.

Lily fills her vacant spot. But I soon leave her, open-mouthed, to join Celestine below and continue our conversation at the buffet table. 'What more do you want?' I ask. 'My blood?'

'What I want is a family like yours. I want to come home after a good day at work with money in my pocket and eat a proper dinner together, not some crap out of a tin on my own every night.' She runs a finger around the edge of a plate, driving the remains of hollandaise sauce into a corner.

Members of the party briefly come back into focus. They've been absent in my mind's eye for a while, but now the floor fills up with them. On Aubrey's lap Rose balances the photograph album Colin and Rebecca have put together and flicks through the pages. But Aubrey isn't responding as hoped to forty years of photos. 'Come on, love,' she says. 'Looking at photos is good for the digestion.'

Colin and Jerry, Rebecca and Julia come down from

the upper deck where the band has been silenced. Colin claps his hands slowly and quietens the gathering. Lily watches me like a hawk as she begins her tribute.

'I've been elected to say a few words of appreciation. I want us to raise a glass in a minute to Rose and Aubrey, but before we do I just want to say a few things. We are all here to celebrate love. The love between husband and wife and what they created out of that love . . . children, grandchildren and good friends. I want to say, for so many of us Rose and Aubrey have been role models. Forty years together is an unbreakable bond, welded by compassion, respect and companionship. It started off as romance and grew into something profound and inspiring. Rose and Aubrey, I salute you. You are the stars that light up our lives.'

Celestine leans into me. 'Ain't that sweet. Pity it's all a lie.'

'What business is it of yours whether it's a lie?'

'It *is* my business. This is my chance to do something good. I can see a purpose at last.'

'What purpose?'

'To clear your conscience.'

'Clear *my* conscience?'

'. . . Let us raise our glasses to Rose and Aubrey.'

'I want to establish a true marriage for you, Mark. I want everything for the best, for you and Lily.'

'You don't know the difference between ideals and lies.'

'I'm going to exalt you.' She swings two empty wine goblets off the table, clips them together and draws everyone's attention on to us.

Here comes the bitterest moment of my life.

'I want to make a speech too,' she says. 'As the outsider, the rebel in this family, I got a few things I want to say about love. I don't know Rose or Aubrey but I appreciate you've done something right in your life just seeing all these people come together and live it up. But what I want to say is some people go down when life keeps throwing shit their way and never come back up again. While there are others who float to the surface no matter how deep the shit is. I'm one of those who don't come back up, I guess. Sorry I didn't bring a present for you, Rose and Aubrey. But I brought something else instead, something for you all.' She turns to me and says clear and loud, 'You want to tell them or shall I?'

I turn the flick-knife around in my pocket, my palm sweating on the grip. 'What she wants to tell you, for her own poisonous reasons is, she and I did something when we were children which I've never disclosed to this family. But it can wait until tomorrow. Tonight is Rose and Aubrey's night.'

'No! Say it now, or I will,' Celestine shouts me down.

Flora and Eliot's faces are hollowed out by candlelight. I see Lily put her arms round both of them, protectively and possessively. I already feel the coldness of them being withdrawn from my life.

'What's going on, Ray?' Lily's voice tunnels under the roaring silence.

I seize Celestine by the arm and march her away. The guests form a parting, allowing us through to the companionway. From the upper deck I push her into the wheelhouse. She protests to the crew with a string of expletives. The skipper is an old seadog retired on to the Thames and doesn't appreciate us in his domain. He has a dangerous job to do without such interruptions.

'Get this fucking nonce off me, would you?' she says.

'This is my mother-in-law's party,' I say, 'and I want this gatecrasher off the vessel. You'll be passing East India Dock in about half a mile. Let us off there.'

'Both of you?'

'As soon as you can, please put us ashore.'

The skipper brushes against a wall near the East India Dock basin and I escort Celestine out of the wheelhouse on to the foredeck and off the vessel. Then we begin walking inland without a single backward glance at the blazing eyes of my family.

24

After a short while we find ourselves on the towpath of the River Lea. The old industries along the way look tired and wan from breathing in their own smoke for so long. I walk a step or two behind her, to think straight. I have a navigation plan even if she doesn't. We head west along Limehouse Cut and leave the water for good on Bow Common Lane in the direction of Globe Town. The school we pass is my old one, outside of which I first met Celestine. It's now a carapace of broken glass in a windswept field, and that's all I want to see, all I want to remember. We duck under washing lines and telecommunication cables. The scent of the night combines bleach with caramel. The heat is sharp and the street lights pointed as we journey into an African village displaced to Bow Common, where turbaned women carry buckets on their heads, children on their backs and scrawny live chickens by the neck. It is said that when the assassin journeys to the killing he clings to the scenery along the way, and the world out here is a harsh space, its horizon buckled as though by an earthquake – all pitted hollows and trembling rock under a fire-yellow sky.

I am going to kill her this time, at the site of my original crime. In the abandoned grounds of the social club where we played and where I killed among the blackberry bushes, I'm going to lay this terror sister in the ground. This thing must die tonight. I'll fold her deep into the soil. And bury the past that has cast a dark cloud over my life.

Getting fresher in my mind as we near the location is that memory of Celestine, aged twelve, sitting on the roof of the corrugated iron lock-up garage in the club grounds, her legs dangling over the side and drinking Fanta. She was there as I arrived, watching like a bird of prey. She saw me use the matches and then the fire going out of control. When I ran away, she stayed on the garage roof to watch.

I blurt it out. 'You stayed to watch her die.'

Celestine turns her head sideways to catch my eye. 'Run that by me again?'

'You stayed to watch her die. You didn't try to save her.'

'Oh. That old chestnut.'

I alter course by a couple of degrees to help me think from a fresher angle. I was caught after my first killing because I needed to be. Killing was my act of emotional breakdown. I do not feel any emotional breakdown now. I can see the three stages of killing ahead of me as clearly as a riverbed on a chart. If I stay clear-headed, before, during and after, I'll never be detected. Scene-of-crime police look for evidence left behind from the moment, the ten seconds when a killer loses his nerve or reason. When you lose nerve or reason, you scatter your DNA like chickenfeed.

Twenty-six years ago my killing raised a hue and cry across the land. But who will shout this time? Who will miss Celestine? Who will care when she fails to turn up for work in the asylum of the gamblers? It won't distress the towpath homosexuals not to have her shoot them with an air rifle. She'll never again disrupt the domestic routine in my house.

The other thing that makes me feel I'm going to manage it right is the absence of fear. I am not at all afraid of what I am about to do. My children can sleep soundly in their beds. Lily will sleep soundly in hers. I may even get to lie next to her, albeit awake. Even if I am apprehended and my wife gets to know what I once was (and am about to become again) she and my children will be able to put this episode behind them in due course. When that day comes, these past twelve years will be seen as an aberration. After all, what is twelve years when you can live for a hundred?

About a mile from the site, Celestine picks up the scent of my intentions. 'What are we going here for?'

'I want to see the club.'

'Well I don't,' she says, taking back control. My dominance drains away quickly.

I struggle to say, 'You're coming with me.'

'Since when did you become the boss?'

'I was the boss the night Miles disappeared.'

'You said you never did anything to Miles.'

'I didn't. But he's dead and so will you be if you don't do as you're told. As you've reminded me, I've had the practice. I've got the experience.'

'You think that frightens me, Ray? What is it you want to see anyway?'

'I want to see where we did it.'

'Where *you* did it.'

I don't answer this time, and on and on we go, beating against the wind, until finally we arrive. Or do we? I know this is the right place by virtue of our bearings, with the Royal London Hospital at 275 degrees. But where are the woods? Where are the ruined tennis courts, the asphalt slopes, blackberry bushes, bog, lock-ups, trench, the rope that swings across it, the little pond, dens, coves, caverns and hideouts in the treetops? Where are the *trees*?

I'm thunderstruck. All has been covered by a housing estate. The property developers have got in here and turned it around. Kings like my father have bricked over my memory. They have turned my former adventure playground into a mock-Georgian housing estate. There is nothing left of the wilds where my sister took her final walk of her life, where my future was set.

I can't take Celestine out now, nor take the foul seconds back. Without its location I cannot see the past. It won't work without one. So she escapes my wrath again.

'Why are you looking at me like that?' she demands to know. 'You're trembling, Ray, like a dog with the flu. What is it, a spasm?'

'Did you know about this?' I ask.

'About what?'

'Did you know they built houses here, over where I killed . . .'

'What did you expect, a blue plaque?'

'I expected to see the bushes and the trees, the lock-up garages.'

'Nothing stays the same, Ray. Now let's fuck off. I've had enough of this day. I want to sleep it off and start again tomorrow.'

With killing still on my mind like unrequited desire, I walk away from my childhood further into the looming night.

25

It takes a little under three hours by train to reach the seaside town of Oystermouth, where Tom Reeves spent his happy childhood and I'd spent mine by wishful thinking. Three hours is not so long, yet it feels like the other side of the world we're travelling to. I worry that the map in my head won't tally with the real place. I don't know what we'll do when we get there, having planned no further than our arrival. The circumstance of our exodus from London hangs over me. We leave a scorched earth in our wake. Flora and Eliot should be in school and I should be running up-river on the Thames. Neither their mother nor my towage manager is aware of our global position. This could be my final fling with them, at the end of which I can hear the howling wind.

The carriage is half-full, what an optimist in my situation might call half-empty. There are no other children on board but my own. A stuffed hold-all is wedged into the rack above our heads and on the table is a single Walkman to which the children are connected via two sets of earphones. They listen to a story tape – Jacqueline Wilson's *The Suitcase Kid* – and every few minutes burst out laughing or gasp with incredulity at the same time;

an empathy between different personalities that only a good writer can achieve.

I'm setting out to find happiness, a last-gasp happiness in a land of make-believe. I'm kidnapping my children to whom I may not have a legal right. My life has never been my own. My *sperm* is not my own. But see what it has created – two children real and true, despite the lies fed to them by their father. In their innocence they are as beautiful as they are true. Realising such beauty is the first intimation of terror.

Eliot shouts over the story tape. 'I'm hungry!'

I click off the Walkman. 'Hey!' says Flora.

'I'm going to get a sandwich from the buffet car. What kind do you want?'

'Tuna fish,' says Flora.

'Can I have a cheese sandwich?' Eliot adds.

'Sure. Stay put till I get back.' I turn their Walkman on and slide out of the seat.

The doors slide open with a hiss each time I enter a new carriage and one in three travellers stare at me. There is no shade for me to hide my face, no wall to shoulder. I catch the sound of shrill mobile phones, like migratory birds gathering in an autumnal tree. The stray, shouted and common phone refrain: 'I'm on a train!' sounds to my ears like 'Mark Swain!' and I wonder if I'll ever get to complete my journey. In the last carriage before the buffet car there are just three passengers. A boy and a girl of about eighteen sit next to one another hunched over a mobile phone, sending a text message. They giggle healthily, are rosy and bonny-faced. By their deportment they seem more like siblings than lovers; students returning home from university with a month's dirty laundry in their bags. The third passenger is a few years younger than the other two, and all alone. Something in her expression beneath the visor of her padded silver cap reminds me uncomfortably of Celestine. The difference is, this girl is black.

At the buffet counter I buy one tuna and two cheese sandwiches, two cans of Coke and a tea, which the waiter fits into a single bag with geometrical precision. I wonder for a moment about his life, where he lives and with whom. What are his secrets? Does he have one family waiting for him in Oystermouth and another at the opposite end of the track?

The teenagers are still texting on the mobile and the black girl has gone from her seat. At the end of the carriage I bump into her as she emerges from the toilet and nearly lose my purchase on my bag. I apologise. There is no response from her, just dull, cold fire in her brown eyes.

Flora and Eliot are plugged in and rocking. I remove the sandwiches from the bag, lay down napkins and open cans of soft drinks. Flora sinks her teeth into her tuna sandwich, while Eliot first removes the onion and tomato from between the slices of bread. I sip my tea but have no appetite and leave the third sandwich in its wrapper. Outside the window the country unravels at a hundred miles an hour. A flat steel-grey sky presses down upon ploughed brown earth. Crops of potatoes, cabbages, beetroot and rape have yet to break the surface. On the edge of the field is an estate of council houses, the walls scored with graffiti, and on to the soil drops a murder of crows. Surely, all these things are saying, you do not come here to live. You come here to die.

Somewhere near Bristol the train makes an unscheduled stop. I hear police-car sirens and brace myself in the seat. The right thing to do would be to forewarn the children in the time left, blurt out the truth that would alter the course of their lives for ever. But I can't bring myself to break into their cassette-story reverie. The worry burns me like a streak of lime. Then two policemen appear, running along the platform. They look into our window but don't stop. Another policeman comes, carrying a black rifle, a stun gun pointed to the ground. Yet another arrives with a German Shepherd on a leash. They all run in the same direction. Passengers in our carriage begin speculating about terrorists, enemies of the people moving among us using false identities. A middle-aged man, who has been briefing a young French au pair about his children's routines, now gets off the train. He stands on the platform and lights a cigarette. A mountainous railway guard shoulders his way through the train in the opposite direction to the police. The passing minutes accumulate.

Flora takes out her earphones. 'Why are we stopped?'

'I don't know,' I say. 'Something's happened further down the train.' Time means less to Eliot than to his older sister and he remains happily connected to the Walkman. 'I'm going to take a look,' I say to Flora. 'Stay here.'

I join the man smoking on the platform, who thinks there's been a mugging on the train. He says a knife was involved. I don't know how he knows this. But I do see the teenage boy and girl who just moments ago were texting on their mobile. They stand on the platform chaperoned by one of the policemen, their previous casualness all gone. The girl scaffolds herself inside her rigid arms. The boy's face has collapsed. By and by the black girl I recognise from her silver cap is escorted out of the train in handcuffs. A plainclothes policewoman runs her hands down the girl's body. The German Shepherd strains its leash as she checks the hems of the girl's jeans. Even the silver cap is searched and then replaced, the same rakish angle restored.

My accidental companion observes: 'How dumb can you be, to mug someone on a moving train?' He draws pensively on the cigarette, his mood softening as he exhales. 'Look at the way those police work. It's like they're *parenting* her.'

The girl is moved off, past her two victims standing with their chaperone. Their heads revolve slowly, taking one last look at their antagonist, seeking answers that are invisible to the naked eye. As she passes me I see only blunt stone. The armed policeman is last to leave the platform. He carries his rifle across a shoulder and the girl's weapon gingerly by the tip of the blade – a common vegetable knife, probably from her mum's kitchen drawer.

When the train moves on again I check my watch. We have been at this station for thirty-five minutes, which have the restorative power of a short vacation. I've been innocent of an offence nearby. Two more stops further down the line the train terminates for good and we have to complete our journey by coach, owing to maintenance operations on the track.

It is early evening as we walk away from the station through the town that *is* as Tom described – damaged beyond repair by the Luftwaffe and rebuilt by criminals. An ancient Wessex colony, former medieval frontier of fire and destruction, erstwhile smelting nexus of iron, lead, zinc, nickel, copper and magnesium.

In the heavy, weeping air, Eliot pauses on the pavement. 'Is this is where you grew up, Dad?' His voice is full of incredulity.

In the distance an edge of the crescent-shaped sea glitters like silver. 'It gets prettier the further we get out of town. The beaches you'll enjoy, I think.'

'Where are we going to stay?' Eliot is concerned still.

'We'll find a bed and breakfast.'

'I wish you could drive, Dad. It would be much easier.'

In truth I want to walk to get the measure of this town, and as we wear down shoe leather I check off the real place against the blueprint I've held in my imagination for more than fifteen years. The children are good walkers, seasoned by our own Kent marshes, and make no further complaint as the High Street becomes Wind Street and then Chapel Street. There is a sort of lull in the life of the place, between the end of a working day and the muezzin calls of the nightclub-converted chapels that I see every few hundred metres. Large glass storefronts refract the red sky across the road that shimmers like a river or a pond, and makes me feel like I'm sailing my children through town rather than walking their little feet off.

We reach the entrance to the docks and from inside I hear a familiar sound of marine engines charging up ships' batteries. Tankers setting keel for open sea are oracles of light playing upon the oily water. We are on several borders at once, between heavy industry to the east – gasworks, oil refinery – and the golden beaches to the west; between night and day; between good and evil. I find the Regency Port Authority, Customs House and Chamber of Commerce in the vicinity where a future probation officer attended a nursery beneath a top-floor brothel.

A footbridge takes us across a sluggish river. On the other side is a blue prison singing out of tune and a virginally white law court. The arched stone gateway into a well-groomed park gives me such a powerful *déjà vu* I steer the children inside. Along the winding avenue of ash trees I hear their footfalls on the soft macadam. The rustling of encroaching foliage dampens them into silence. They are walking scared, while I seek out the tranquillity in all this regimented order.

We sit on a bench, and as the light continues to fade

I put my arms around the children, pulling them closer. Eliot produces his Top Trumps and shares the pack with Flora, using my lap as the deck. But this game, which you win and lose on the basis of supercar performance statistics, fails to distract them. Still disorientated, they watch instead a platoon of park-keepers fan out of three separate doors in a green octagonal hut. Even Flora and Eliot recognise, by their stride, that they are going home, even if we cannot. Their work here is all done, their achievements displayed in the flowerbeds bordered with chain loops, in grass verges edged with a spirit level, in the straitjackets that constrain the sycamore saplings and in the stream swept clean of algae that runs silently into a glistening pond. A bowling green with a military haircut seems incongruously lush against the dead white lawns dried by weeks of unconscionable heat.

The humidity is ominous as a plague even at this time of evening as I make a move. Walking back the way we came, the children are stunned into an even deeper silence by the vague outlines of trees bordering the undulated path, by blue hydrangea-covered walls and by the eyes of nocturnal animals staring at us from down by the pond. The little wind there is racks the foliage and makes a sound of water running on corrugated tin.

We follow the road west between school playing fields and golf links, with sand dunes opposite. A disused railway line runs alongside the dark pulsating sea. Telegraph wires cut the sky into shreds. Beyond the Territorial Army hall is Tom's old school, Emanuel. The buildings scattered around a grass arena fill me with such deep longing, I ignore my children's need to be settled somewhere for the night and steer them into the grounds. But the school has been abandoned and left to rot. All that remains of this Christian school, that took the children of missionaries as boarders, are three grey, pebbledashed schoolhouses called Bethel, Sharon and Galilee. Pillars crumble with age, windows are broken, the lawns are waist deep and weeds grow up the sides of walls. The science laboratory I locate in a single-storey prefab building. Putting my eyes to a window I can just make out the shape of maple worktops with their sinks and taps and Bunsen burner gas fittings. A presence of the chemistry teacher, that sexual predator who kissed the sixth-form girl in his car, moves between the benches in a white coat.

I can't stop myself from saying, 'This is the old science lab. In the summer term, kids raced out of here at four with hands burning from chemicals and plunged them into the sea.' They display little interest, looking through the dusty panes into nothing with sorrowful, bleary eyes. 'We'll be at the sea tomorrow. Now let's find an inn for us to stay.'

It's another epoch before we find such a place – the Seaview guest-house in a terrace along the front. The landlady has a vacancy in a 'family room' with one double bed and a single. Decorated with flock wallpaper that curls at the cornices, the room feels ghosted by a thousand former guests. A smell of mothballs clings to the air. Net curtains lift in the breeze over the open window. As I rifle through our bag, I realise I've forgotten to pack toothbrushes and toothpaste and pyjamas for the children in my rush to be away. Too tired to complain, they take off their clothes and go to bed in their underwear. They fall asleep instantly in the double bed.

I plug my mobile phone into the electricity supply and lie on the single bed. The phone, which has been off all day, suddenly jams with voicemail and text messages from their mother. I can't afford to know what they say and instead listen to the kids sighing in their sleep, to the starched duvet cover rustling in the dark. Eliot kicks his leg free, which lands across Flora's belly. She moans, turns to face the wall. The same question keeps droning in my head. What do I hope to find beside the sea, the closest you can get to another world?

Beyond the window, stars fall out of the sky. Everything out there is in eternal conference. The past, present and future coexist simultaneously. I seem to have reached a point where my personal time is going round and round on a loop. There can be no new surprises, no new experience for me. My wristwatch synchronises with the dead seconds. The true realisation I've been fighting for so long is I belong alone in the world. My children are simply visiting me. Plagued by this thought, even they seem to vanish into the night. I can no longer hear them sleep. They do not move in their bed, become like dishes in a rack, or friezes on the wall of a prehistoric cave.

Will this hot summer night never end? I grow listless upon the bed. My head pounds and my mouth is dry. I close my eyes and think of winter but my imagination fails me. I open my eyes and the furnishings shift, move and multiply. The room begets new rooms to resemble a doll's house, with my children asleep in the nursery.

The children wake me with the sound of the television. Flora is searching the channels for cartoons, but settles on the news. Eliot protests. I don't know why she wants to watch the news either. Maybe the news from elsewhere takes her mind off where she is. The American President is saying something outside his Texas ranch about supporting Israel in the road map for peace. They show pictures of Jewish settlements in the West Bank.

'This is boring,' Eliot says and lunges for the remote control.

Flora maintains her possession of the control and turns

to me as I'm heading for the open bathroom door. 'Does America support Israel building houses in Palestine because that's what they did to the Red Indians' land?'

I stop at the bathroom door and concede she's made a viable connection, recalling the President once saying, apropos the hunt for Osama Bin Laden, 'Bring him in dead or alive, like those old posters out West.'

Flora continues, 'They put the Apaches and the Sioux in reservations, didn't they, like the Israelis are doing to the Palestinians?'

'They stole land from them, yes. You're on to something. Clever girl.' I look at my watch. 'For seven in the morning.'

I complete my mission to the bathroom. Returning a few minutes later I find Eliot has given up his attempts to change the channel, beaten less by Flora than his own fierce appetite. He flops back on the bed and holds his stomach. I do not care to stop here for breakfast, want to keep moving, so help Eliot into his clothes while Flora dresses herself with her customary care, slipping on a Gap shirt and flared jeans. They use the bathroom in turn and we check out by eight.

Further down the same street we find a café open. Crushed down one side of a booth the kids eat strawberry and chocolate sundaes. Drinking weak, milky coffee I sit opposite and watch them. Flora compares the taste to Häagen-Dazs and Eliot thinks it's the best ice cream he's ever had. 'That's because you've never been allowed ice cream for breakfast before,' Flora suggests.

'This is like a holiday, when all the usual rules get broken,' I say. 'We'll have a proper lunch.'

Flora asks: 'Dad, why have you and Mum had a row?'

'Not exactly a row.' It is more serious than that.

'I don't mind if you did. Eliot and me are always rowing.'

'Mum said you ruined Grandma's anniversary,' says Eliot. I can tell it still shocks him, how I left the party with Celestine, alighting on to a jetty on the north shore. 'It was horrible when you left. I thought you were never coming back.'

'It was worse than horrible,' Flora adds. 'I thought my life had come to an end. Why did you leave? Why did she say those things about you?'

I don't know how much revelation they can take. But they're going to be told sooner or later by Lily, who will now be in conference with members of her family. Maybe she's summoned Celestine to the house to give an account of herself. My half-sister might be having her full hour in the spotlight finally, clearing *my* conscience.

If they are going to be told, let it be me who makes the first mark. Such an opportunity may never come round again. 'Celestine isn't my cousin,' I say. 'She's my half-sister.' Difficult expressions lock on to their faces. 'Same father, different mother.'

'Why did you say she was your cousin?'

'Because when she and I were your age we did something terrible together.'

'Did you steal something from a shop?' asks Eliot.

'It's much worse than that.'

Flora glances quickly at Eliot – if seeking a moment's solidarity against me, I cannot tell. But she knows my crime is serious without knowing *how* serious. Something is making more sense to her than to Eliot, who is two years younger. I've also talked to her more than to Eliot.

The café is deserted at this time in the morning and the young servers are yawning behind the counter. Our little drama in the corner goes unnoticed.

My desire to clear the air grows stronger with every passing second.

And because it feels good, it must be moral.

I begin again: 'I've tried all my life to make up for it . . . by loving you both and your mum.' Their silence thickens when I mention their mother. They don't know if that subject is taboo or not. 'I don't know if your mum's ever going to forgive me for something I did before we met, before you were born.'

Eliot tries to assimilate this revelation that I was once a bad boy. But I'm not convinced he really wants to know the details and go no further with this. I already feel the heat of hell on my face. I'm not so sure now if this is moral.

'I'll tell you another day,' I say.

But Flora is not Eliot. 'Tell us now,' she insists. 'Did you go to prison?'

Our eyes lock over the surface of the table. Everything in the café evaporates for this moment. I catch Eliot's expression as it changes down. I can see in his eyes, machinery overheating trying to cope with the load. Nothing in his short life has prepared him for this.

'I've been punished as was proper. I don't forget what I did.' I leave it there, don't tell them any more. How can I? How can I explain that their childhood has served to remind me every day of the girl I killed, whose birthdays I mark in a private seance? Flora even looks like Olivia, with the same wavy blonde hair. Or how to explain the way I watch girls of the same age as my sister when she died – in the streets, supermarkets, playgrounds. It is a condition of my character now, this deep hunger that can never be satiated. I see eight-year-olds with their mothers and imagine Olivia in both hosts, as child and as the mother she might have become. How would they understand the years that have passed so slowly in my life, that I stole from her? 'So,' I try to sound refreshed. 'That's all you need to know. And that I've tried to be the best father I can be.' I begin to smile but kill it, in case they regard me as being carefree.

Eliot says: 'And Mummy is the best mummy in the world.'

'And Mummy is, of course.' Life in the café switches back with a hiss of steam from the coffee machine.

From a chemist near the square I buy three toothbrushes and toothpaste before finding a bus whose destination chimes with one of my borrowed memories. We ride in the top front seat and twenty minutes later land at a beach. With the hold-all slung over my shoulder, I go down to the sand with a child's hand in each of mine. To any observer we may look like a happy family, rather than a father hanging on to his children by his fingertips. What I *don't* feel in this Neverland is my old fear of someone approaching to ask me to help them remember where they've seen me before. A child actor . . . An old school friend . . . The slackening of that terror allows me to promenade the children gaily along the beach. A crescent of green beach huts facing the sea is fronted by manicured lawns and palm trees. This is order on the ground. I've never seen a place so benign. We've hit it at the right time too, in summer on a school day, the sort of day when truant boys are playing in the surf when they should be in a science lesson. The beach is cut in two sections by a large rock where boys are leaping off into the sea, as they have done for all time. Also on the sand is a clapboard café called The Surfside where the kid called Janway Davis once smuggled out money from the till inside ice-cream cornets. I notch that up for a lunch venue before leaving it to our stern.

Where the huts end the cliffs begin. It is wilder here, with ferns and thorn bushes hanging over the footpath. We walk before the wind with the sea to port, and at the headland watch the swell sweeping round the point. These swells with hard-muscled backs swing into the bay from one end to the other. I am a river man out of my depth, but so excited I request to them that my ashes be scattered on this headland overlooking the bay.

They both protest. Eliot in particular seems worried that I'm going to die at all. Not now, he's implying, not when Mum's not here at least. I have not talked to Lily for twenty-four hours, the longest silence we've ever sustained.

We sit on the white grass. Flora makes daisy chains while Eliot prises stones out of the ground to throw into the sea. Both are slightly perturbed by the moaning of air forced by the swell through a blowhole in the rocks. Nothing could be simpler than this, inhaling ozone rising off the sea, and I want the children to feel my pleasure. If I really had grown up here the sea would run in my veins, whatever my final destination on the earth.

They seem to take pleasure from wasting time. Wasting time in such a spot is consuming time well, as healthy as meditation.

Or are they simply taking stock?

They *are* unusually pensive. I can hardly expect anything else. Maybe time is rushing through their heads after all, as they consider an uncertain future. It begins to worry me, and I start to crave their conversation as a vital sign. I point to the flashes in the sea where guillemots have just dived, to sails on the horizon and to the sun breaking through cloud to shine like a torch upon the water. All this does is create minimal sounds and gestures back.

What they really want to do, I discover, is eat, and within thirty minutes we are back on the beach, sitting around an oval plastic table on the patio of The Surfside, gorging on fried egg, beans and chips and drinking Coca-Cola. It's a number one hit in a number one venue with a view of the sea and the day begins to look like a winner.

'What's four apples add seven apples, Eliot?' Flora asks.

He counts on his fingers. 'Eleven apples.'

'What's seven carrots and eleven carrots?'

'We haven't done carrots in school yet.'

With her face lowered Flora shakes her head. I'm so pleased they're bickering again, just hours after I've confessed to a major crime, just as I'm pleased to hear Flora complain that she has to wear a frightening costume for a forthcoming dance performance. Maybe I am winning in this gorgeous place.

'How is it frightening?'

'Because it's got a sequin top and trousers that *have no flare*! And a green stripe.'

'If you dance well,' I advise, 'no one will notice the costume.'

There are two young men at the table next to us smoking cigarettes, evoking an unpleasant memory of two different men smoking in an Italian restaurant. As her mother would, Flora is disapproving of their smoke that drifts our way and reads the health warning off their packet of Camels: *Smoking can harm the unborn child*.

'Esther in my class said that smoking when pregnant is good for you because smoking makes the baby small and easier to get out.'

Eliot chips in: 'My friend Charlie goes on Instant Messenger with people he doesn't know.'

'That can't be Instant Messenger,' says Flora, 'that's a chat room.'

'Yeah, well a chat room then. You know what one of them said? He sneezed when he was about to kiss a girl.'

'When are we going home, Dad?'

'I don't know.'

'Then where are we going to stay tonight?'

'In the next bay over, in Hareslade.'

When they finish lunch and drain their cups we walk the same way as before, with the wind to our tail, up to the slick headland that affords the grandstand view of the swell. Rather than linger in the same spot we continue around the cliffs to where in faith I believe we'll find Hareslade a few miles away. The land becomes wild and the path narrow, forcing us into single file. I watch the children go ahead of me, and only when I look back do I realise we've been walking over a hollow cliff for the last two hundred metres; the path a fragile lip over thin air. This is dangerous stuff, but it's the bees that scare Flora, who runs away down the path.

The tide is receding now. Sticking out of the sand below are the wooden skeletal remains of an eighteenth-century shipwreck. Tom Reeves told me the story of this ship and I pass it on to the children – how she was bound from South America, carrying the dowry of a Spanish princess who was to marry an English nobleman. The ship was lured on to these rocks by locals showing her a false beacon, and then was plundered of its cargo of coins. There are still silver dollars under the sand, and about two hundred elephant tusks.

What we encounter around the next bend comes without prior warning, as the wind is blowing from behind. The cliffs are on fire. Oxygen-gorging flames switch and snake as they climb the gradient, consuming everything in their path – gorse, heather, white bladder campion and thrift. I can feel the heat on my face from half a mile away. Smoke rises into the sky and ashes drift out wide on to the sea. We meet our first strangers on the path, moving away from the fire and advising us to turn round. One is full of bitter accusations about youths starting the fire. The other suggests it's a controlled fire set by the local council. But how can this be controlled? Within half an hour of our watching, the fire moves over the top of the next headland, leaving behind winking embers. Flora grabs my shirt-tail as three horses run along the spine of the headland with their manes on fire.

I don't want to turn back, like I don't want to return to the past. I want to go on, make it to Hareslade. Since the tide is outgoing, I decide to use the strip of drenched sand and begin to look for ways down the cliff. 'You hold on to one another.' I start to prepare the kids. 'Eliot, you hold on to me.'

The going is steep, and we stumble and slide on the loose scree, but make a ledge just clear of spindrift. In its ghostly spiralling atmosphere Flora whimpers. But going back up now would be harder than continuing and I coax her to keep up the good work. We scramble some nesting gulls out of the fissures and they flock around our heads, counter-attacking with a flurry of wings. Flora's whimpering develops into full-throated sobs until we finally reach the safety of the sand. I kneel in the wet sand to comfort her, while Eliot flexes his muscles like a fledgling commando and mocks his sister for her fear.

Another mile along the edge of the sea and we come to a small cove. The cliffs each side are scarred and strewn with massive boulders, and hidden in a tangle of ivy is a brace of derelict stone cottages. The beach itself is backed by a ridge of stones: the remains of a limestone quarry. We scramble over the shingle and find a small black lake. Eliot and Flora skim stones across the still water.

The isolation provides a safe haven, yet is filled with melancholia. The caw of gulls and the hiss of the sea work on separating me from all hope. We can and should only be visitors here. Its yawning holes are too big to fill.

In the lee of the eastern cliff are a couple of furnished but empty cottages and a small guest-house where we book a room for the night. I disturb the receptionist manicuring her nails to ask if there is something we could have to eat. But she is unhelpful. I even detect a little pleasure in her voice when she says they do not provide dinner. She tells me our options are to walk two miles through the enclosed wooded valley into the village, where a small shop stays open until seven. Or wait for breakfast. The young woman is clearly unhappy we're here at all, the only guests. I lost the right to protest twenty-six years ago, and let it go.

We venture up to our room, which like last night's has a double and a single bed. We play Top Trumps for a while on the big bed and then a few rounds of hangman on the guest-house stationery. Flora neatly lays out her clothes for the morning over a chair, then undresses and lies in bed. I pick up Eliot's clothes where they fall off him and place them next to, but not on, Flora's. It is still quite early in the evening but they are tired, and sleep is all we have left to do. I regret that we brought no books. So I tell them a story of how this bay was once used by smugglers, who'd come at night with packhorses and wait for the stab of blue light to appear on the water, announcing the arrival of the Frenchmen with cargoes of brandy and hogsheads of tobacco. But I misjudge their mood entirely. Rather than entertain, the story makes them insecure.

My next is a love story, and that relaxes them. 'When you were laying out your clothes just now reminded me how your mum does it in the morning. She stands in her underwear, spreads a blouse and skirt on the bed and smoothes each one flat with the palm of her hand. Then in front of the full-length mirror she puts on the blouse, then the skirt, fastening the zip at the back. She lifts the hem and pulls the blouse down and straightens the skirt. In summer she pulls the curtains in the bedroom and the light shines through her cotton dresses. I love watching her. Like when she brushes her hair and pulls the long strands out of the bristles afterwards. She has healing hands, long and thin. After all these years she still wants to hold my hand when we walk somewhere and twists the wedding band round on my finger. You know that way she covers her mouth with her hand when she laughs too loudly? I love that too. Her laughter escapes through the gaps in her fingers and slips through me. Her gaze is a blessing. I count in her eyes. I matter to her. She's my best friend.'

My lullaby has put them to sleep. I kiss them lightly on the forehead and go downstairs, through the kitchen and into the rock garden. In my hand is my mobile phone and as I reach the beach, making a call to Lily becomes irresistible. I want to feel her voice slip through me. I tap out our number and wait. The sea is calm under the encroaching night. It shimmers and whispers. Lily answers on the second ring. The sound of her voice sheds light on to the sea, for a second.

Then: 'Where are they?'

'They're here.'

'Where's here?'

'They're asleep. They're all right.'

'How can the kids be all right?'

I wade into the sea up to my knees with the phone clamped to my ear like a shell. 'No, listen, Lily, please listen to me.'

'I'm not listening to you until you bring them home.'

I think about that, where home might be. And she really is not listening to me. 'They better be back here right NOW, or . . . Do you want me to call the police?'

Does she know? What does she know? Who told her what she knows? What I know is I cannot return with the children, and must keep moving them around this sea path to the end of the world. It will be a long journey by the time we return to the beginning. They'll be grown up, and I'll be dead. We'll all be dead.

I hang up on her, an unforgivable thing to do, unthinkable just two days ago, and make my way back to the bedroom.

In the morning I wake before the children. With the volume turned low I listen to the shipping forecast on the alarm-clock radio: winds variable 2–4 from the southwest, veering later; visibility twelve miles; mercury rising in the glass. I part the curtains and the clear blue sky confirms the forecast. Then I listen to the news for any mention of two children gone missing with their father, the former child-killer, Mark Swain. Then Eliot wakes up and looks around the room uncertain of where he is. I turn the radio off, lower my head and kiss him. His hair smells of the sea. Flora stirs but remains lying in bed with her eyes wide open.

They stay subdued as they dress, and keep their counsel while eating a full English breakfast in the hotel lounge, served by a different woman to the one who refused us a sandwich last night. I stare out of the window to formulate a plan but get nowhere at all, and end up staring at magpies in a hollow tree, shaking out their wings and diving on to the squirrels.

Within the hour we are packed up and on the cliff path. We leave behind a still smoking slab of hillside, rocks cracked and scarred by fire, grass and heather charred into stumps, and push forward. We follow the contours of the cliffs. The tide is out again and the relentless gulls are massing on the sands, cracking open the hapless shellfish proffered up by the sea.

'Are you all right, kids?' I ask after we've been walking an hour.

'Yes,' they say in unison, but their lack of dissent is uncharacteristic.

I am wondering if they've become frightened of me when I see what looks like a wooden carving of the human form at the base of the cliff, with smoke curling around one end. Screwing up my eyes I see it's a real body. What I thought was smoke is white hair moving in the wind. I order the kids to stay on the path and clamber down the steep cliff. An old woman lies motionless in a gully of trapped seawater. I'm assuming she is dead, but test for a pulse in her neck nonetheless, and a weak Morse is returned through my fingers. Don't write *me* off. My own pulse starts racing. I check for head injuries, lifting her eyelids for signs of cerebral fluid. She doesn't seem to be haemorrhaging. Her breathing is soft. Her limbs are where they should be. She's lying on her back so I can't inspect her spine.

Then I feel her hand on my arm, a probing motherly touch which makes my head swim. I look into grey eyes. 'Can you hear me?'

'Yes, I can hear you.'

'Where are you hurt?'

'My back . . . I can't move at all.' She sounds unnaturally calm, calmer than I am at least. She also seems to intuit my need for reassurance, seems to be judging whether my troubles override her own.

'How long have you been here?'

'Since yesterday afternoon.'

'Yesterday!'

'I fell off the path.' Her voice becomes shrill recalling the trauma, from remembering the difficult past.

I have nothing to give her. All I have is the mobile phone in the bag. 'I'm going back to the path. I can phone for help. Don't move till I return.'

'I'm not going anywhere.' She smiles but her eyes register the fear that I won't return.

From the path, the children's white faces peer over the edge at me. 'An old lady's hurt herself,' I say, too out of breath to elaborate. I dig into the bag for the phone. 'We're going to call for help.'

I open the phone but don't have a signal. Above me the cliff soars another hundred metres and I begin to climb until my phone records a small signal. I tap in 999, ask for the ambulance service, give our co-ordinates and impart information about the casualty. Then I return to the kids.

'Let's go and keep her company, shall we?'

I help the kids down the cliffs to where she lies. Her eyes are closed, but open as we approach. The presence of my children seems to comfort her. 'Hello,' she says and the kids say nothing.

'This is Flora and Eliot, my children.'

She inhales deeply and breathes on the name, 'Grace.'

'Did you hurt yourself?' Eliot is first to ask.

'Yes, dear.' She sounds calmer again, now we are here, as though all she was short of was company. 'How old are you?'

'I'm eight,' Eliot says.

'Ten,' Flora adds.

'Not in school today?'

I answer for them. 'We're having a few days together.'

'I have grandchildren about your age.'

I sit down on the rocks beside her and take her hand in mine. I can feel the rough skin of her palm and a worn wedding ring. Her nails are broken and caked in dried blood. Her old face is still beautiful with plenty of light left in her eyes.

'Oh, I feel so much better already, now you've come along.' Her voice trails off. She can only manage one sentence at a time before needing to take a deep breath. It's the only indication of the pain she must be suffering. 'I thought I was going to die here from boredom.' I can see her searching my face for what lies beneath.

'You may have damaged your spine.'

'I can't feel anything. Can't move at all.'

'I'm sorry I have no water to give you.'

'You are good enough, and your lovely children.' She squeezes my hand in hers. 'If I never walk again, it'll be a blow. But at least I'm seventy-one, not seventeen.'

'You might be okay.'

'Let's hope so.' She addresses the kids. 'Have you seen my little dog?'

'What kind of dog?' Flora asks.

'A little fox terrier, about as old as me.' She stares down the beach. 'He wandered off sometime in the night and hasn't come back.'

'Shall we go look for him?'

'His name is Jake and he comes when you call him.'

I tell the kids not to go too far or climb the cliffs and they wander off together along the sand, calling out the dog's name.

Out of the blue she asks, 'Are you local?'

'I used to be.'

'What school did you go to?'

Still in character, I answer, 'Emanuel.'

'Ah, Emanuel. Closed down now.' Her chest expands. 'My son and daughter both went to John Ellis School. Know anyone from there?'

'Not really, I don't think.'

'I'm only asking because I'm sure we've met before.' She pauses. 'What's your name?'

'Ray Greenland.'

Grace looks at me, then averts her face as she manages

her pain, then delivers a monologue that has to cost her dearly. 'I think I'd remember a name like that. But your face is very familiar to me. I have such a good memory for faces it's almost a disability. I've seen a face in the street and ten minutes later remember it's the waitress who was rude to me once a long time ago. I have children about your age, Ray, and I do know you, you know. Even if it might take me ten minutes before I remember from where.' Her whole torso shrinks like a balloon losing its air.

'The air ambulance should be here by then.'

'My children's names are Sarah and Vaughan. I used to call them down for dinner, "Sarah Vaughan" – like the jazz singer. That always tickled my husband. He died three years ago. We were married fifty years, a rare thing, even in my day. What about you?'

'My wife's at home.'

'Where is home for you now?'

'It's . . .' I don't know how best to describe it, or where it is. 'On the Thames.'

'Is it brackish, where you are?'

'It is, Grace.'

'You know what I like about rivers and seas? There are no borders between them, anywhere. All rivers run into the sea and all seas run into one another. Are you happy there, beside the Thames?'

'Yes. Or I was.'

'Oh dear. Has something gone wrong?'

A cloud of sea mist floats above us like a teenager's wedding veil. 'Don't worry about me, Grace. Save your strength. You're talking too much.'

'Worrying about you stops me worrying about myself. Something gives me the feeling that you and your wife are apart. Am I wrong?'

'I wish I knew.'

'Well, you have beautiful children. You should try and fix it up with your wife.'

The children are no longer in sight, but I can hear them calling Jake. 'I've known my wife for twelve years and we've been very happy. It's my life before we met that's the problem. People just have to know what you did and who you once were.'

'Everyone wants references, don't they?'

'I think it's more a case of discovering my references are forged. I got the job on false pretences.'

'I was so happy with my husband, and yet my son and daughter are both on their second marriages.' She pumps my hand inside her own. 'In constant battle in and out of the courts over their children. I don't know why that is. Can't fathom it. I've even wondered if there's something in the water supply.'

'Could be.' From the east a sound of helicopter blades chopping the air makes me feel depressed. I like talking to Grace, just like I enjoyed talking to Tom Reeves, and all too soon it's going to be over.

I look up into the sky, shielding my eyes from the sun as the helicopter appears. The children run back into view. Flora starts apologising that they haven't found Jake, but Grace can't hear. Eliot tips up his head to watch the helicopter. Its rotary blades flatten the sea and rake Flora's hair around her face. The pilot puts his bird in irons, head to the wind. Minutes later a paramedic in red overalls and helmet is winched on to the sand by cable. The paramedic is a young woman. She unclips herself and asks me for information about the state of Grace's injuries. We are all shouting. After I tell her all I know she speaks to the pilot on a short-wave radio. The cable is retracted and another paramedic, a male this time, descends to the ground with a rigid aluminium stretcher.

The helicopter gains some altitude and parks over the sea to allow the paramedics better conditions in which to stretcher up Grace. They talk to her as they secure her body with canvas belts and wooden slats. Then in one smooth action they lift her on to the stretcher. The woman speaks on the short-wave radio and seconds later the helicopter flutters down to close the gap. The stretcher is clipped on to the cable shackle by four straps. Grace lifts her face off the stretcher and beckons to me. I disengage from the kids to approach her.

'I told you I don't forget a face. But it's not your face I remember, it's your eyes.' She snatches my hand and squeezes it a little before letting me go.

I stand back as she rises off the ground. She keeps on rising into the sky until reaching the mouth of the helicopter, and is tugged into the bird. One after the other the paramedics return by the same means. With Eliot and Flora by my side I watch the bright red helicopter dip its nose and then climb into the sun whence it came.

Two hours after Grace leaves by helicopter, the kids complain about their hunger. There's nothing I can do, except keep them marching. The earth heats up as the day grows older and our path keeps vanishing into a mirage. The slick and oily surface of the sea is buckled by a ground swell. The swell marches to shore in orderly fashion, even though it comes from disorder, from some storm raging out at sea. It arrives chaste and silent but is born out of chaos. What the eye can't see is its fantastic propensity for violence.

At the next bay along I suggest a dip in the sea. We have no costumes, but the small beach looks deserted. Our underwear should suffice. As we strip off on the warm sand, Flora reminds me of how frightened she is of water. She is a non-swimmer, like my father was a non-swimmer; something I wish to rectify, but with too much haste.

Eliot rushes into the sea and the waves shiver and collapse at his feet, sucking up stones on their retreat. As we near the water's edge, Flora pulls down on my hand as though trying to anchor us in the wet sand. My idea that she should enter this volatile sea appals her. But all I want to do is demonstrate my love in a form more solid than words. I want to help conquer her fears while I am still around to do so and cajole her into the water in her underwear. Immediately the undertow tears violently at the backs of our legs. The tension in her neck and shoulders communicates down her arm and through her hand that clasps mine in a vice-like grip. I seek out Eliot and with my other hand grab hold of him. A wedge of white water canters towards us. I dive under the surface, pulling them under with me. It's very cold and ragged. Both my holds remain good in the turbulence, but when I break the surface all that is visible of Flora is her umbilical arm connected to my own. I yank her to the surface and watch her scrunched-up face for the euphoric smile, but it never comes. She has trusted me with her life. What better show of love is there than that? Another, larger wave bears down upon us. I go under as it disembowels itself upon the stony floor. But it's a force too strong, and both children's hands are ripped out of my grasp. In the pitch-darkness I have no choice but to submit to the power, the undertow, the invisible forces of nature, and I'm flipped over backwards several times. It's a fight I can win and I scramble for the surface. When I finally come up there is chaos all around, caused by the rip hitting the waves. Eliot is floundering a few metres away but Flora is nowhere to be seen. I turn in circles like a corkscrew. The sea boils around me, lustily stirring up the brown sand. I do not lose faith that I will see her again, but it is eroding fast. The sea is an inscrutable thing. I spy a flash of white cotton and Flora inside it, floating face down, prey to the rip about to spin her out to sea. I dive and swim, my arms like windmills until I crash on top of her. I get a purchase around her waist and will never let go. I see that Eliot has made it to the beach.

In the trauma of being parted from me Flora thrashed her cold and tense limbs so violently under water that she's sprained a muscle in her leg. She limps in to shore with my assistance, pummelling my back with her fist like she did that time I lost her in a department store.

The three of us sit shivering in the sand, drying slowly under the sun. Flora sits beside me but her soul is two hundred miles away. Her withdrawal of trust crucifies me. I am trying to think of what to do or say when we get an unexpected visitor in the raggedy shape of an old fox terrier.

'Jake?' Flora asks the dog who almost smiles at the sound of his name, shakes his mane and wags his stumpy tail. Either that, or he simply knows how to be the dog Flora wants him to be. 'It *is* Jake! Oh Jakey boy. Good *dog*.' Flora puts her arms around the dog's neck, her face in his face. 'Good boy!' Eliot embraces the dog around the back legs. 'Eliot! For God's sake, don't do that. He'll run away again. Good *boy*, Jake. We found you!' She loops her fingers inside his collar. 'Can we take him to Grace?'

'I don't know where she's gone, Flora.'

She holds back the tears. 'Then what can we do? We can't leave him here. We *must* take him home.'

Eliot agrees. They want to take this homeless dog home. I know what taking the dog home means to them, even if they don't, and it's such a strong conviction it has to be resolved somehow.

Jake runs off. Flora screams and jumps to her feet to give pursuit in her soggy underwear, limping as she runs. Eliot soon gets ahead of her. I bag all our clothes and follow them up the beach. The dog has run into a copse and I see the kids disappear into the foliage. I catch up with them in a grassy clearing behind the copse, where Jake is sitting on a tartan blanket between a man and woman. The woman sits up and looks curiously at our wet, semi-naked forms until I explain about the dog.

At the same time I assess her partner for risk. He has an uncanny resemblance to one of the two men in Franco's. Sweat runs off his sunburnt nose on to his neck. He keeps his waterlogged eyes upon me as she tells us about the dog appearing at their cottage door last night. 'We made the mistake of feeding him,' she says. 'And now he won't go away.' They had tried taking the dog for a long walk and hiding from him behind a tree. For fifteen minutes the dog ran up and down and finally disappeared. When they got back to their cottage, Jake was sitting on the front doorstep, waiting for them.

The dog looks very happy with his new sponsors, his hind legs on their blanket. Flora and Eliot approach him tentatively, low to the ground, and Jake plays hard to get. 'If you return him to his owner you'll be doing us a favour,' the woman says.

I think about Grace not being able to walk again, or walk the dog. Jake might be better off staying where he is. 'I'm afraid we're just passing through.'

'On holiday?'

'That's right, on holiday.' I look at the kids shrinking from cold, hunger and tiredness. 'Do you know of a guest-house near here?'

'A guest-house?' The woman's voice sounds querulous. 'There's nothing until you get to Cheriton.'

'How far is Cheriton?'

'About eight miles along the coast.'

At the sound of eight miles, the children stare up at me like beggars, like Jake. I think of Flora's limp. One mile would be too much in her present state.

'That's too far,' I sigh. 'We won't make it.'

Then the woman holds out a lifeline. 'We do B and B at the cottage. We haven't really opened up yet for the season, but we can take you, if you don't mind a bit of a mess.'

'That'll be great.'

'The house is just back there beyond the woods.'

We pull on our clothes over wet underwear as they gather their blanket and slip on sandals. Soon we are making our way in single file along a path through the woods. Jake runs ahead on point, sniffing into the undergrowth for rabbits. I am as wary of the man as he is of me. To allay this, I tell him my name, and he introduces himself as Richard and his wife as Clare. They have one son, Mathew. He gives the impression that every word he speaks costs him dearly, that he's told me too much already, so I hit upon a different subject, the bush fires on the cliffs. They still haven't been put out, he says. He worries the fires might spread to his cottage. But that is all he does say and clams up again.

Five minutes later an isolated house materialises and I see what he means, as there is no fire-break at all between the house and the surrounding trees. Nor can I see how they attract business in such a remote spot. But it's a fine establishment, with clematis growing down the whitewashed walls. It also occurs to me that no one will find us here. Perhaps that is why Richard likes it too.

When Jake tries to come indoors with us, Richard lifts him off the ground using his foot and the dog rolls off into the grass. His son is just home from school and waiting for action in the kitchen; a short, soft boy of thirteen in a crumpled white shirt and school tie noosed around his neck.

He eyes up Flora and by way of a greeting, offers her a cylindrical tin.

'Open it,' he says.

Flora prises open the lid and releases a stream of orange snakes into her face. She screams and drops the tin. Coiled at her feet are three snakes made of dyed cotton wrapped around metal springs. Not even Mathew laughs. He kneels down and methodically replaces the snakes, compressing their springs against the bottom of the tin. 'Why don't you show Eliot and Flora around?' his mother says. My children walk off forlornly with Mathew as I follow his mother in the opposite direction.

B&B is a woman's work in this household. As Richard retires to the lounge to watch TV, Clare shows me up to our room. Clare is overweight, out of breath after climbing one flight of stairs, and struggles to make an apology for the room not being en suite. She points down the hall to the bathroom.

I stare at three single beds and a wash-basin. 'I know this is probably irregular, but could I trouble you for a sandwich for the kids? I'll pay of course.'

'Oh, no worries. Would they like something more than a sandwich?'

'If that's not too much trouble.'

'No trouble at all. I'll be making Mathew his tea soon. Do they like fish fingers?'

I feel a pang of sorrow. I'm on the verge of saying: 'Flora prefers chicken nuggets,' but instead reply, 'Yes, they do.'

'And can I offer you something?'

'I'll have fish fingers as well.'

'Are you sure?'

'Yes, absolutely.'

When Clare leaves me all I can think of doing is to sit on one of the beds in the musty room. I am so clean out of ideas, reduced to begging in a stranger's home. I am saved from myself when Flora and Eliot appear.

'Mathew's mad,' Eliot begins as he bounces on one of the beds. 'He's got an air rifle.'

'He's a horrible boy,' Flora adds. 'He was going to shoot a jay.'

Says Eliot: 'It was so freaky, Dad. He opened the window to stick the gun out and the jay started making screeching noises in the tree. Then it flew at the house. Actually landed on the gutter above the window and started hissing at him.'

'The jay knew what he was going to do,' Flora concludes.

'He shot a squirrel too.' Eliot is now sitting on the bed beside me. 'He's making a trap with a spring and he's going to put the squirrel in a box, and when some-one opens the box it will jump into their face.'

'I don't like it here, Dad.'

'We have to stay one night, Flora.'

'Jake is depressed. They're feeding him pasta and bananas.'

'Are you hungry? You're going to have some fish fingers in a minute.'

'I don't like fish fingers,' she says.

'Your mum would make you eat them. We don't have much choice.'

In the event, Clare cooks enough oven-ready chips to satisfy Flora and I eat her fish fingers. I keep my eye on Mathew who is so obviously dangerous. The nerves in his face keep jumping below the surface of the skin as he thinks of fiendish plots. No wonder he likes springs under his surprises. He looks like a machine himself, waiting to be turned on. What that machine is capable of worries me. 'Mum,' he says, 'can Flora and Eliot sleep in my room tonight?'

'If they want to, dear.'

Eliot and Flora plead silently with me. 'They're tired and we have to leave early. I think they better stay in their own room tonight.'

His mouth shows impatience with me. If only he knew who he is dining with. Part of me wants to tell him this. He's a kid who needs to be scared.

'Can I have that dog to sleep in my room then?'

'Certainly not.'

I am eager to get out of this kitchen and my children away from this boy. I don't like it here either. Jake barks outside the back door in a pitiful way. Perhaps he's regretting now being so promiscuous with his affections.

I sit on the edge of the bath while the kids splash around in the water. They are subdued, and mournful about Jake's fate in this new home. 'That boy will probably shoot him. Poor Jake, I wish we could take him back to Grace.'

'I think Jake will be okay, Flora. He's being fed and that's more than he might have got.'

'Yeah, but bananas, Dad! Whoever heard of a dog eating fruit?'

'That lady will miss him,' Eliot sighs.

'Yes, she will.'

'She was nice, wasn't she.'

'I liked her.'

'And she was very brave.'

I get the kids out of the bath and take them to our room. I go to pull the curtains to create the illusion of night before the sun has gone down, and see smoke rising from the direction of the headland. The wind is driving our way. I squeeze the curtains shut and all natural light disappears from the room.

They are still pink from the hot water and their hair damp on the pillows as I read to them from a book about wrecks and maritime enigmas that I found downstairs. I settle on a chapter about ghost ships – derelict vessels that drift in and out of the world's ocean lanes, contributing hazards to navigation, ramming other ships in fog or in the dead of night before disappearing again – like the *Parr* of Nova Scotia that drifted 2700 miles across the Atlantic after being abandoned by her crew. An Elder Dempster liner sighted her off Liverpool and put out a boat to set fire to the derelict; a noble ambition that failed when the mate dropped the matches in the sea. But the oldest ghost ship still on the waters of the world, according to this book, is the *Dunmore*. Abandoned in 1908 in mid-Atlantic when her cargo of timber started to shift in a storm, she was seen recently drifting in the northern ice floes.

'I find that hard to believe,' Flora says.

'Listen to this one then, about the *Carroll A. Deering*. She drifted on to the Diamond Shoal three-quarters of a mile off Cape Hatteras . . .'

'Why are ships always "she"?' Flora interrupts.

'I don't know why they should be feminine. Anyway, all sails were set on the *Deering* and the crew all gone when she was found. Suggestions were made of a Bolshevik piracy. Maybe an oil-fired submarine chaser waylaid the crew and took them to Russia for interrogation.'

The kids develop their own theories about the *Deering*. 'Maybe they're still out there now,' Flora believes, 'in little lifeboats, eating fish.'

'Maybe they were kidnapped by Martians,' says Eliot, and seeing him yawn, I close the book.

I lie with them on the bed until they fall asleep and then pad downstairs to return the book. I sit in the lounge for a while, staring out of the window at Jake asleep on the lawn. He's trying to survive a bad day too.

Then an hour later Flora comes into the lounge, her eyes full of sleep. 'I couldn't find you,' she complains, then adds casually, 'Eliot wants you.'

Back in the bedroom Eliot is sitting up in bed. 'You remember when we went . . . we were at a place where you had to guess which key fitted a lock?'

'I think that was your school fête.'

'No, it wasn't my school fête.'

'Then Flora's school fête. You had to guess which key opened a glass box with a five-pound note inside.'

Eliot alarms me when he begins to cry. 'Oh it wasn't that. I can't remember.'

'Try again, darling. There was this lock and key . . .'

'I sat on your lap. It might have been the science museum. I sat on your lap and this box was . . . we opened it with a key and there were fish swimming around.'

'Oh yes, I remember,' I lie. 'The science museum, you're right.' It could have been the Aquarium that Eliot always refers to as the fish museum, but I am more concerned to settle him.

'Well,' Eliot says, 'I've got the same stomach ache as I had then.'

'You've got a stomach ache?'

'The same one I had in the science museum.'

I've always taken the children's physical complaints seriously. But on this occasion I don't and tell him to try to go back to sleep. After he settles I return to the lounge and turn on the TV to calm myself, and get drawn into a lurid face-off between a woman and a man who claims to be the father of her twenty-year-old daughter. The whole thing is played out in front of a studio audience and the presenter's sincerity is about as genuine as a pimp's Rolex. I listen to how these two people met when they were sixteen. Her cigarette complexion and his armful of tattoos testify to a long, abject life. 'We still drink in the same local' is the only way he can describe the quality. The daughter, whose lineage is under investigation, stands on the sidelines, wan and tearful, repeating how she loves them both and wishes they'd stop fighting over her. The mother ignores her to shout at the man: 'Where were you when she was on drugs?' He replies reflexively: 'You wouldn't let me see her since I got out of Borstal.' If he sees the girl around the estate, he says, he tells her he's her dad. And that, according to the mother, had to stop, because he wasn't. The finale, promised after the commercial break, will be the result of a DNA test. The presenter waves it at the camera in a sealed envelope.

Waiting for the DNA results, I hear footfalls overhead and then a thumping noise. I run upstairs into our room to find Eliot's bed evacuated. 'Where's he gone?'

Distractedly, Flora says, 'In the bathroom.'

In the bathroom he is sitting on the toilet and being violently sick on the floor tiles. His trajectory is alarming. He manages to say, 'I'm sorry.'

'No, I'm sorry, Eliot. You just relax.' I kneel beside the toilet and put my arm around him, possessing him. 'I've got you.'

Flora appears as I am trying to rub out the muscular tension in Eliot's belly. 'Doesn't anyone care about me in this family?'

'Oh Flora, please!'

'It's because I'm first-born, isn't it?'

He vomits again on the tiles, his whole body screwing into a tight ball. 'It's okay,' I whisper. 'It's got to come out. Good boy.' Flora storms out of the bathroom.

'I'm sorry, Daddy,' he says again.

'You've got nothing to be sorry about.' His face burns with a fever. He is pale and limp, and his naked back is covered in a film of sweat.

'It's not my house and I've made a mess on the floor.'

'That's okay, really. I'll clear it up.'

I carry him back to the bedroom and lay him on the bed, then run downstairs to the kitchen where Clare is putting family photographs into an album.

'Hello,' she says. 'You settled in all right?'

'My son has been sick. Do you have a mop or something? And a bucket for his bedside?'

'Oh dear, the poor thing.' She gets up from behind the table and from a pantry removes a mop in a bucket. 'I'll give you a bowl for his bedside.' She hands me what looks like a plastic salad bowl.

Upstairs I place the bowl beside Eliot's bed. He's already asleep, but struggling, his knees tucked into his chest, hands trembling. I tell Flora to keep an eye on him and go to clean up in the bathroom. I fill the bucket in the shower and as I am mopping up the tiles, Flora appears. 'He's being sick again.'

Eliot hangs off the side of the bed, projecting into the bowl. I don't like this at all. I sit beside him and hold his shoulders and feel him shuddering through my hands.

Another ten minutes later he is sick again. This time he screams in pain and there are streaks of blood in the bile he produces. Flora cries, for her brother this time. He has a high temperature. I stand up abruptly and go seek out Clare.

I find her in the kitchen. 'How is he?' she asks.

'I'm going to have to take him to the hospital.'

'Oh dear. I'd ask my husband to drive you but he's drunk a shedful.'

'Could I borrow his car?'

She looks uncertain. 'I suppose so. He's so out of it, I doubt he'd notice if you did.'

I get Eliot out of bed. He shivers as I dress him in his Gap jeans and t-shirt. I wrap him in a blanket. He is sick one more time before we can leave, with the same accompanying screams of pain.

I carry him outside and, as Clare holds the car door open, put him in the front seat. She is giving me directions to the hospital as Flora gets in the back. From the twilight Jake appears and jumps on her lap. 'No,' Clare says to the dog. 'Out.'

I can see the comfort he gives Flora. 'Would it be okay if the dog stayed?'

'Yes,' she says. 'Perhaps you can drop him off on the motorway.'

We close all the doors and only when I get into the driver's seat does Flora realise something. 'Dad, you can't drive . . .'

'Yes I can.'

'Since when?'

'Since a long time ago.'

It doesn't matter that she doesn't believe me. Jake getting to ride with us means far more. I drive through murky country lanes with one hand on the wheel, the other on Eliot's shoulder. I can't really call it driving. The transmission is automatic and I just steer through the lanes, taking out a lot of hedgerow with the wing mirror. 'Can you tell me where it hurts?'

'My tummy hurts and my chest.'

'How does it hurt . . . is it a sharp pain?'

'Yes.'

'I'm taking you to the doctor, okay? We've got Jake with us too. We'll be there in about fifteen minutes.'

Holding Lily in my thoughts makes it harder still to drive. This crisis needs her. Eliot needs her. Children need two voices in their lives. I am depriving them of one another. Lily will be suffering badly. I picture her sitting in the house, with Celestine maybe, listening to a blow-by-blow account of my criminal career.

The country lanes give way to a suburban swell and that's where the hospital is located, close to the park where we sat on our first night here; an eight-storey modern building overlooking the sea. I drive right up to the entrance of Accident and Emergency and stall the car. Eliot is sick again, producing a stream of yellow bile in a prolonged seizure. He cries in severe pain and when it is over, falls limply across the seats into my arms.

I carry him up the flight of stone steps into the A&E, followed by Flora, who has rigged up a leash out of her Moroccan cloth belt and leads Jake into the hospital. We sit in the waiting room, empty apart from a young woman handcuffed to a police officer. Flora stares at the steel chain linking the two and then at me, making her own private connections. She looks back at the prisoner who catches her out this time, lifts her arm theatrically and rattles the chain. Flora blanches with fear and the prisoner laughs at her. When the assessment nurse ushers us through to an examination room Flora moves so fast she and Jake slide into the automatic glass doors before they have properly opened.

Eliot is sick again as the doctor arrives. The doctor is young with dark rings under his eyes and as he holds a stethoscope to Eliot's chest, Jake begins to strain on the leash. The doctor doesn't care for the dog in here and asks Flora to take him to the waiting room. She looks at me in wide-eyed horror. I know she's thinking about the prisoner in there, but something is worrying me more and I tell her to go.

The doctor thinks it's probably gastroenteritis. I tell him that Eliot had some blood in his vomit. 'He's straining himself. It's quite normal. I can't give him anything orally for pain relief because he won't hold it down. Gastroenteritis has an active period of about eighteen hours. How long has he been sick?'

'An hour, hour and a half.'

'We can keep him in overnight.'

'I'm not going to leave him. We're all a long way from home.'

'You can stay with him too.'

'I have a daughter as well.'

'And a dog,' he smiles.

Flora, Jake and I follow a staff nurse into the children's ward. I refuse a porter's wheelchair and carry Eliot in my arms. In a small and empty room I lay him in bed and help the nurse take off his clothes that are beginning to smell, and roll the sheet over him. He moans softly, rubs his stomach, arches upright and retches. The nurse is swift in producing a syringe tray and holds it under his chin. With her other hand she smoothes down his damp hair. 'Poor little lad. We'll take good care of you.'

I have to fight against the tears. 'Can the dog stay too?' I ask the nurse. 'They're a bit inseparable.'

'A dog . . .' She frowns at Jake.

'He's lost,' Flora pleads with the nurse.

'You'll have to take him out before the consultant comes through in the morning. Or I'll be fired.'

In Eliot's room are two squat armchairs. Flora curls up in one with Jake, to whom I would now pay good wages if I knew how to explain it to him. The blinds are open and the room has a view of the sea, upon which a ferry sails with its lights blazing. Cardinal buoys wink every few seconds and a lighthouse beam swings over the black water.

I stay awake tending Eliot when he wakes every half-hour to retch. Then around 02.00 he sleeps and stays asleep. The time left before morning I spend worrying about Lily. I know I should be calling her, but don't want to be a messenger of even more bad news.

When Eliot's eyes open again in the morning something of their former brightness returns. He is limp and soft but his fever has lifted. The sheets he lies in are damp with his sweat.

He guzzles water from a paper cup as a doctor examines him. Flora has exited from the room with Jake, lingering somewhere outside in the corridor. I stare at the dandruff on the doctor's lapels as he checks Eliot through a stethoscope. He advises me that Eliot can go 'home' but should rest for twenty-four hours. Meanwhile I should feed him on thin soup and water.

I dress him in clothes that smell of the illness, since all his spare clothes are back in Clare and Richard's house, along with my mobile phone. He is unsteady on his feet as we walk, and says nothing until he sees Jake on the end of Flora's belt. 'Jake!' he cries, bending to the ground to embrace the dog.

Everyone wants to go home. It's clear as the light of day. Then it occurs to me that Grace is likely to be in this same hospital. On the ground floor I ask at reception about her, but with only a first name to go on the receptionist can't help me. I even describe the circumstances of Grace's arrival by ambulance helicopter, confident no one would forget that. But she's only been on duty since 07.00 today. Seeing the disappointment in the children's faces, she quickly realises how important this Grace is to them and picks up a phone. We hear her ask the control clerk in the porters' mess if someone answering to the name of Grace came in yesterday. Her face retains its gravity until the last second. Then, replacing the receiver gently on its cradle, she says, 'Room 307.

There's a woman in there fits the description.'

In room 307 on the third floor we find Grace in traction. She is staring up at the ceiling as we arrive. Jake also sees a familiar face and strains at the leash. Flora lets go of the belt and he scuttles down the squeaking rubber floor to leap on to Grace's bed. Both kids laugh and Grace laughs too as Jake licks her face. She turns her head on her otherwise immobile body and sees the three of us standing in the doorway to her room.

'I never thought I'd see him again,' she says. 'Or you.'

'Hello, Grace,' I say. 'How are you?'

'Fractured the base of my spine. Old Jake here's going to have to wait a long time before he gets a walk from me.' She frowns at Eliot. 'You don't look so well yourself, old chap.'

'I've been sick,' he says. 'I had to stay in hospital all night.'

'Oh, my dear. Are you any better?'

'Yes, thank you. A little.'

'And are you going home?' Grace looks at me. Flora and Eliot look at me. I look at the dog.

'Yes, we're going home,' I say. 'On the next train out.'

26

'This might have happened to you twenty-six years ago, but I've just found out. It's very fresh in my mind. I'm feeling sick just thinking of what you did, what the father of my children did. It makes my flesh crawl to think about it. Disgusts me, you touching me all these years, I can't look at you now. This name you've cursed us with, Greenland, the children's name . . . How could you have done this?'

She has overlooked that I was twelve years old at the time and speaks as though the moment of the offence was yesterday. I say, 'Would you have married me, had my children, if you'd known?'

'What's the point of asking me that? You should have told me when we met and taken your chances. It was cowardly.'

She will not call me Ray. Her face is strained and heavily taxed. We've both had a sleepless time of it, these past few days.

We are sitting at each end of the kitchen table that is stretched at full banqueting length with the two leaves pulled out. A vase of blue hyacinths between us seeps into the room a strong scent of the wild.

'What is it you want me to do?' I ask.

'Do? I'm still figuring out what you *did*.'

'Celestine is our immediate problem.'

'Celestine is *your* problem. *My* problem is how I protect the children. That's my job now.'

The kids I can see playing in the garden. They are under orders not to come indoors until called. 'What I mean is Celestine told Miles who I was, and I don't know who else. I just want you to be aware of that.'

I want her to be aware but only to a point. For instance, I don't confess to losing Miles in the river, however 'accidental' it was. It's still far more instinctual for me to keep things hidden. It's not so easy to reverse a way of life in an instant.

Lily is thinking in the opposite direction to me and demands complete transparency. Despite her repulsion she asks specifically for an account of the action from twenty-six years ago. She wants me to revisit the moment of the offence.

I'd hoped I'd never have to go there again, but can see this is the only way forward. Can the truth hurt more than the lies?

Through the window I watch Eliot receiving Flora into his tree den with unusual graciousness. They seem to know that this conflict between their parents is so serious, it inhibits them from creating one of their own. Cowering in the tree den, in the habitat of the birds, they wait for the storm to pass, unaware this is an eternal storm. What Lily wants from me now I have only told Tom Reeves, and my head spins and my throat contracts. Thresholds of silence lie stretched between each of my heartbeats. I draw a few breaths of fresh air from the open window and take a fix on my beautiful children.

* * *

And I'm saying to Olivia, You want to see a secret place? Where there's elves and stuff. I hook her hand in mine and pull her up this asphalt slope. We climb through a hole in the blackberry bushes and she's nervous of getting pricked by the brambles. I say, If you hold my hand I'll lead you through. The thorns are pricking her legs, making her scream. I'm telling her to hush up, *Shhh*. Look, there's wild rhubarb and I start smashing the rhubarb, you know, with a stick. Celestine is sitting on the tin roof of the garage. The whole structure wobbles from her excitement, agitation. Stashed inside a hold-all in the bushes is the woollen sweater with the hood, the red one with a hood. I think it was red, the one with the fur collar and cuffs wet with lighter fuel, four cans of lighter fuel, and I say Put it on. Olivia starts complaining it stinks. *Put it on!* Or I won't show you the secret place. I don't want to put it on. You have to put it on or the elf won't let you through. She is rambling on and crying and that's when I start to feel really bad. But it's too late. That's the thing. It's too late to turn back. I am convinced, adamant that turning back now would make it worse. She's taken off her yellow PVC mackintosh, feeding her hands through the arms of the sweater. She snivels putting the mackintosh back on, over the petrol-soaked sweater. I didn't tell her to put the mackintosh back on. I have to light her now. I have to strike the match without her seeing. To keep the rain off the matches I have to light one inside my coat. Olivia has only one arm inside her mackintosh as I touch the end of her woollen sleeve, the fur, with the lighted match, and it goes *whoosh*. I'm so surprised. I thought the fire would just creep up slowly. I thought there'd be time for Celestine and me to discuss it with Olivia, explain that it's our father we're trying to get. But now Olivia's charging around, straight into the blackberry bush and out again and the flames are climbing up her back and chest and arms and start to engulf her hair. I start to run like the clappers. I am running away and I don't care if Celestine is following or not. I run all the way home.

I can't sit still for a minute and take off again back to the club, where Olivia's face down in the mud and it's raining on her and in the grass. It's very quiet, only the sound of the rain falling on the grass. There's smoke rising from her clothes, but no flames any more. Her PVC mackintosh has melted into lumps sticking to her neck. I sit with her. I don't know what I'm feeling. A black and windy emptiness. I feel a draining off of normal things. The light is low, I think. It's getting dark. No, it can't be that. It's still light, at four o'clock. It's because the fire's gone out. The rain is rustling in the grass, like someone whispering. I keep hearing these words in my head: *Who's going to stop the rain from talking?* I lie next to her. I'm hoping if I stay here they'll find me. And Olivia will wake up. Then we can have supper when she gets better. And my mum will come back from the mental home. I never imagined my sister would not reappear when I willed her to. Didn't the existence of Celestine sort of prove how sisters could just appear willy-nilly? I get up and walk to the canal and I take a swim. It's dirty and freezing but I'm already so cold it doesn't particularly bother me.

I drift back home again and change into my pyjamas. The house is so quiet I turn on the TV, but all I can hear is rushing, like wind in my ears. There were wild flowers, yellow and blue flowers, around Olivia where she lay. And then the flowers get very bright as my dad comes home and asks, *Where's Olivia?* Not, How are you, Mark? But, Where's Olivia? It's the sound of her name that brightens the flowers, makes everything grow light, and I think it's going to be okay, Olivia's going to be all right. He begins asking me why I collected Olivia from after-school club and why I'd told the teaching assistant he'd given me permission to do this. Then he asks again, Where is she? It's six o' bloody clock. I say, You don't love me, you only love her. He hits me with his open fist. *Where is she, you little fuck!*

Why don't you ask Celestine!

At the mention of this name, his face falls. He tries to say something but no sound comes out of his mouth.

I don't know when it happens but the police come round to the house, two of them. They ask me questions about where I think Olivia might be. I go stiff with tension and tell them she might be playing down the club. And then I'm being put into the back of a police car, a coat over my pyjamas, and a policewoman is asking me to show them where this place is. I like her, so take her to the club, and it's got a lot smaller since I was last there. It's also dark now and they carry flashlights. I take them to look at the corrugated iron garages first. I tell them to look on the roofs. Then I say, I think she might be playing near the blackberry bushes. And that is where we find her, and she's not moved an inch. In the background is the sound of a train on the Stratford line. The police are very quiet in the rain.

27

One component of the inshore navigation certificate I took inside prison was a first-aid course. I learnt my resuscitation ABC on a dummy with rubber lungs in my cell. I tested myself relentlessly on respiratory, circulatory, nervous, skeletal and digestive systems: the way the heart pumps in de-oxygenised blood and pumps out oxygenised blood; how the sensory nervous system stores information and makes decisions. I appreciated this knowledge as descriptions of what it is to be human, and how to cope when the mechanism breaks down. I learned what to look for in cases of asphyxia – *the skin may be ashen and the lips may be blue* – sucking wounds, air hunger.

According to my books there are two ways of dying: losing blood and losing breath. On coming across someone unconscious you have to find which of the two systems has failed. Is it a coronary thrombosis or some interference with the function of the brain? Is she bleeding, or is there a lump of hamburger stuck in the windpipe? What you don't do is hang around and pray. You get down on your knees and work. Mouth to mouth, heart massage. If the casualty's starved of oxygen for more than five minutes she's going to have brain damage when she recovers, if she recovers at all.

But before you do anything, you first you have to check the environment. Let's say the casualty's lying on the floor in a ship's engine room. You won't necessarily know it, but she might still be attached to the 440-volt live cable that put her there. Touch her and you'll go up in a puff of smoke. Once the environment's safe, the first thing is to check the airway's not blocked. Feel for a pulse (weak, irregular, zero); signs of head injuries (cerebral spinal fluid in the eyes . . . pink tears); haemorrhaging (arteries pump, veins seep). If she's bleeding, find the site of the laceration, incision, puncture or sucking wound (paradoxical breathing). Stem the bleeding at the pressure points (i.e. the femoral artery). Then put in four breaths with the head back and airway open before checking the pulse (carotid). One breath, and if there's no pulse, five massages to the heart. Then every three cycles check pulse, eyes and breathing.

I liked how this language seemed to invigorate the human form (pink tears, pumping arteries, paradoxical breathing). The vocabulary of first aid is an elegy for the sick and injured and brings them back to life. I worked myself into quite an emotional state learning how to treat burns caused by wet heat, fire, sun and chemicals. Other words were so clearly rational: 'The serum leaks out of the circulatory system into the burn area and forms blisters. Shock develops when the blisters burst. With full-thickness burns, the skin appears pale and waxy, sometimes charred.'

And what better prose than this: 'When treating someone whose clothing is on fire, if the accident occurs indoors prevent the casualty rushing about or going outside, as movement and breeze fan the flames. Lay her down to prevent the flames sweeping upwards to the head. Douse her with water, or wrap her in a coat or blanket. When all flames are extinguished, gently remove rings, watches, belts from the injured area before it begins to swell, but remove nothing actually sticking to a burn. Don't apply lotions, ointments or fat. Don't break blisters or remove loose skin. Cover the injured area with unmedicated dressing. For facial burns make a mask from clean, dry sterile material, such as a pillowcase, and cut holes for nose, eyes and mouth. Immobilise any badly burned limbs. Give sips of water to a conscious patient to replace lost fluid. If the breathing and heartbeat have stopped, begin resuscitation immediately. Any burns to the mouth have to be treated as very serious because the tissues in the mouth swell quickly and can close the airway. The danger then is asphyxia. If she panics it's going to get worse. Remove jewellery or tight clothing around neck and moisten the lips with water . . .'

But it was these words that made me finally break down and weep:

'Deep burns are relatively pain-free because the nerves are damaged.'

Pain-free.

28

Lily's introductions agency is a honeycomb of lavender-smelling, pastel-coloured consulting booths. She sits in a swivel chair as far away from me as possible. Her skirt is tugged over her knees and her bare legs clamped together. Beyond the door I hear the rustle of chiffon, and a client's baritone from another booth.

Lily is in charge of this industry, the captain in a sea of love. But she's having trouble staying on course. She looks at me with that other expression normally reserved for clients, then stares through the window, alighting upon the Anglican spires in the city. 'Marriage is a very unnatural act. I should have known this before, but I didn't. I don't believe in this job any more.'

'Lily, I . . .'

She waves her hand to silence me. 'Love is very insecure, isn't it? That's why we get married, to lock up this insecurity. But marriage doesn't protect anything. It's a false sense of security. At worst it's a prison, and then you get divorced. Divorce might have been seen once as a good thing. But nobody thought through what effect it would have on the children, did they? Oh, they said things like, kids are adaptable, natural survivors. But now those kids have grown up and they're not saying, "Oh we adapted all right, we're natural survivors." Because they know how terrible it was; how damaged they are. Marriage is an unnatural act. But divorce is a disease that kills our children.

'What happens when these kids grow up? They cling to the first person to be nice to them, settle for less than they should. They fear being alone more than making a bad marriage and killing the children all over again. That's what you've done. You've wrecked the children's future. Just as your childhood wrecked yours. Don't say anything. I've learnt nothing. I know nothing about marriage and love, no set of facts, like a set of keys that fit one lock and no other. I know less than nothing. I've been ladling out advice for years without knowing what I've been talking about. My life has been one big lie. I can't go on with this business.'

'You're talking about separate issues.'

'Don't you dare advise me.'

From the other booth we hear peals of female laughter. The man inside is practising his charms on one of Lily's colleagues. Perhaps she's only pretending to be charmed. This much I do know: there's no laughter in our booth, real or false.

'What the hell were you thinking? Marrying me and not telling anyone. It's a recallable offence . . .'

'Who told you that . . . recallable? How do you know what that means?'

'I've taken legal advice.'

'Oh, have you?' I'm shocked to hear this. A lawyer's job in these instances is to muddy the clear waters. They are a train running backwards.

'It was a breach of your licence to kidnap the children.'

'I didn't kidnap them.'

'Call it what you want, it was still a breach of your licence.'

'Everything I do is a breach of my licence.'

'I'm giving out advice on who should marry who and the whole time I've been married to a fucking killer. Listen to me, I'm even swearing like a stevedore.'

'That's okay.'

'Don't tell me what's okay, all right? What do you mean, everything you do is a breach of your licence?'

'I didn't tell my probation officer about us. That was the first violation of the licence.' The soft folds of her linen blouse draw my eyes, the delicacy of her hair lying on her shoulders. 'The embargo on the press reporting on my whereabouts expired a long time ago. But if we go to the Home Office they'll reimpose it.' These words feel rough on my tongue. The language abuses, mocks our love, a love that is slipping from my grasp. 'The Home Office will protect the kids' anonymity is what I mean.'

'That's convenient for you.'

'How is that convenient for me?'

'They'll have to protect your anonymity to protect theirs. But I'm not sure I want your name any more . . . You've made us illegitimate.'

'My love . . . that's not illegitimate.'

'Your love is founded on lies.'

One of her team knocks before walking into the booth. She sees me. 'Hi, Ray, sorry to interrupt.' I'm relieved to hear my name again. An assisted blonde, her very dark brown eyes smile in perpetuity. She has no idea that what is transpiring in here is a marriage hitting the skids, as she tries to make a fresh one in the adjoining booth. 'I need Maureen Chabrier and Sharon Johnson's files. I think they might get on with this guy in there.' She pulls open the drawers of a chrome cabinet against the wall.

Lily raises her arms from her lap. 'Oh, I've taken Sharon off file for four weeks while she's seeing someone.'

It encourages me to see her return to business, when only a moment ago she claimed it could no longer be done. Her colleague takes a file from the cabinet. 'Maureen's better for him, anyway.' She flutters her fingers at me and says, 'Bye Ray,' before mincing out.

Lily waits for the door to click shut. 'This is not over. Not by a long way.'

'I'm going to see my probation officer. It's something I have to put right, for all of our sakes.'

'I'm not sure if there is an *our* any more.'

'What else do you want me to do? I'll do it.'

'You're talking about the future. But it's the past that's the problem. I told you before, this might have happened to you twenty-six years ago, when you were a child, but I've just found out about it. It's very vivid in my mind. I don't know when I'll next have a proper night's sleep.' She massages both eyes with her thumbs as if to illustrate. 'How does this kind of thing happen to people like me? This is meant to happen to other people, people with desperate lives, on the other side of the tracks. Criminals and trailer trash. Not middle-class women like me. I thought I knew who I was. Now I'm just frightened . . . of my own judgement.' She sighs, gives me what I take to be the first sympathetic glance since I've been sitting in here, then says, 'You're going to have to move out, while I decide what to do.'

29

There are three others besides me waiting for appointments. Two women, defeated by their own weight, sit and watch a teenager move around the reception area. He paces as though on the point of stampeding. It's been more than a decade since I've felt that smouldering anger in the heavy stare, seen head-to-toe charity shop clothes, or smelled the stubborn stench of penal institutions. Every few minutes the teenager goes up to the counter, his neck flaring red, and demands to be seen by his PO. Each time he receives a passive stare from the uniform behind the glass partition. He flicks his cigarette into a corner and lets it burn. He leans against a wall that is smeared with greasy shadows, the imprints of hundreds of probationers. When my name is called and the security door buzzes me through, the teenager tries to gatecrash the offices. He is shouted at and threatened with action by the receptionist before he retreats back into the room.

I have not forgotten my way round this warren and climb three sets of stairs to the third floor. It is almost pleasurable to be back. But when I walk into Tom Reeves' office the shock of discovering a woman in Tom's chair leaves me speechless. Even his calming Monets have gone from the walls. She tells me Tom has retired from the Probation Service and introduces herself as Frances Rodriguez-Smith, my new PO. Towards her I feel a child-like insecurity, and a lot of resentment. I recognise my Crown Prosecution Bundle on the desk and feel crushed. I haven't seen those files for a long time. I'm definitely back where I started.

Not quite back where I started. The files are twelve years out of date. They document only the bad news. It takes me the better part of an hour to bring Frances Rodriguez-Smith up to speed, summarise what has happened since I last sat in this office with Tom. She writes notes the whole time, occasionally asking for clarifications, is vigilant where there is equivocation, maintaining a formal but warm tone of voice.

Frances is a small woman, under five feet. But height doesn't come into the bargain when you are sitting across from one another. And she might be tiny but she talks like a giant and delivers her sentences at great speed. Unlike Tom, she even volunteers bits of information about her private life, including an account of the chemotherapy she had recently for breast cancer. She repeats certain verbal expressions. After her hair fell out she had *shades of the prison house* about her. Her husband during all of it was a *prince among men*.

Maybe it is this scrape with death that makes her so frank. She finishes telling me about her ordeal then admonishes me sternly for failing to make a disclosure about Lily. She calls it 'ignorant optimism' to imagine I'd get through my whole life without the truth leaking out.

After I bring the story up to date she lets her pen cool off on the edge of her desk. My supervision will have to be reimposed at the very least, she tells me. A recall to prison might be considered by the Multi-Agency Public Protection Team, when they meet in a week's time, but she doubts they'll recommend it. 'After all, you haven't broken any law. It's your children they'll be more concerned about now. You've left them exposed all these years. Not to tell us about them, that was irresponsible, to say the least.'

'If I'd made that first disclosure to my wife my children wouldn't exist.'

'Possibly not.'

'I've worked hard to earn my wife's love. Worked hard to cancel out the past.'

'None of us can cancel out our past, Ray. We are governed by it.'

'I'm not talking about all of the past, just one single mistake I made in childhood. I have no right to be a parent, isn't that what you're saying, because of that one mistake?'

'You had no right to be a parent without our permission.' She repeats the words I'd hoped never to hear again: 'Your life is not your own.'

An electric fan in the room moves around the dead air. The breeze flaps under the collar of Frances' ice-blue shirt and makes my skin shiver. Only my flesh, it seems, is penetrated by the cold climate in here. I revolve my hands and examine them, despairing at how such small extremities once had the power to cause so much ill will. At the age of twelve they were half the size but more than twice as cruel.

We have reached an impasse in our discussion. I ask her advice on how to deal with Celestine, explaining how she has threatened the security of the family and blackmailed me.

'Can you prove it?'

'I've had to give her thousands of pounds.'

'She might say you gave it to her in good faith. Is it her word against yours?'

'More or less.'

Tangentially she begins telling me about her husband, *a prince among men*, and what he thinks about life. 'Juan says he likes the company of men because they comfort him. He likes the company of women because they teach him things he doesn't know. Would you agree with him?'

'I agree with the second part. Men don't comfort me at all.'

'Does Celestine, your half-sister, teach you things you don't know?'

'She teaches me things I don't *want* to know.'

'And she still exerts power over you?'

'Yes, in a way.'

'Why do you let her?'

'Isn't that obvious?'

'How can you stop empowering her then?'

'When one of us dies.'

'I don't believe that. You're very resourceful, Ray, to keep up a pretence for so long. You may have to call her bluff. See what she does, if anything, and then deal with the consequences.'

'It's not only me who'll have to deal with the consequences.'

We discuss how long it will take before the courts re-impose a reporting ban on the press and whether Celestine is likely to approach a newspaper to sell her story and disclose my whereabouts before they do. 'There is the Internet,' Frances says. 'That's not regulated. She could make it difficult for you in all sorts of ways, like telling parents at your children's school, the mates you work with. There's no end to it.'

At least I do not pose any threat to the public, we agree on that. What I pose is a threat to my family, and for the meantime Frances suggests I live apart from them.

'That's what Lily said. So that's it, that's the solution,

the one I've always denied. I separate from my wife and children to protect them, to keep them safe. My fears are finally confirmed. What do I tell my children then, why I'm not living with them?'

'That's more difficult. I don't know.'

'How long for?'

'I don't know that either. But if someone tries to seek you out, vigilantes or someone else, you won't want to be home at such a time. We can arrange safe venues if you want to see your wife and children. And we'll assess the situation over the next six months. In the meantime you need to start looking for a place to live.'

30

At the house I knock on the front door. I knock on my own front door. A moment later Lily opens up and I read in her face that this is exactly the protocol she expects from now on. *Your home is not your own.* She leads me on to the threshold and then stops me going further in, retraining me to act like a visitor. This is a very hard but not completely new feeling. In a sense I've always felt like a visitor in my own house, as I've been a visitor in my own name.

She beckons for me to follow her into the kitchen. Walking down the hall I look up the stairs, which seem to taper off into darkness at the entrance to the kids' bedrooms. Entering the kitchen I immediately lose my bearings. I don't understand what I'm looking at, but then I do: a turnout from Lily's brothers. They are gathered as though at a funeral, in suits and ties. Jerry doesn't say anything and his stare sheers away from me. Only Colin says hello, but that is all he says. Not, 'Hello, *Ray*.' No one wants to call me by that name.

I feel it's up to me to break the silence. 'I'll pack a few things, shall I?'

'That's been taken care of,' Lily says.

Now Jerry speaks for the first time. 'Your suitcase is in the living room.'

'Thank you, Jerry.'

'Right,' says Lily. 'Let's get this over with.'

She leads us all out of the kitchen and into the living room, where once more I'm disorientated, this time by finding Rose sitting stiffly in an armchair with her hands spread across her lap. I brace myself for a barrage from her. Surprisingly, she says nothing.

Lily takes a step to the mantelpiece and picks up a photograph. 'I forgot to pack this . . .' She holds it gingerly by the pewter frame. 'I presume you want your father's picture.'

'It's not my father,' I say, but take the photograph anyway. One of my fingers touches the back of her hand in the transfer and the sensation spreads rapidly through my whole body.

'Who is it then, if it's not your father?'

'I don't know.'

'Well, I don't want it here.'

'I'll bin it if I may.'

'Not in my bin, you won't.' Her voice rises in temperature. 'I'm surrounded by your lies aren't I? How many lies have you told over the years to protect that first one? Like that one about your father dying six months after your mother, after they killed your sister in a car accident. Jesus Christ! So what other heirlooms in our house are fakes? The things you've told the kids all these years about their grandparents. It's a big web of lies. We're caught up in a web of your lies.'

There comes from behind me a familiar sound of Rose in condemnation mode, her special note of moral rectitude. But she is not condemning me. She is condemning her daughter. 'Come on, Lily. Don't be so harsh.'

Lily ignores her mother to berate me further. 'What

should I tell the kids when they ask where that photo has gone?'

'Where are they?' I ask, suddenly feeling their absence in a most visceral way and wanting to see them, smell them.

'Not here.' Lily sounds almost pleased to announce.

'They're at my house,' Jerry says. 'With Julia.'

I'm waiting for Colin to join in the baiting game, for the whiplash to fall upon my back, when I hear Rose's voice again. 'Give him a chance, for heaven's sake.'

This time Lily doesn't ignore her. 'Why are you defending him, Mother?'

'Because Ray's a good man. And you all know it. You should be ashamed of yourself, acting the almighty judge and jury.'

'What he did . . .' Jerry shakes with emotion. 'What he did, he could do again. You want to take that risk?'

'Are you going to be stupid all your life, Jerry? Ray's never going to hurt anyone because he knows what it can do. Surviving what he did as a boy has made him more of a man than you. Good Lord, if we judge people on what they once did wrong as children, the world will never progress. And Lily, shame on you too. I'm shocked that you can treat a man who loves you in this manner.'

'It's love founded on falsehoods. He's not who I thought he was.'

'He knows who he is better than you know yourself. Besides, love is often founded on all sorts of murky waters. Look at your father and me. What with that other woman of his.'

'What are you trying to do, Mum?'

'Save a good marriage.'

I pick up the suitcase from the floor. 'Where are you going?' Rose asks.

'I don't know, Rose. I'll stay in a hotel until I find somewhere to live.'

'No need for that. You can stay with me, at least for a while. We've got plenty of room.'

I feel the air contract as Colin, Jerry and Lily all inhale together. 'He's not staying with you, Mum,' Jerry declares.

'Don't order me about, Jerry.'

'He can't stay with you . . . right, Colin?' But Colin keeps his silence. 'I mean, if someone tries to get him when he's in your house . . .'

'And what, Jerry? I'm an old woman with a few years left in this world. Do you think I'm scared?'

'What about Dad?'

'Oh please! He's got even less time than I have. When you get to our age, Jerry, you care more about leaving things behind you in some sort of order.'

For the first time Colin looks me in the eye. I wait for the fall of the axe, but instead he addresses me with a measure of his former warmth. 'How long were you in prison?'

Grateful for the frankness, I say, 'Nine years and ten months. Followed by four years' probation.'

'Four years' probation . . .' Lily ponders aloud.

'It took them four years to assess risk. My supervision was suspended when I was no longer regarded as a threat. That's when I met Lily.'

Lily has the final word. 'Then I think it might take me four years to decide if you're a risk to me.'

31

'Don't think because I saved your bacon you can get round me, Ray,' Rose is saying in her kitchen. 'What you did was unforgivable, unforgivable. You didn't tell her when you should have. I mean, really. Lily might not have run a mile then, but she will now, because of the children. My God, what did you think you were doing? Don't answer that. I'm very angry with you, Ray. And it'll probably send me to an early grave, worrying about the effect this is having on my grandchildren.'

I listen to her from the table, having been coerced into a chair. I'd offered to help make supper, but no man has ever helped her in the kitchen and it was too late to start now. 'The thing is, I remember all this, I remember reading about you in the papers and I thought at the time, What will become of that boy now? Not for a second did I imagine he'd turn up as my son-in-law. I want to wring you out to dry, Ray, I really do. I think it's going to take *me* four years to come to terms with it as well. If I live that long.'

When supper is ready, Rose asks me to fetch Aubrey. She protects Aubrey from damaging truths as I do my children, and has told him that Lily and I have had a row as a way of explaining my presence in their house. Aubrey simply raised an eyebrow after receiving this news and said to me, 'Women! Can't live with them, can't live without them.' In the living room I lock his wheelchair at right angles to his armchair then remove the padding around him – the four cushions to the side and down the back. I lower my centre of gravity and hook his arm around my neck. With my muscles trembling I raise him up on to one leg, screw him round and take all his weight as I transfer him into the wheelchair.

I catch my breath. 'Does Rose do this every day?'

'Of course,' he says as though I'm a fool to ask.

In the kitchen she explains, 'I know you're a bit of a *cordon bleu* chef, Ray, but we eat simply here.' She has laid the table with plates, cups and saucers. A white porcelain teapot is hidden under a knitted caddie. I position Aubrey so his knees tuck under the table and he snatches up a fork in his fist. When Rose serves up the stew she has made in a pressure cooker – mutton that falls off the bone, carrots and white barley – Aubrey sets to work immediately. His manners are as bad as Celestine's. Rose gives me a generous portion, says grace, then pours out the tea. Before she begins to eat, she cuts the meat and slices the carrots on Aubrey's plate.

We eat in silence. By and by I say, 'This is a nice stew, Rose.'

'Don't be a flatterer, Ray. Nothing but the truth from you from now on.'

'Well it *is* nice, although a bit salty perhaps.'

'And no criticism either.'

When supper is finished I get out of the way and go sit on my own upstairs. My body aches all over and makes me wonder if I'm starting the flu, or have a parasite from the river. What worries me most is being too ill to work in the morning. Without work I have nothing.

I have made my nest upstairs in Lily's old bedroom, with dolphins and heavenly constellations stencilled on to the pink wallpaper. I sit on the single bed, sinking into a mattress covered with a brown and itchy army-issue blanket. My clothes hang in the oak wardrobe next to her school uniform and a couple of party frocks. I sit on the edge of the bed reminiscing about the punishment 'awards' I received in prison: fourteen days of solitary confinement. I couldn't see the future then, and I can't see it now.

I'm aching for the children, I soon realise, and not with flu. It's at this hour I'm usually reading to them in bed and my body knows it. For the same time it would normally take me to settle them, I experience withdrawal symptoms.

Then I hear the telephone ring and Rose shouts up the stairs that it's Flora wanting to talk to me. The kids have been having their own withdrawal symptoms.

I find the telephone stretched from the living room into the hall. I lift the receiver off the chair and hear the tremor in my daughter's voice. 'Why are you staying at Grandma's?'

This is so difficult. I left it to Lily to explain why I'm not there and I'm crippled by the question. I want to be truthful, but truth received is a different animal to truth told. I have to weigh up what to say against what she can take. 'You remember when you asked why I'd had a row with Mum? Well that's just it, you see.'

'I want you to come home.' I hear the tears in her voice.

'Believe me, if I could I would. But this is not Mum's fault, okay? And my love for you here is as strong as it is over there.'

'I don't understand that.'

'Let me say hello to Eliot.' I hear the telephone being

transferred and my son's subdued breathing down the line. 'Are you in your pyjamas?'

'Yes.'

'What book are you reading tonight?'

'*Guinness World Records*.'

'Excellent.'

'I want you to read it to me.'

I begin again. 'Touch your heart with your hand, like I'm touching mine. Okay, that completes the circuit. I'm sending all my love down this telephone wire and it's going straight from my heart into your heart.'

'But I want you to kiss me goodnight.'

I try to make the sound of a kiss but my lips are too dry.

Lily comes on the phone. I hear her shooing the children away before she says in a dulcet tone, 'This is really difficult, Ray. The kids don't understand what's going on. They've got me over a barrel. If I don't let them see you, they'll think I'm an ogre.'

She called me Ray! I take heart from that, even if it is over the phone. 'Then let me see them soon, Lily. We can arrange a place and time, at your convenience.'

'I'm scared of what will become of us, all of us. It's like a curse.'

'What about the day after tomorrow. Can I come see them then?'

'Okay. Come over after they finish school.'

'Thank you.'

'Ray?'

'Yes, Lily?'

'Just this. It isn't easy for small things in this big world. I know you suffered too, for what you did.'

I can hear how softly she replaces her receiver and keep holding mine to my ear for a while longer, enjoying the gentle purring tone, feeling myself levitating off the hallway floor on a carpet of her words.

Rose is about to lift Aubrey out of his wheelchair into the armchair as I take the telephone back into the room. 'Here,' I say, 'let me help you.' She allows me to take her place. Standing in front of him I put my arm behind his back and he throws his useful arm over my shoulders. I bend my knees and lift him. He shakes, standing on one leg as I swivel him on to the armchair. No sooner is he settled than he asks to go to the toilet.

'Oh, Aubrey. Why didn't you say before we moved you into the armchair?' Rose sighs.

'Shall I take him to the bathroom, Rose?'

'You know the way.'

I lift him back into his wheelchair and take him to the bathroom in the hall. As he hangs on to me, I kick the wheelchair away and loosen his belt with one hand, unzip his trousers and pull them down as far as I can. He reverses backwards, hopping on one leg. I seat him on the toilet with his trousers down to his ankles, then he says into my ear, 'Fire in the hole.'

The word 'fire' burns me.

'What do you mean, Aubrey?'

'Got to drop a log.'

'Oh. I'll wait outside then.'

As I stand in the hall I'm tempted to think of this as my punishment, but that would be unfair to Rose. And I've served my time, I remind myself. I play back those last words of Lily's in my head until I hear Aubrey calling me. Sliding open the door, the stench is almost unbearable. Wiping his bottom, his skin feels like paper to my touch. I hitch his trousers over his knees, raise him on to his foot and pull them over his sagging belly.

I'm lucky to be able to participate in my family at all. Until Lily forgives me, I'll be grateful for this much.

32

I've never taken the route from Rose's house to work before and I'm late for the first time in my life. I run on to the jetty where the rig is waiting and find Noel in the wheelhouse, executing preliminaries on my behalf: checking the instrument panels, the weather fax. Sunny spells with scattered showers expected later. The GPS and radar are up and the engines running, monitored by the two engineers below. After checking the worksheet I set keel for Canvey Island.

Noel is in a talkative mood. 'There's a tree that needs pollarding outside my flat and no one does anything about it but me. I complain to the council. The tree is actually outside the house next door. But the woman in there I never see from one month to the next. I think she goes away all the time. That's what I call a good neighbour. My neighbours in the flat below, they're in all the time. Talking all the time. I hear every word. It's like they live with me, waking me up. And the planes, they come over one after the other. We're not meant to be on the flight path down there. I want to float a big helium balloon up to the pilots that reads, *Get off my roof*.' Then he remembers something. 'Oh yeah, your visitor's back. Without the drunk this time.'

Why am I not surprised? Frances Rodriguez-Smith warned me she'd come after the men at work. She can't seem to live without me, or is driven by a quest for my destruction, her father's son. As the ship courses through Lower Hope Reach, I find her on my bunk, staring at the empty space on the cabinet where my television used to be.

I stand in front of her. 'You're beginning to annoy me.'

Her eyes look mean. 'I think I kind of want to know what happened to Miles.'

I worry about Miles too, for different reasons. I may yet be undone if he turns up in a different form, like a corpse. Undone *again*. I feel guilty about him, a blemish on my second nature. Maybe he'll be the subject of another disclosure to Lily one day, when I am feeling safer. 'You didn't need to come here to ask me that.'

'Would you prefer if I came to your house to ask?'

I don't mention I've moved out of the house in case it works to her advantage. 'I don't know what's happened to Miles. Last I saw of him was on Lambeth Bridge.' I turn my back on her and walk out of my cabin. It is very difficult to act disinterested.

We are running past Stanford-le-Hope and the Mucking Flats. On the barren grassy shore is a pirate loading ramp and travelling crane, a rusting container beside an idle gantry, and off the port quarter a few cows and sheep nose around the edges of a wheat field.

Noel is at the wheel, meditatively whistling to himself. After a few minutes he says, 'Everything all right with your visitor?'

'Can I be frank with you, Noel?' I have never used this tone with him before. And his response is new to me.

'My boy, is there any finer way? I think the world of you.'

'I've got trouble with her.'

'I thought you'd got a soft spot for her.'

'I said I've got trouble with her. Not got her in trouble. I haven't knocked her up.' The confusion almost makes me laugh and then I see her rising up the companionway into the wheelhouse like a curse. Noel looks searchingly at me.

'You have a nice view from up here,' she says and I know it's a prologue, the opening of a can of worms. 'Better than mine anyway. Have I told you my boat needs to come out of the water? Going to cost seven hundred quid.' She leans against the chart table with arms held back. 'I was wondering if you'd like to invest, Ray.'

'You are a scum-sucking pig.'

My answer puts a shiver down Noel's back. As it travels to his waist he screws the wheel.

'Then I guess I'll have to spill a few words in your mate's ear.'

Noel's bum steer now affects our course, and he has to correct fast to prevent us mowing through the drying flats. 'Someone calling me?' he asks.

'The name Mark Swain ring a bell with you?'

'Can't say it does,' says Noel.

'Who do you think your skipper is? He's a child killer. Killed his own sister . . .'

Noel takes his hands off the wheel completely and for a few seconds we drift at the mercy of the current. He focuses all his attention on her and suddenly begins to laugh. This laughter has no apparent end. I have an unimpeded view of the insecurity passing across her face. Noel finally stops laughing just long enough to manage: 'And I'm Uriah!' before laughter gets the better of him again.

'It's *true*!' Celestine shouts.

'Yeah, it is true.' Noel's laughter turns into a sour smoking cough. 'I am Uriah. Oh, God. Excuse me.'

He disappears below while I correct the mistake on the wheel, bringing us back on course.

Who's Uriah?

We are near our destination at Canvey Island where the spirit tanks and gasworks on Scar's Elbow come into focus. On the south shore are the Cooling Marshes beyond Egypt Bay, where Lily and I took Flora and Eliot on a bicycle ride in another lifetime.

She has got to Lily. The rest now is nothing. I say to the hazardous cargo: 'How's this going to end, Celestine? What's your plan?'

She stares at me, breathing heavily. 'How did it end for Miles?'

'Miles jumped off Lambeth Bridge.'

'You mean he was pushed.'

'No, he definitely jumped. There are two witnesses who saw it, who'd stopped their sports car on the bridge. So you can tell who you like. They'll know what they saw.'

Celestine stays her ground. I wonder what she intends to do next and what I'll do to her as we cruise past Deadman's Point. On the other side of the floodwall is a caravan park. The St George cross flies from every caravan roof. So this is where the English ended up, at the point where the river ends and the sea begins – marked by a dark grey stripe. The tide burns into the river along a north–south axis. White sails mark the horizon like fence posts. Jet-skiers dart in and out of sluggish container ships.

What I want to do to her will have to wait as another, different risk takes precedence over everything else. We are in a dangerous moment, when lives can be lost through careless handling. In the vicinity of big ships carrying munitions and gasoline oil I easily dispatch Celestine to the corner of my mind. She is nothing among this company.

A spirit tanker waits at the yawning, toothless mouth of the sea. I talk to the master on Channel 68 and circle in to get her. But she does not require a tow in this height of tide. The tanker loosens her purchase on the swing buoy and I lead her to the gasworks jetty through the foul areas.

We have four hours to kill before she'll need an escort back to sea.

I drift upstream on the incoming tide. Celestine sits on the chair beside me, smoking. She looks tired, with rings under her eyes. Noel reappears with the first and second engineers. The last time I saw the engineers in the wheelhouse was on Christmas Eve. We have worked together as a crew for eight years.

Noel says, 'Here she is, boys, upsetting our skipper, putting the ship at risk.'

The first engineer stands close enough to Celestine to inhale her spent and anxious breath. 'It's unlucky having a woman on board.'

She holds her ground with the engineer. 'Your skipper's the only risk around here.'

Noel suppresses another fit of laughter. 'Of course, our skipper's a killer.' He points to Celestine. 'I guess one more won't make a difference to you then will it, Ray?'

'Can she swim, Ray?' the first engineer asks. 'Instead of killing her we could leave her on a buoy to wait for a ship to pass.'

'Immaterial if she can swim or not,' says Noel. 'Current will take her straight out to sea. Won't even touch the sides.'

'Deepwater Street out there,' the second engineer says. 'Avenue of Remembrance.'

Celestine crosses her arms, plants her foot on the chart-table tree and pretends to yawn. 'You're really scaring me, guys. Bloke in the office knows where I am.'

'Sure he does. But why do you think he made you sign an insurance waiver? Can't see from his window what happens here.'

She doesn't take our threats seriously. It's my crew not

taking *her* threats seriously that enrages her. She is pinned against the bulkhead and lost for words. I discover a whole new respect for my crew. I am moved and humbled. They have not judged me on what they hear about my past, don't even question it. For there are certainties they know for sure, such as that in my capacity as their skipper I make no mistakes. I take them out and bring them home safely again. This is what they understand, and appreciate. Why my family can't be as generous as my crew is really the difference between love and work.

Looks like I'll always be in a job.

Four miles up-river from where my shift ends I go looking for some breakfast. My half-sister walks behind me like she once did as a child and follows me into the café. A breeze slips in with her under the old oak door and swings the ceiling lanterns. There is an anchor in a corner, framed knots on the wall, fishing nets slung across windows, a compass embedded in the serving hatch.

I buy us breakfast but can't eat mine. I push my bacon, eggs and beans to the side, sip my tea and watch Celestine clean her plate. What can our future hold, when we share less than six months of the past? What is it she wants to share? All that I once had, what she might have wanted, I've probably lost.

As she wipes her mouth with her sleeve, I say, 'You have no dignity. I'd give you money to go away, but you're a bottomless pit.'

But she replies with 'Something in this café's making me uncomfortable.'

I have my back to the room and heave round to see what might be bothering her, making her uncomfortable. I've been coming here for years and the usual crowd of merchant seamen fills up the tables, showing off photographs eight years out of date, of their children. The room smells of diesel oil and the sea. At 8.30 in the morning there are no shadows in which to hide a guilty secret. The customers are all men with no homes to go to. The cooks and servers are all women.

I turn back to face her. 'I'm not responsible for what our father did to you.'

'I know that.'

'Then stop punishing me.'

'I can't. I don't know how to.'

And then something happens. Something goes off. One of the women servers opens the counter hatch and walks over to our table. I can feel the force of gravity shifting along the floor. 'Sorry to bother you,' she addresses Celestine, 'but I'm sure we know one another from somewhere.'

'Doubt it. You might think you know me, but you don't.'

'Must have one of those faces then.'

'What you mean, one of those faces?' I hear the beginning of fear in her voice, something I recognise well. 'I've got no quarrel with you.'

'I didn't say I had a quarrel with you. Perhaps we went to school with one another.'

I reach across the table to place my hand on Celestine's trembling wrist and explain to the woman, 'She didn't go to school around here. Do you know Oystermouth?'

'Never heard of it,' the woman says.

I say, 'It's a little town on a crescent-shaped bay with sandy beaches all around . . .'

'Oh yes,' Celestine turns her arm over on the table and takes my hand, enclosing her cold fingers around my wrist. 'Oystermouth is the best place in the world. To be a child there was a blessing.'

And a beautiful place to return to when your life is not your own.

Acknowledgements

Texts I have drawn from include: D.G. Wilson, *The Thames: Record of a Working Waterway* (London 1987); Francis Sheppard, *London: A History* (London 1988); Ben Weinreb & Christopher Hibbert (eds), *The London Encyclopaedia* (London 1993); Hermione Hobhouse, *Lost London* (London 1971); Gitta Sereny, *Cries Unheard* (London 1998).

Thanks also to Chris Woodman and the crew at Adsteam Towage, and to Bridget Hinkley of the London Probation Service for clarifying what the real procedures would be in an imaginary situation.

Richard Beswick, Derek Johns, Linda Shaughnessy, Rob Kraitt – I salute you too.